"A diabolical arsonist sets a fire too hot to put out, and he's on the loose, killing firemen. Hopkins who-done-it will keep you turning pages to the end. And just when you think you've got it figured, the author speed shifts into high gear with a twist that will leave you breathless! Don't start this book on a weekday!"

Books in print by Bradd Hopkins

Navassa
(Russell Dean & Company, 1998)

Forthcoming Books by Bradd Hopkins

The Morningstar Papers
(Russell Dean & Company, Fall 2000)

Mandelbaum's Donut
(Russell Dean & Company, Spring 2000)

The Smiling One
(Russell Dean & Company, Fall 2001)

To order additional copies of <u>The Fourth Corner of the Ninth Room</u>, or
copies of <u>Navassa</u> by Bradd Hopkins, call toll free

1-888-438-4115

Or write to:
Russell Dean and Company
P.O. Box 349
Santa Margarita, California 93453

THE FOURTH CORNER OF THE 9th ROOM

a novel by
Bradd Hopkins

RUSSELL DEAN & COMPANY, PUBLISHERS
Santa Margarita, California, U.S.A.

First Printing : October, 1999

Library of Congress Cataloging-in-Publication Data.
Hopkins, Bradd
The Fourth Corner of the Ninth Room/ Bradd Hopkins p.cm.– (Russell
Dean fiction –novel)

Library of Congress Catalog Card Number: 99-90709

ISBN 1-891954-22-9
1. Novel.   2. Arson   I. Title.   II. Series.   1998-1999

Dust jacket/cover design by Liselotte Bjorck-Posson, Betula Productions, 8340 San Marcos
Road, Atascadero, California 93422. ©1998 Russell Dean & Company.

Printed in the United States of America.

ACKNOWLEDGEMENTS

Once again, the usual gang has proved instrumental in bringing this work to print. The biggest problem seemed to be getting the manuscript back from the various readers. Rebecca Hopkins and Kezia Letzin avidly encouraged and supported the daily efforts necessary to the creation of The Fourth Corner of the Ninth Room by demanding to see the next chapter as soon as it was written. To my readers Courtney Cable, Teresa Damas, Dawn McCaleb, Mark McCullough, John and Carol Carson, Norm and Cindy Hammond (nee Winter-there was a marriage last year!), Cathy Hudson, Barbara Arnold, and Don Plotkin I wish to acknowledge my debt and my gratitude.

Thanks also to Zandra Zimmerman, and all of the others who, knowingly and unknowingly pushed, prodded, encouraged and educated me during the course of the labor.

Perhaps the most significant thing for me was that I read the final draft to my father as I sat with him during his last days, and he liked it.

B.D. Hopkins
January 4, 1996
Santa Margarita, California

THE FOURTH CORNER OF THE 9th ROOM

a novel by
BRADD HOPKINS

RUSSELL DEAN & COMPANY, PUBLISHERS
Santa Margarita, California, U.S.A.

CHAPTER 1

The door splintered and gave way to the force of the prying tool. It slammed open with a crash as it hit the end of its hinge travel. Three men crouched outside the doorway, masked and swaddled in flame retardant bunker gear. They waited perhaps fifteen seconds. Intently, they watched the light pall of gray smoke to assure that it did not draw back into the building. It did not.

"Let's go!" ordered the officer, laying the Halligan tool aside. "Let's find it!" Captain Mike Sutcliffe emphasized his command with a squeeze on the shoulder of the man in front of him, who relayed it ahead to the nozzleman in a like fashion.

Crouching low, the nozzleman entered the darkened warehouse. He dragged the dead weight of water in the stiff, charged inch-and-three-quarter diameter fire attack line with the assistance of the man behind him.

It was cooler than they expected and relatively easy going to the next doorway. The middle man on Attack Team One pulled off a glove and laid the back of his hand against the top of the door. He found that it, too, was cool to the touch. He put on the glove he had removed. He opened this door as well, which

1

was not locked. All three men watched and waited again for a few seconds. They tested the air currents with eyes and ears, every sense straining and intensely alert, reaching into the smoky darkness for information. It was there. The demon breathed inside.

A flickering, lazy, orange glow through the low haze of smoke betrayed the presence of the fire near the center of the open warehouse space. The high ceilings had allowed the smoke to rise. A nearly clear layer of breathable air remained stratified at almost six feet above the floor. The smoke rippled at the bottom like the waves of an inverted, oily ocean. This would be easy. The hose team moved toward the orange glow keeping low.

The nozzleman, Larry Barent, was a new guy. He was green, untested, fresh from the rookie academy. This was his first real interior attack. He found here in the dark spaces of the smoky warehouse the strange mixture of fear, pride, and exhilaration that firefighters take like a drug. It was for this, he knew now, and not the money, that he had studied and competed. It was for this he had applied repeatedly and accepted repeated rejection all over the state, persevering, hammering his disappointments into resolution, until he triumphed, and was offered a job. Now, he was doing it.

The third man on the hoseline, Captain Mike Sutcliffe, was a veteran officer of some twenty years.

He felt edgy as his crew made its way to the heart of the fire. Something seemed wrong; something was not as it should be. He slowed the advance of the team by dragging back on the hose line unconsciously against the advancing nozzleman, to buy time for his gnawing uneasiness to take real form, to buy time for the fire ground commander to deploy another hose team to back them up. He knew the orders had been given. From monitoring the radio traffic on the tactical channel, he knew that the second team was was on its way. Johannsen and the crew from Engine Four would be in place in two minutes or less. He knew a lot could happen in two minutes. An orange glow danced ahead of them, projecting the shadows of a drunken, whirling gypsy on the walls.

As they approached the dancing orange glow, it changed. It sputtered, made a single popping sound. Rapidly, it brightened to white, then bluish white, and began to roar like the afterburner of a jet. The heat suddenly doubled, then trebled in the space of a breath. A blinding, white-hot column of fire shot suddenly toward the ceiling. Nozzleman Larry Barent looked down across his chest in stark amazement as the front of his bunker gear burst into flames. Instinctively, he opened the bail on the nozzle to let a stream of water free to quell the flame at its source, the blinding white column. His action, in virtually any other situation, would have been the correct one: quench the flame. Kill the heat. The bunker gear he wore would self-extinguish. In this case, it proved exactly wrong.

As the stream of water, flowing at one hundred seventy-five gallons per minute, struck the column of white heat, the component molecules of hydrogen and oxygen were ripped apart by temperatures of over five thousand degrees Fahrenheit. The elements recombined instantaneously above the fire, producing a powerful explosion that knocked the men to the ground.

The seasoned officer, Sutcliffe, crouched farthest from the tremendous heat that had suddenly developed. Crab-like, keeping low, he scrambled blindly back towards the door where they had entered. Dazed and disoriented by the shock of the explosive blast, he followed by instinct the charged hose line toward safety. Hand over hand along the hose line he scrambled, scrabbling along the floor in the smoke toward the waiting back-up team. Briefly, he heard the horrible screams of the other two men in his team, and scrabbled even faster. Then, his burning ears captured the sudden, awesome, mind-numbing silence amidst the roaring conflagration. The back of his bunkers burst into flames.

The back-up hose team froze temporarily outside the second door immobilized by the sudden change in fire conditions. The men found themselves unable to advance and unwilling to retreat; there were other firemen inside. As the officer in charge of the back-up hose team fumbled for his radio to report the change in fire conditions, his nozzleman was astounded to see a ball of flames rushing toward him along the floor, out of the smoke, lumbering like a blazing bear. Before he could react, the ball of flames tumbled through the doorway and bowled him over like a charging fullback. The nozzleman realized, on contact, that the ball of flames was a man.

Slowed by his contact with the nozzleman on the back-up team, the ball of flames was tackled by the second man on the back-up hose line. The second man held him down as the nozzleman found the nozzle that had been knocked from his grasp. Frantically, they doused the flames that were consuming the protective clothing of the officer.

"Get him outside!" yelled the team leader. "Get him out!" He keyed his radio, trying desperately to calm his voice.

"IC, Interior Two," he spoke into the radio, placing the device against the plastic face piece of his breathing apparatus for better clarity of transmission. The hard plastic of the face piece acted as a sound amplifier. His breath came in harsh gasps, and he inserted the words between breaths.

"This is IC; go ahead." The Incident Commander acknowledged the transmission.

"IC, Interior Two. We're pulling out! We have an injured man. Severe burns. The interior is untenable! We can't hold it! Repeat, we're pulling out! Have medics meet us at side one." The professional calm of the voice, the professional calm of a man who was used to communicating coolly in emergencies, belied the emotion of the message.

"Negative, Interior Two. Back up Team One as you were assigned. Withdraw with Team One. I'll send a rescue team for the injured man."

"IC, Team One is *gone*! We're coming out. Recommend you withdraw all teams and go defensive."

"Copy, Interior Two. Break! All units withdraw and move to defensive attack. Objective: surround and drown. Interior units check in with IC on safe withdrawal. Everybody out! Ventilation team, off the roof! Evacuate! Evacuate! Evacuate!"

As the radio transmission died away, air horns from the several fire engines and trucks deployed around the warehouse bellowed four sustained blasts three times, the audible signal for evacuation of the interior of the building.

***

The pump operator on the fire engine supplying Interior Team One noticed the pressure drop substantially on Team One's line. Puzzled, he increased his engine speed to compensate. *They must be flowing lots of water*, he thought. As the engine speed went up, the pressure did not increase. In a panic, his mind searched for what was wrong. He rechecked the position of every valve and selector on his control panel. He knew that losing water pressure on the interior line could get a hose team into trouble; it was his job to assure that never happened. But the second line to the interior showed an increase in pressure commensurate with the increased engine speed. By this he knew the pump was in gear. The compound gauge, showing incoming hydrant pressure, was steady and ample. He tapped the face of the oil-filled discharge gauge quickly, sharply with his gloved knuckle several times to make sure the needle wasn't stuck. The needle did not change.

With mounting concern running through him like an electric charge, he tried to raise Interior Team One on the radio. They didn't respond. As he cleared the airwaves, he listened in mounting dread to the radio traffic for the Incident Commander coming from Interior Two. That traffic, combined with his inability to raise pressure on the line, could only mean one thing. With a nauseating sense of apprehension like a stone in his gut, he realized that a line was either ruptured or burned through.

As the Incident Commander completed his evacuation order, the pump operator left his control panel and went to the engine's cab. There he laid on the air horn in four sustained blasts, repeated three times. Then he returned to the panel. He checked his gauges one last time. They confirmed his worst fears.

In frustration and rage at his helplessness, he struck the discharge gauge violently with the flat of his fist, breaking his hand. The pain shot up his outer arm, but it did not help. He leaned there for a few seconds, pressing his forehead into his hands against the panel. Dully, with a tightness in his throat, and a frustrated, blind rage in his heart, he reached up with his good hand and closed the valve that supplied water to Interior Team One.

***

Two paramedics with armloads of medical gear came around the corner of the warehouse at a dead run as Interior Team Two emerged from the doorway carrying between them a smoking bundle that was Captain Mike Sutcliffe. They lugged him away from the building and laid him on the pavement of the parking lot outside the collapse zone, where the medics could care for him.

At first glance, covered with the charred tatters of his bunker gear, the man was not recognizable as a human being. The lead medic stifled a wave of nausea as he drew his bandage shears and began to cut away the stinking, burned fabric from Sutcliffe's body. As he cut the chin strap to remove the burned man's helmet, he noticed that the back of it was deformed by heat. The fiberglass-wrapped, high pressure air bottle was severely burned. He cut away the straps of the breathing apparatus and cut through the low pressure line from the regulator. Air escaped with a loud, continuing hiss as he backed away some thirty feet. The extruded aluminum bottle might still contain as much as two thousand pounds of air pressure. In its damaged state, with the reinforcing fiberglass wrapping destroyed, there was no telling whether it would continue to hold its pressure, or explode at any instant. They dared not move it, or treat their patient, while it held a charge.

The paramedic firefighter ordered everyone away from Sutcliffe while the bottle's air charge drained down. When the hissing stopped they moved back in to resume treatment. The second medic broke out two one-quart plastic bottles of saline solution from his pack, and began to place soaked dressings on the areas of Sutcliffe's body that were exposed as the charred bunker clothing was cut away with scissors. He set up an I.V. against the fluid loss they anticipated in their patient.

Captain Sutcliffe regained consciousness during the needle stick that established his first I.V. He asked very coherently where his men from Interior Team One were.

"Don't worry about them," said the medic. "You've got some bad burns, and you need to remain quiet."

"It doesn't hurt," countered Sutcliffe. "I've got to find those guys." He tried to rise.

"No way, man," declared the medic, gently pushing him back down. "You're still in shock. You'll be in a lot of pain in a few minutes." He held a syringe up against the brightest background light on the scene and forced a drop of amber liquid from the point of the needle.

"Oh, God! Oh, God!" moaned Sutcliffe, as the pain sent its first messengers through his nervous system. Then it emerged, as from behind a curtain, pervasive and intense, a predator tearing at his skin. His every nerve ending howled in outrage. He sucked in a sharp breath in response to the onslaught of the agony, and screamed. He wanted *out* of his body. He wanted to die if it would stop the terrible pain—or at least pass out—but the pain would not release its hold on his consciousness. He sought his God to strike a bargain, but God was not dealing. The pain swept through his mind like a raging flood.

The medic inserted the needle into the large muscle of the man's thigh and slowly depressed the plunger. The wave of relief as the morphine sulfate entered his body was so intense that Sutcliffe passed out again. He remained unconscious as he was lifted onto a gurney and slid into the open maw of the waiting ambulance.

The medics picked up their gear where it lay scattered on the pavement about the silhouette of Captain Sutcliffe. A column of sparks and flames tumbled high into the night sky as the roof of the burning building fell in. They turned from their work for a moment to watch it.

***

Battalion Chief Albert Digby, Incident Commander of what would come to be known as the Wellman Warehouse Fire, watched as the roof collapsed inward, bathing the nightscape with a surrealistic radiance of spewing sparks and embers. He wondered to himself if something he had done, or not done, had caused the deaths of the two firefighters on Interior Team One. They were certainly dead, for they could not have survived the roof collapse. He reviewed his command decisions mentally, trying to assess the impacts of the fatalities. There would be an investigation, an inquest; of that much he was sure.

That the fire had gone through the roof so quickly amazed him. It was beyond his experience. The timetables of fire evolution, born of years of command experience, seemed to be suspended on this particular fire. His crews had been playing catch-up from the moment they arrived.

That he was in command of a fatal fire distressed him. Firemen didn't die that often in fires, and he had well-trained crews, top-notch officers. What had gone wrong? And how, in the name of God, could he ever face the surviving men, and the families of the men who had perished? It was a small fire department; he knew the families and the children of each man. What could he possibly do to set things right with the families? He did not know, and wanted desperately to go home.

CHAPTER 2

The consciousness of John Randolf Barent struggled upward inside a long, cold well shaft, fighting for light and awareness in response to the insistent beeping from a pager on the bedside dresser. The dreams it left behind, and the intervening oblivion, had been warm and comfortable. The sweet, warm oblivion begged his waking mind to return, beckoning it back down the shaft, away from the light. Oblivion clutched at the departing consciousness like a living thing, entreating it to return, if only for a while, to dream some more.

The mind of John Barent had seen it all before, and knew that discipline was the only way to escape the siren call of sleep. He mustered it and came awake, groggy and irritated —but awake. A headache banded his forehead and fenced with knitting needles behind his eyes as it always did when duty roused him from a dream.

He swung his feet to the floor, sat for a few moments with his head in his hands, faintly nauseated. He rubbed his eyes. Jessica stirred next to him.

"What is it?" she queried into the darkness.

"Callbacks. Hide your eyes." He reached for the lamp on the nightstand and flicked the switch. The

13

light hurt for a moment, then his eyes adjusted.
Jessica burrowed under a pillow. She had only just
gotten to sleep, having worked late the previous
evening.

"Shit." Her voice was muffled but distinct. "Don't
answer."

"Got to. Besides, it's overtime." Barent had not
turned down an offer of overtime since his divorce,
almost three years ago. His finger was already
punching up the number of the dispatch center. The
call was answered on the first ring.

"Consolidated Police/Fire Dispatch." John recognized the female voice. He knew it only as Stacey.
He had never seen her.

"This is Barent. What have you got?" Barent
reached for a pack of Winstons® on the nightstand,
fished one out, and lit it with an ancient Zippo
lighter his father had carried in the war. He looked
absently at the Seabees insignia on the lighter as he
dragged deeply on the smoke. His nausea increased
briefly then vanished as the nicotine reached his
bloodstream. He exhaled a sustained jet of smoke.

"Structure fire at 1910 Sacramento. There are
two possible fatalities. John, they're firemen."

"God." His heart filled with black, steaming
dread, like poured molten lead. "Who?" Any name
Stacey could give him would be the name of a
friend. His stomach knotted and squirmed like a ball
of rattlesnakes.

"We don't know yet."

"I'm on my way."

He rummaged urgently through a pile of rumpled clothes on the closet floor, extracted blue jeans and a shirt. Jessica had once commented wryly on his laundry classification system. He maintained that there were many acceptable levels and degrees of "clean" that were less than fresh. There was no point in doing more laundry than necessary, he'd argued, if you could handle the matter administratively.

He found clothing of a suitable degree of cleanliness. He fished fresh underwear and socks from a drawer in the night stand and dressed. He eschewed a glance in the bathroom mirror. It would have reflected a lean, triangular face that badly needed a shave. It would have urged him to run a comb through the tousled, jet-black wavy hair. It would have suggested to him that some Visine® was in order to calm the flaring red whites around the black pupils of his eyes.

From underneath the socks in the nightstand drawer, he retrieved a Browning® BD380 automatic. He pressed the release and dropped the clip into his waiting hand, checked it. He drew back the slide and checked the chamber for a live round. It was empty. He released the slide on the empty chamber, and reinserted the thirteen round clip, driving it home with the heel of his left hand.

He grabbed a Raiders® jacket from the hall closet on the way out the door and stuffed the little automatic into the right pocket. Department policy clearly stated that sidearms would be carried in holsters at all times, if the investigator chose to carry a sidearm at all. John Randolf Barent tended to ignore policy in favor of personal preference whenever he thought he could get away with it.

He had left the car keys, by some odd chance, in their proper place. He snatched them from their hook on the wall near the door. It had been less than four minutes since he climbed out of the well of dreams. He performed a quick mental inventory, then stepped out into the cold morning darkness. The air was brisk and clear, as still as the night before Christmas. The old car, a superannuated Alfa Romeo ragtop with a manual choke, started at the first turn. It idled roughly, grumpy while it warmed up. He backed out of the driveway, flipped on the headlights and headed for town, for the address Stacey had given him: 1910 Sacramento. It was twenty minutes away.

The fire scene was south of the downtown district in a light industrial section of the city. It was a big building, fairly new, or at least less than a decade old, he surmised. He parked the Alfa Romeo at the curb half a block away from the barricades and flashing lights of the fire scene and walked the remaining distance.

Andy McCabe, who was the Fire Marshal and his boss, intercepted him as he ducked under the yellow barricade tape labeled "Fire Line-Do Not Cross". Other eyes paused from their work, looked at him oddly as Andy caught his sleeve. Barent had notorious hair which, on waking, inevitably looked like he had combed it with an eggbeater. He dismissed mentally the odd looks. He figured he must be wearing a particularly comical coif. He should have consulted the nagging mirror before he left the apartment. Mentally, he shrugged. He ran his left hand through his mop in a cursory attempt to impart order.

Andy McCabe, on the other hand, looked like he had just stepped off a men's fashion page. Barent marveled at his boss' ability to look freshly pressed at all hours of the day and night. Underneath the man's blue work coveralls with department insignia on the left shoulder a crisp white shirt and a power tie reflected the light of the fire scene. Not a hair was out of place. John Barent wondered briefly how he did it and briefly hated him for it.

"What have we got?" queried John of his superior. He expected a quick briefing, and an assignment to head up the cause and origin investigation. Instead, McCabe surprised him.

"Go home, John. We don't need you on this one." McCabe's tone was uncharacteristically gentle.

Barent was stunned. This was a serious fire, and he was their acknowledged best investigator. It wasn't as if there were plenty of investigators; it would take the entire staff a few days to complete the investigation on this one. He looked at McCabe in puzzlement.

"What in the hell are you talking about? Stacey told me we lost two guys, and now you're telling me you don't need me? What's going on, Andy?" It hit him like a pile driver as McCabe opened his mouth to reply.

"It was Twos, John." McCabe watched Barent carefully as the import of his announcement soaked in.

"Larry...?" His voice uttered the name, low and apprehensively. His nephew, his brother's oldest son, was assigned to Engine Company Two.

McCabe nodded.

The flashing lights of the emergency equipment played off the building surfaces, reflecting from glass and masonry to give the scene a surrealistic cast. The roar of engines and generators blended with the roaring in Barent's own ears as he absorbed the information. His mind raced through the facts, looking in panic for reasons why McCabe would lie to him. His eyes darted about the scene wildly, searching for his nephew's name on the reflective coats of the firemen working on the mop-up. Finally, his mind brought him Larry's face, like a hologram projected on the chaotic backdrop of the fire scene. With obvious and painful effort, he drew himself back to McCabe. Control. McCabe would send him away if he lost control. He took a deep breath and steeled himself, looking for a way to at least appear rational.

"You're sure?" The question was absurd, but it bought time to recover from the emotional shock of McCabe's utterance.

"We're sure," said McCabe quietly. He hoped his relief that Barent hadn't gone berserk didn't show. "Larry and Mark Stevens were on the interior line with Captain Sutcliffe. Sutcliffe made it out, but he's badly burned. He may not make it."

"God..." A wave of electric horror pulsed through Barent, grounding on the pavement.

"Want me to get somebody to take you home? There's nothing for you to do here." McCabe was carefully solicitous.

"No!" Barent was adamant. "I'll be O.K.; just give me a few minutes. I can help with the investigation. You need me. I need to do it."

"Forget it. You're not doing anything tonight but going home. That's final."

"McCabe, listen. If you don't let me do my part here, I'll come unglued. This may be murder as well as an arson investigation, if we find out the fire was intentional. You need me. I have to do it. I'm not going home. And that's final!"

"I can have you removed. Don't make this any harder than it already is."

Barent glared at McCabe, fire and malevolence blazing from his eyes. He lowered his voice, speaking through clenched teeth. He spat the words venomously at the Fire Marshal.

"You son of a bitch! Your authority ends at that barricade tape. Eject me, but I will stand right there, on the other side of that line, and watch. And I'll make your life a living hell in any way I can until the day you retire if you do this to me. You owe me!"

McCabe backed away from the confrontation, muttering words to soothe the beast that he had seen emerge from Barent. He decided that the beast would be a greater problem than any other he had right now. He acquiesced, just a little. If compromise would ease the conflict, compromise was the answer. McCabe had a nearly pathological need to avoid conflict. He moved to placate Barent. He was careful not to seem to relinquish his authority.

"John," he murmured persuasively in conciliatory tones, "you're upset. I'll ignore the threat. You're upset, you didn't mean it. Back off until we have removed the bodies, and I'll put you in charge of the C & O investigation. I want Castaneda to do the fire death investigation. Aaronsen will handle the photos and documentation. Go get a cup of coffee and come back in two hours. It's for your own good."

Barent bristled at the last comment, but concealed his rage by looking at the ground. Every time anybody had ever done anything for his own good, he wound up inevitably regretting it. Still, if he would compromise, McCabe said he could do the cause and origin work. It was a concession, he now realized, that few bosses would make, and one that McCabe might come to regret if he, Barent, couldn't control himself. McCabe would only be pushed so far, and if he opted to kick the decision upstairs, Barent knew he would be cut out of the investigation altogether. At least this way he would be on the case.

He looked up at McCabe. He drew in a deep breath, let it out. In as calm a voice as he could manage, he said simply, "O.K." He looked again at the ground. McCabe remained silent.

Barent drew his collar around his neck as he suddenly became aware again of the pre-dawn cold. He turned away from McCabe without another word. He left the control line, and went to his car. The Alfa started on the first turn of the key, and he drove to the office to retrieve his evidence collection equipment for the investigation.

As he drove, he considered calling his brother to tell him of Larry's death. He decided he had to make the call. He did not know enough yet, but the painful call couldn't be deferred until later, until he had his own feelings under firmer control. The call was one that couldn't wait for the cold, official information through channels. His relationship with his older brother would be harmed by any postponement. Bill deserved the unsoftened truth, brutal as it might be.

Under the stark, green-tinged glare of the over-head fluorescent lights at the office, he sat down at his desk. He stared at the phone for long minutes, composing his thoughts, trying to imagine how it would feel to receive the call he was about to make. He had no idea how to begin, what to say. He knew only that family loyalty demanded that he make the call. In flagrant violation of office policy, he lit a Winston®. Somehow he derived resolve through the contact with his father's ancient Zippo® as he flipped open the cover with its satisfying and pre-dictable click, and completed the lighting ritual. With trepidation, he reached for the phone, dialed Bill's area code and number from memory.

"Hello. Bill Barent." Bill was already awake. His voice had the cheery clarity of someone on his third cup of coffee and ready to leave for work. Bill was an operator for the All-American Pipeline. He lived in Blythe, near the Colorado River.

"Bill, it's John."

"Hey, Bro'! What's up? Isn't it a little early for you to be on line? Something wrong?" His greeting edged away from cheerful as he caught his brother's tone.

"Bill, I've got bad news. There's been a fire here. A bad one. Larry's been, uh...Larry didn't make it. He's dead. His crew got into trouble on an interior attack." The words tumbled out like dice from a cup. Barent felt his throat tighten.

The stunned silence from the other end of the phone was the hardest thing John Barent had ever endured. He forced himself to remain quiet while his mind ran through a litany of explanations and apologies, wanting to make his brother's pain go away, and to ease his own discomfort by explaining away the terrible fact of their loss. He said nothing.

"How?" The word dropped like a rock into the still pond of silence.

"I don't have all the details, yet. Bill, I'm sorry. Jesus, I'm sorry. They're still at the scene. It would have been hours before they notified you through official channels. I'll be working on the investigation. I'll call you as soon as I know more."

CHAPTER 3

A seam of brilliant orange laid open in the dawn sky like a bleeding wound on the eastern horizon two hours later, to the minute, as an icy and detached Barent arrived back at the fire scene. McCabe eyed him guardedly as he presented the customary briefing to the assembled investigation team. Barent learned with the others everything they knew and suspected up to that point. Other members of the staff hovered at the edge of the group gathered for the briefing as well, so that all would have the same body of information from which to proceed.

Castaneda was absent, having gone with the bodies of the deceased firefighters to the morgue. Jim Aaronsen stood by with cameras and bags of equipment festooning his person. He looked very much like a prospector's pack mule. One other man was present, whom Barent did not know, a gangly man half a head taller than Barent. The stranger had 'cop' written all over him.

"The call came through dispatch by automatic alarm at 0232 hours," McCabe began. "A standard first-alarm assignment was dispatched, and Engine Two —Captain Sutcliffe —called a second alarm on his arrival before he left the cab of Engine Two.

"Sutcliffe committed to interior attack, and turned over command to Chief Digby in order to make a quick attack. Digby coordinated the resources from that time. Dispatch logged the transfer of command at 0239 hours, two minutes after Sutcliffe was on scene. We haven't been able to talk to him yet about what he saw on arrival. He's at Monte Vista Hospital.

"The warehouse stored paper and office supplies. It was protected by a rate-of-rise heat detection system, and had full fire sprinklers. The sprinkler system was engineered, and the calc plate says the density was 0.22." Barent knew this referred to the gallons per minute per square foot the system was rated to deliver. It should have been enough to extinguish the fire at the incipient stage, and he interrupted to ask McCabe why it hadn't. McCabe sent him an irritated glance and answered as a continuation of the briefing.

"The system was shut down, the main control valve was closed, and we are still trying to figure out why we didn't receive a tamper alarm," McCabe continued. An electronic device that signaled any off-normal valve position supervised the valve. Law required such supervision for all sprinkler system control valves.

"The fatalities are Larry Barent and Mark Stevens." McCabe scrutinized Barent as he said this, searching for any reaction that might suggest Barent would not be able to handle things. Barent controlled with effort the sinking, sickening feeling in his stomach. The public acknowledgment of his loss added weight to the growing realization that it was real. Barent suppressed the welling up of grief that threatened to overwhelm him by biting the inside corner of his mouth. McCabe had been watching. Satisfied, McCabe went on.

"It looks like Sutcliffe might not make it, either. They're saying sixty-eight percent." He referred to the area of Sutcliffe's body damaged by third degree burns. McCabe hurried ahead before any of the men could address the connection between Larry Barent and John Barent and offer their sympathies.

Barent was grateful with half his heart, and hated him for it with the other half. His outward expression remained indecipherable.

"I've called in the State Fire Marshal to assist in the investigation," McCabe continued. "Deputy Caulkin will be assisting Captain Barent here with the cause and origin investigation. He'll be here by mid-morning." It wasn't unusual for the SFM to be called in on larger fires. Barent had worked with Marty Caulkin on other fire scenes and had come to value the man's expertise. Caulkin was good, very good. Barent was briefly thankful that the internecine jealousies that sometimes hindered cooperation in the police department investigations did not seem to apply to work on fire scene investigations.

"One last thing before you go to work. Dave Brooks, here, will be assigned to this investigation for on-the-job training. Take care of him, Barent." McCabe indicated the heretofore-unidentified man present with a glance in the man's direction. The casual introduction was replete with meaning. Brooks was, indeed, a cop.

Barent suppressed an urge to challenge Brooks' presence, thinking better of it. If he resisted Brook's assignment to the investigation team, his own slot might be placed at risk. This was political. McCabe's private agenda was to try to hand over the fire department's investigation and prosecution responsibilities to the police department, and stick entirely to fire prevention and education. The underlying budgetary savings would look good to the city fathers, and enhance McCabe's developing reputation as a fiscally savvy manager. That Barent believed such a move would castrate arson prosecutions—cops were uncomfortable with arson, and did other stuff first—was beside the point. It was a good career tactic for McCabe, who actually knew little about investigation, and cared even less. Barent realized that his own tenuous position on the investigation team had given McCabe an opening that he dared not move to close. McCabe was dumb —like a fox.

"Have we got consent to search?" asked Barent. That this was probably a crime scene made consent a requirement at the very least. Administrative consent was a formality at this early stage of the investigation, but Barent's excellent track record had been made going by the book. Barent knew that when he uncovered the first evidence that the fire was intentionally set he would have to freeze the operation and obtain a criminal search warrant. Once a crime was discovered, the perpetrator had rights. To continue to search without that warrant would render unusable in court any physical evidence they might discover. It would violate the arsonist's 'reasonable expectation of privacy'. Under the liberal California courts, reasonable seemed anything but reasonable. Barent had always wondered at the thinking that said a crook had a reasonable expectation of privacy in a building he burned down.

"Right here," said McCabe, pulling a signed form from a pocket inside his coveralls. "This is from the plant manager. It's enough to start, and we really haven't relinquished control of the scene."

Barent shrugged, taking the proffered document and checking the signature and date.

"Alright. Let's do it."

Barent began a walk around the outside of the structure with Brooks following mutely, and Aaronsen, the photographer, bringing up the rear.

He described into a tape recorder the sights that presented themselves, the damage, the broken windows and the intact ones, and their locations. The substance of his description would be used, if a warrant became necessary, to identify the premises to be searched. His description was precise and detailed.

"It is 8:45 a.m., October 13, 1999. Speaking is Investigator John Randolph Barent, in process of conducting a cause and origin investigation of a fire that occurred on these premises approximately six hours ago. The premises have been controlled by the fire department since the arrival of the first fire fighting units on scene, and this investigation is proceeding on consent signed by Walter Meyers, the warehouse manager.

"The structure is a high, one-story tilt-up, unpainted concrete edifice, with the numbers "1910" attached to the building on the side facing the fronting street, which is Sacramento Avenue. The front part of the building contains office space, and there are signs of forced entry at the front door consistent with fire department emergency ingress..."

Barent stopped his monologue from time to time to direct Aaronsen to photograph what he was describing. Aaronsen had experience, and took only one photo of each item Barent indicated. He knew every photo would have to be labeled, logged into

evidence, and catalogued. Wasted multiple photographs, taken only to assure that a good shot was
obtained, would multiply the workload. Failure to
include all photographs would be challenged by any
good defense lawyer. Experience had shown Barent
that it was generally better to lose one to poor lighting or camera movement, now and again, than to
take unnecessary or redundant pictures.

They worked their way into the interior, donning
respirators against the potential of harmful products
of combustion that might linger in the closed areas
of the interior. Barent turned on the GX-82 carbon
monoxide detector, and slung it by its strap from his
shoulder. It would give an audible alarm if dangerous concentrations of the gas were detected, and
they could withdraw. He couldn't count on the respirators to remove the carbon monoxide they might
encounter, but many of the other trace chemicals in
the smoke would be trapped in the activated carbon
filters.

The front offices were relatively intact. Barent
sealed the file cabinets with lead-wire seals, paper
tape, and tags as he passed them. They might contain evidence of use at some later time. Financial
records were always potentially evidentiary if the
fire was determined to be arson. Economic gain was
the single greatest motive for burning commercial
property, and the files might show motive. Barent
sealed the files routinely against this eventuality.

They would be removed later from the premises.

The team now entered the main warehouse space through the same door that Sutcliffe had made his ill-fated fire attack mere hours earlier. The sun of the young day lighted the interior at a low slant through the open roof. Wisps of smoke and steam wafted upward from the charred rubble. It looked like a garden at the gates of hell, with twisted bars of blackened metal reaching like barren, leafless plants toward the sunshine streaming in through the collapsed roof. The smell was unmistakable, of wet ashes and cold fire.

Barent headed for the fire sprinkler riser in the far corner of the devastated warehouse, walking carefully across the debris. There stood a large valve assembly that controlled the sprinkler system's water supply. McCabe had said the valve was shut off, but no signal had been received. Such systems had two alarm circuits, which operated independently of each other. The first was a paddle switch in the water pipe, which tripped if water flowed, and sent an alarm. The second alarm circuit supervised the control valve, and triggered a distinct, separate, silent alarm if the valve was moved to any position but fully open. This valve was closed, yet no alarm signal had been sent, and Barent wanted to know why.

It only took a glance to see the problem. A cover had been removed from the electrical conduit and the circuits had been bridged with homemade bridge wires. Somebody who knew precisely what they were doing had intentionally defeated the alarm system circuit. Barent froze the investigation and ordered everybody out. The simple discovery of the intentional defeat of the alarm system made this a crime scene, and made the firefighters' deaths murder. It was now critical that he obtain a criminal search warrant before continuing.

"This one's by the book," he explained, mostly to Brooks, who asked peevishly why the investigation was halted. "If we continue now, we have to protect the bad guy's rights against unlawful search. Now that we know he's involved, we have to safeguard his interests, and his right to privacy. Even though we don't know who he is."

"That's nuts," Brooks was astounded. "How can we...? How can the suspect have a right to privacy in a warehouse he torched?"

"Read Michigan versus Tyler, and Michigan versus Clifford. You can do it while I make out the warrant, and I'll answer your questions when you've finished." Barent referred to case law from two Michigan arson cases that set the nationwide standards that dictated his cessation of the search. Anything they found now, any evidence they seized now without a warrant, would be suppressed in court under the "fruit from the poison tree" doctrine. Any evidentiary fruit from an illegal search was inadmissible at trial.

Barent stopped to speak with the Incident Commander, and told him that they were stopping to get a warrant. He asked Chief Digby to maintain a watch on the premises until he could find a judge to sign the warrant and authorize the search. Digby had grudgingly agreed, not entirely convinced of the need to do so, but obviously too preoccupied with his own problems to offer more than token resistance. Both men knew that Digby's command, his tactics, strategy, and decisions would be reviewed in detail. A Board of Inquiry would scrutinize his decisions because of the deaths of the two firemen. It hung over Digby like the sword of Damocles, and the outcome would hinge on Barent's findings to a large extent. Barent never ceased to be amazed at how much Chief Digby didn't know about his own job.

CHAPTER 4

Barent always felt stupid when he executed the knock-and-notice provisions of a search warrant service on a burned out building. It meant that he had to stand outside the open —usually jimmied— door of the burned out hulk of the building, with birds and bugs flying freely through the broken windows and out through the open roof. He must knock, identify his authority, and announce in a loud voice that he was serving a search warrant on the premises. The grunts always got a charge out of it. Sometimes, they hollered, "Hey, nobody's home! Come back tomorrow!" or "The door's open!" or some such derisive mouth work, gleefully watching Barent's wry discomfort at being told the obvious. He endured it only because he had a case thrown out once, long ago, for his failure to dutifully comply with the instructions of a warrant. The experience had ultimately embarrassed him much more deeply that the inane song and dance of knock-and-notice.

Now began the true drudgery of the criminal investigation; the collection and recording of physical evidence that would show the fire was intentionally and willfully set. Equally important was the determination of who had done it, and why, but that was usually difficult to determine based on physical evidence alone. Often, it was not even possible. While the investigators might discover beyond a reasonable doubt who the culprit was and how the deed was done, proving it in court was something else entirely. The nationwide arson conviction rate hovered somewhere below five percent.

Barent started where he had left off. The beanpole cop Brooks trailed along like a faithful puppy, always in the way, always an annoyance. Someone had indeed defeated the sprinkler system tamper alarm with a high degree of skill. The signal wires had been bridged with a resistor fashioned from alligator clips and a couple of pieces of wire. The circuit thus manufactured fooled the alarm circuitry into thinking everything was hunky-dory while the perpetrator closed the water supply valve. Aaronsen took the photographs, and Barent carefully cut away the wiring to leave the bridge wires intact and connected. Brooks was tasked with bagging the evidence, and logging it into an evidence log which would describe every piece of evidence the investigators collected. Barent described the bridge wire in detail, and its removal, into a microphone on his collar connected to a tape recorder on his belt.

They worked their way painstakingly to the point of origin by looking at and assessing numerous indicators that told the trained eye where the fire had come from. Remaining wood and paint were more severely damaged on the side that was exposed first to the fire. Inferentially, that was the direction from which the fire had come. Wood was particularly helpful where it remained. Douglas fir commonly used in framing charred at about three-quarters of an inch per hour of burn time, white pine, a little faster. The actual depth was less important than its comparison to other pieces of charred wood of the same species that remained in place. By inserting a knife blade into the char and comparing the depth of penetration to solid wood with other such measurements, it became possible to determine approximately how long a specific piece had been exposed to flames. The deeper the char, the earlier in the fire the piece had been exposed. There were other indicators as well.

The job of stabbing the charred wood with a knife blade was given to Brooks. It was not reliable in and of itself as a method to determine the point of origin, but it would correlate with other indicators. And it would give him something to do. Brooks took a knife from the evidence collection kit, and after a brief instruction on the technique, began comparing depth of char as they moved through the structure. It made him feel useful, and kept him out of Barent's hair while Barent looked at other, more critical indicators.

When they finally arrived at the point where all the indicators showed the fire had originated, they found precisely nothing. There, in the middle of the warehouse floor, nothing remained. The floor was clean of debris, and the metal roof supports were completely burned away. Not just bent and deformed by heat, but completely gone. Vaporized. Barent was baffled.

"Here's one for the books, Dave." Barent couldn't force himself to say, "Here's one for the books, Brooks," and was compelled into an undesired familiarity with the cop who had been assigned for training.

"Fire almost always leaves something at the point of origin that will indicate what started it. The bottom of a plastic trash can under the ashes, or even the remains of a device, if one was used. This is our point of origin; look at the indicators. But there's nothing here. It looks literally swept clean. So, what do we do now?"

Brooks was mystified. "I have no idea. I've been absorbing the stuff on the indicators, and it's made sense, but now I couldn't tell you where to go next."

"Look at the floor," Barent instructed him. "What do you see?"

"It looks like glass, greenish glass, is melted there. And there are chips in the concrete around it."

"Where did it come from?" queried Barent. "How did it get there?"

"It fell from the ceiling?"

"If it fell from the ceiling, where is the debris it would have fallen onto? All of our indicators point to the floor, in this area. Look at it closer."

Brooks got down on his hands and knees, and peered at the molten glass. "It's part of the concrete!" he exclaimed. "How can that be?"

Barent got down on his knees, and reached for the knife he always carried. It was gone. He must have forgotten to drop it into his pocket when he left the house, still groggy in the pre-dawn hours. He patted himself down quickly, but found no bulge that might be his knife. He shrugged mentally and turned to Aaronsen.

"Got a knife, Jim?" Aaronsen let his camera dangle while he fished in his pocket, coming up with a pearl-handled pocketknife. He handed it to Barent, who snapped it open and knelt over the patches of green glass on the floor. Using the blade, Barent scraped at the edge of the melted glass. It didn't come free from the concrete; it was *part* of the concrete. Aaronsen winced at the use of his blade for such a purpose.

"Hey!" he cried.

"Sorry. Can't find my own."

"It's probably busted somewhere if you use it like that! Give it back."

"Picky, picky." Barent snapped the blade closed and gave it to Aaronsen. "I'll buy you a new one," Barent lied. Aaronson made an obscene noise and inspected the blade with exaggerated concern before he snapped it closed and dropped it into his pocket.

"That's molten concrete," Barent said, almost to himself. "It's been fused into glass. That's hotter that anything I've ever seen. What in the hell could have burned here that would melt concrete?" He continued instructively to describe what they were seeing for Brooks' benefit.

"The chips around the fused part are common in very hot fires. They're called 'spalling'. It happens when the moisture trapped in the concrete flashes to steam from the heat and explodes. That usually means accelerants were used; otherwise, the moisture cooks off too slowly to do that. If that's so, we should be able to pick up traces of flammable liquid vapors from the concrete. Let's get the sniffer."

The sniffer was a hand-held machine that took air samples and analyzed them for flammable vapor content. If a flammable liquid hydrocarbon like gasoline or diesel fuel had been used to accelerate the fire, traces would almost surely be detectable above the concrete floor. Also, there would be a burned pattern, made of residual carbon, where it had been poured. There was no pattern here, but it was still worth checking with the instrument. Aaronsen left his camera bag, and fetched the sniffer from the car. It produced nothing. No flammable vapors were present. This didn't mean that flammable liquids hadn't been used, just that it would be harder to prove. It was clear that some sort of unusual accelerant had been used to start the fire. If they could determine what had been used, they would be a leg up on finding their culprit. Taken along with the tampering discovered at the sprinkler valve, they could establish one of the elements of the crime of arson—the element of intent.

"Jim, I've seen all I need for now." Barent said to Aaronsen. "When Castaneda gets back, I want you guys to get a shovel crew and take it to the bare floor. I'll tell Digby to grab some firemen to help you. Brooks and I are going back to the office with the business files."

CHAPTER 5

"Can I talk to you for a minute?" Aaronsen stuck his head into the office where Barent and Brooks pored over the business files from the Wellman fire. "It's kind of important." He was covered with ashes and soot. A smear of blackened sweat and carbon traced a streak across his right cheekbone. His blond hair was filthy, and he smelled of the fire scene, acrid and damp.

"Yeah. Come on in."

"J.R., I need to talk to you out here. Come with me."

"Good grief!" Barent commented wryly, rolling his eyes back into his head in an exaggeration of pique for Brooks' benefit. "I'll be back." His best Arnold Schwartznegger imitation wasn't very good, but recognizable. He trudged out on Aaronsen's heels, following him to the parking lot.

"What's on your mind, Jim?" Barent asked when Aaronsen stopped and turned to face him.

"Recognize this?" Aaronsen held out a plastic evidence bag, sealed and tagged. It contained a pocket knife, covered with wet ashes. Barent didn't like the set of Aaronsen's jaw.

"It looks like my knife. Thanks! I thought I'd lost

it."

"I found it while Castaneda and I were cleaning the Wellman building to the bare floor."

"Thanks. Where was it?"

"I found it in the sprinkler control room. Under the ashes. You want to tell me how it got there?"

"I must have dropped it. I really don't know. It must have been kicked under the ashes, or it got ground in when you guys were tramping around. I don't even remember taking it out, but I must have. I was kind of preoccupied when we first started, what with Larry and all..."

"I said I found it *under* the ashes."

"Damn it, I told you I must have dropped it. For Christ's sake, give me the knife, would you?" Barent bristled, and his eyes narrowed as he regarded Aaronsen impatiently. Jim Aaronsen was almost as good as he was at reading the layers of ash on the floor of a fire scene. If he said the knife was under the ashes, that's where he found it. Still, it couldn't be his knife. Not under the ashes and debris that fell *after* the fire started. He searched for an explanation.

"Maybe it's not my knife. Maybe it's just like mine, but not."

Aaronsen looked at Barent speculatively, then at the knife. The handle was ivory, with a seal and a salmon in scrimshaw on the handle. He wasn't buying it. He had seen this blade on a dozen fires, and had, in fact, used it himself. It was clearly Barent's knife. Aaronsen remembered when Barent had returned from an Alaska vacation with the tool.

"Then where's yours?"

"Home. Hell, *I* don't know."

"Well, you don't mind if I hold onto this while you find yours. I'm not going to log it into evidence until you find yours."

"Log it. I'll find mine. Log it."

"Whatever you say, J.R."

CHAPTER 6

Deputy State Fire Marshal Marty Caulkin showed up predictably at Barent's office five minutes before noon. He walked past the receptionist, who greeted him as if he was a member of the department and not just a visitor from another agency. She waved him through.

Caulkin carried twenty extra pounds, mostly in the neck and head it seemed, and wore glasses as thick as Coke® bottle bottoms. His eyes held the wild, panicky look of a deeply worried math professor who had found an imaginary number someplace where it shouldn't be. Still, those eyes never missed a detail, and they were the gateways to a formidable intellect. Caulkin shared with Barent a passion for two things: battered Alfa Romeos and chilidogs. He often described his life as a consuming search for the perfect chilidog interrupted by fire investigations, and his waistline attested to his diligence in the search. He was shaped roughly like a bowling pin.

"I presume that you have made arrangements for my usual fee..." Marty greeted them as he breezed into Barent's office without knocking. He shook Barent's hand warmly, and turned to regard Brooks with comically exaggerated suspicion. "Who's the new guy?"

"Dave Brooks, meet Marty Caulkin," Barent made the introductions. "Dave is detached from the Police Department for cross-training. Marty is just detached. He had a loose screw, and it fell completely out." The two, Brooks and Caulkin, standing side by side, brought to Barent's mind a suggestion of Stan Laurel and Oliver Hardy, but the resemblance was too tenuous, too vague to preserve. Brooks was too tall, and Caulkin wasn't fat enough.

"Ah! I thought I smelled pork." Marty said it in a way that Barent knew meant he was kidding, but Brooks was not so sure. Brooks wasted a moment trying to decide if Caulkin's words were an attack or just an insult of acceptance. By the time he decided that a hostile response was not called for, the moment for it had passed, and he was forced to accept the comment as the friendly insult of a brother under the badge.

"What you smell is your customary fee. Chili dogs," responded Barent. "They're on the grill at Frank's Fabulous Foot Long Hot Dogs. You probably could have been here two hours ago, but that wouldn't have been near enough to lunchtime. Let's go eat, and we'll fill you in." Without pause in the stream of words he turned to Brooks. "C'mon, Brooks. Part of learning arson investigation is learning to love chili dogs. A rite of passage, as it were..."

Twenty minutes later all three men were trying to keep chili from dripping onto their shirtfronts. Barent filled in Marty between bites.

"Whatever it was, it burned hotter than hell. The concrete is glass at the point of origin, vitrified. I can't imagine what could have done that. We'll swing by the fire scene on the way back from lunch. You can take a look."

"And the fire sprinklers were defeated?" Caulkin queried.

"Yeah. The tamper switch circuit was bridged inside a junction box. Neat work. Not a skill you find in your everyday fire bug."

"Sounds like you might be dealing with a pro. A torch. What do the business records look like?" Marty referred to a matter of common knowledge among arson investigators. Brooks, intent on following the conversation, swore softly as a dribble of chili from a disintegrating steamed bun destroyed a thirty-five dollar silk tie. Caulkin and Barent smirked transiently while Brooks occupied himself with futile efforts of damage control. Many commercial fires were simply due to businesses finding themselves so deeply in trouble that the idea of selling the business to their insurance company became extremely attractive.

"They're in the black. But they're also into an outfit called the Brave New World Partnership for two hundred grand. It's an unsecured note." Marty's perennially frightened and amazed eyes peered significantly at Barent from over a disappearing chili dog. The eyebrows were raised almost comically high.

"Who are the players?" he asked through the hot dog.

"Four guys with big bucks. A real estate developer, an attorney, a guy who manufactures motorcycle fairings, and a guy who owns several local restaurants." Barent ticked off the names. "Two of them have had fires in town here within the last two years. Also, the motorcycle fairing guy had a major loss fire in his plant in Arkansas. Last winter. It was in the papers."

"Who owns the business?"

"His name's Archie Wellman. They sell business forms. The warehouse was full of paper."

"Printed forms or blank sheets?"

"Why would that be important?" Brooks wanted to know. He'd given up on the tie. And, he wanted to become a part of the conversation.

"Because," explained Barent patiently, "if he claims the forms were printed, he gets insurance reimbursement for loss of manufactured materials, not raw materials. The difference is a substantial profit, if nobody can prove he burned blank paper. It can be a lot of money if the warehouse is big enough. Also, if the forms are outdated, not salable, it's a good way to beat the loss. Make the insurance company buy them, along with a brand new building."

"That's incredible," breathed Brooks. "Who'd have thought of it?"

"Arson has reasons that Reason knows nothing of," paraphrased Marty, philosophically. "Follow the money, and you'll usually find the crook."

* * *

Reeking of raw onions and chili, the three men stared at the unexplainable greenish glaze on the concrete warehouse floor. Marty squatted laboriously and felt the glaze with the palm of his hand. "It's lower than the rest of the floor. This is vitrified concrete. It takes over five thousand degrees to do that. So, how did they do it? What do we know that burns that hot? How would *you* do it?"

"I've been thinking about that," said Barent. "When I was in the Army Ordnance Corps, we used a material called thermite. Well, we never actually used it, but it was supposed to be used, for example, if the enemy was over-running your position, and you needed to destroy files, or tanks, or ammunition. Pop the pin on a thermite grenade and drop it down the barrel of a tank, and presto! An instant puddle of molten steel.

"It's easy to make, if you've got the ingredients, and the ingredients are easy to get. I made some, once, in high school chemistry class. Lit it off and nearly burned the school down. Would have, if I hadn't done it outside. The radiant heat from the reaction was unbelievable. The charge was the size of a soft drink can, and I couldn't get within thirty feet of it. This tale is not to be repeated, incidentally. I don't need the flack I would take if my high school exploits were common knowledge."

Caulkin grinned. "So you think our boy used thermite? That's a couple of notches above the normal technical proficiency of your run-of-the-mill arsonist. Usually it's gasoline and a tossed road flare, or something equally simple. And equally easy to detect." Marty Caulkin was thoughtful. "It's going to kill more firefighters, too, if it catches on," he added, then regretted it immediately. He shot a glance at Barent, who did not wince —at least not visibly.

"It could represent a whole new ball game. If arsonists are getting smarter, our job gets harder. Let's hope it doesn't catch on." Barent offered.

"How would you get it in here, J.R.?"

"I'd bring it in an empty compressed gas cylinder, like on a cutting torch. It'd be perfectly safe, even in most fires. Takes over 2200 degrees just to ignite the mix. It's a dry, metallic powder. Just fill up the empty bottle, wheel it in and leave it until you're ready to have a fire. Then, when the time comes, add the right kind of fuse, and light it off."

"What's the right kind of fuse?"

"Magnesium ribbon works." Barent's statement rang with the conviction of personal experience.

"It's a good working hypothesis. Where would you get the ingredients around here?" Marty rose, puffing slightly from bending over.

"Half a dozen places I can think of, and probably a few I can't. Hell, our perp could have bought the ingredients by mail order. No restrictions on sending the stuff through the mail."

"Let's start checking the local places. No need to make things any harder than they need to be. And let's find out who's bought an empty compressed gas bottle around here in the last month or so."

"Wait a minute!" protested Brooks. "If a gas bottle was used, well, they're steel. Where's the bottle? We didn't find anything remotely like it in the ashes. Not even the base. Solid steel doesn't burn up."

"Vaporized, Davey, me boy," chirped Marty. "Vaporized." Brooks made a face, and kept quiet as the discussion continued. "Everything burns, if it gets hot enough," Marty added.

"So, what's our profile?" Barent invited the hypothecation that would tentatively give them a working set of probabilities. It would be refined in similar sessions as the investigation developed more information.

"It's a little early for that," said Marty. "I think we ought to have a chat with Wellman. Let's see how badly he's broken up about the fire. Let's see what the status of his loan is with the Brave New World Partnership. And let's pull the records of the Brave New World fires and see what they tell us. Let's find out if they kept a cutting torch in the warehouse."

"Well, it looks like a pro to me. Is there any way we can confirm the thermite? All we have now is a negative corpus." Barent referred to the *corpus delecti*, the body of the crime. In arson cases, if you could rule out all accidental causes, inferentially that meant the fire was not an accident. That meant that it was due to human causes, and suggested intent. It wasn't proof, but it represented a beginning. More than one arson case had been lost in prosecution because the investigator had not gone to sufficient lengths to rule out accidental causes, or overlooked a pertinent piece of evidence in the fourth corner of the ninth room that he searched. It was the last place anyone looked, or, in a sense, the first place nobody looked, and thus, could not be ruled out in court.

"We've got to find the folks who sold the ingredients. Then, we've got to identify the person who bought them. Then, we must tie that person to the crime scene, or to the property owner, Wellman. It won't be easy."

"It never is."

"Let's go talk to Wellman."

CHAPTER 7

Sam Sykes Straight Kentucky Bourbon® was the first priority of John Barent when he finally arrived at his tiny apartment home well after the dinner hour. The apartment was a converted garage at the rear of an old house in an older residential section of the city. City planners called it a 'granny flat', but the granny, his landlady Martha Forrester, lived in the front house, was recently divorced and still looked pretty good in a two-piece bathing suit. She lived alone, liked having a fireman around, and had made him a deal on the rental of the place. The place was a dump, but it was cheap. Tattered furniture from the Goodwill Store and cast-off lamps from the garages and attics of sympathetic friends finished out the décor. It was a long way from *Architects Review*, but it was paid for. He dropped two ice cubes into an old fashioned glass and poured himself a generous four fingers of Sam Sykes.

Fatigue from the day, which had started for him in the wee hours, sat on his shoulder like a stone gargoyle and gazed with him at the photograph in a cheap frame atop the television set. His brother, Bill, and himself, and Bill's son Larry stared back at him from the horizontal eight by ten shot of three substantial halibuts hanging upside down by their tails on the rack in Seward, Alaska. It had been the trip of a lifetime. All had shared the limy flavor of Corona beers in the July sun as they bobbed on gentle swells of a flooding tide in the Gulf of Alaska off Montague Island. Each had felt the thrill of the tugging resistance as the huge fish were dragged up from the depths. Each heard the whining scream of heavy duty reels as the fish shot again to the bottom on fishing line tuned bowstring tight.

He thought of Larry, on the float trips down the Colorado River in inflated inner tubes, iced beer in one hand and rod and reel in the other, careless, mindless of time, and insanely happy with the day and the company. Larry, of no artifice. Larry, of fun and future promise, blond hair bleached white by summer sun, electric blue eyes flashing from under the unruly mop.

Larry, his brother's son, was now become a charred hulk of flesh at his most heroic moment. The vision filled Barent's heart with venom, and his mind with pain. Larry was a brother in the fraternity of fire fighting, and he was a damn nice kid. He was dead because somebody wanted to make a buck burning a business to the ground. A goddamned buck.

Barent started in surprise as his second four-fingered glass of bourbon shattered and spewed the amber drink all over his lap. He looked numbly at his right hand. A shard of broken glass had laid it open. Blood welled up and flowed from a long cut between his thumb and forefinger. He realized that he had been squeezing the tallboy glass unconsciously with all his strength. Cupping the bleeding hand against his chest, he hunched into the bathroom and found a clean cloth. With it he wiped the excess blood, and pressed the cloth against the wound as a bandage to stop the bleeding.

When the bleeding was largely stanched, he peeled the makeshift dressing back carefully and looked at the damage. This one would need sutures. *Damn!* He tossed the bloody cloth into the wastebasket and re-wrapped his hand in clean gauze from the medicine cabinet, using pressure from the bandage to hold the open edges of the wound together. He drove himself to the emergency room, having a no small amount of difficulty with the stick shift as he guided the little Alfa down deserted streets to his destination. It never occurred to him that he might be legally drunk with the bourbon on board, and that his immobility was amplified by his intoxication. His mind seemed icy and clear.

From the hospital, after the stitches were tied off, he phoned Jessica. It was troublesome, dialing with his good left hand, but his injured hand barely functioned to hold the phone, and then only with some pain. The local anesthetic was wearing off, and the hand throbbed in measured waves. Jessica answered on the second ring.

"Hello?"

Jessica, it's John." He recognized her voice from the single word. It was unusually deep for a woman, and it gave her speech a sultry quality. It was a bedroom voice if he had ever heard one. "I need some help here, if you've got some free time."

"Is everything alright?"

"Well, I've laid my hand open. Dumb accident, but I can't drive. I'm at Monte Vista Hospital. Can you pick me up?"

"I'll be there in ten minutes."

Barent hung up the receiver, and plodded down the endless sterile corridor to the hospital pharmacy to get his painkiller prescription filled. He hadn't planned to use the prescription the doctor had written for him, but the incessant throbbing as the local anesthetic wore off was causing him to reevaluate his first decision. Arriving at the pharmacy, he pushed the slip over the counter to a bald, pink-faced, white-frocked pharmacist. The man read it, nodded wordlessly, and turned away to fill the order.

Waiting in the hollow fluorescent light of the pharmacy, Barent realized that Sutcliffe was here in the building, somewhere. They, he and Marty and Brooks, were going to talk with Sutcliffe in the morning, but he could look in on the burned fire officer while he waited for his prescription to be filled.

"How do I get to the Burn Unit?" he asked the pharmacist, who was invisible behind some shelving.

"Down the hallway to your right, follow the signs," the voice came back at him. "They're closed now. You can't get in until ten tomorrow morning."

"Have you heard any scuttlebutt about the patient there, the fireman? How's he doing?"

"Who wants to know?" The pharmacist emerged from the maze of shelves and set an amber bottle before Barent. "One every three hours. It may cause some constipation. No alcohol." He looked sternly, significantly, at Barent. He wrinkled his nose and spoke the last two words of his instruction with added emphasis.

"I'm a fireman. I work with the guy, just wanted to know how he was doing."

"You're not one of the paramedics I see around here."

"No, I'm an administrative type. I haven't done emergency medical response in years."

The pharmacist apparently decided Barent was O.K. "He's serious. He's getting lots of strong medication for the pain. They're moving him to Sherman Oaks tomorrow afternoon." The Burn Center in Sherman Oaks was reputed to be the best in the state, if not in the nation.

"Thanks. And thanks," Barent said, holding up

the prescription. "I'll come back tomorrow," he added, as if it mattered to the pharmacist. He wandered away down the corridor in search of a drinking fountain.

Getting the plastic bottle open easily required the full use of both hands, and he fumbled with it impatiently. He cursed the childproof cap. It appeared to be adult-proof, too, if the adult didn't have the full use of both hands, and a doctorate in mechanical engineering. Finally, he managed, nearly spilling the entire prescription onto the floor as the cap came suddenly free. He stopped at a drinking fountain. He popped a pill into his mouth, and bent over the fountain. The water was cold enough to make his head ache as he drank. A piercing pain ricocheted around behind his eyes.

Jessica was waiting for him in the Emergency Room lobby when he returned, and she rose quickly to meet him. Her eyes expressed a combination of concern and relief. She hugged him gingerly, as if he might break, and he reassured her.

"I'm not broken. You don't have to be careful. It's just a cut on my hand, but I can't shift the Alfa. It's beginning to hurt like hell."

"How did it happen?" Jessica wanted to know. "You smell like a distillery." She made a face, scrunching her nose at the redolent odor of bourbon clinging to Barent's clothes.

"I broke a glass," Barent offered vaguely. "Let's

go."

"What about your car?"

"I'll deal with it tomorrow. It'll be O.K. here in the hospital parking lot."

This woman was starting to become an important part of his life, he reflected as they drove away from the hospital toward his apartment. She was always there for him. She was fun, and somehow mysterious. She was twelve years younger than he was, and she was strikingly beautiful in an exotic way. He wondered how much of his feeling for her was true caring, and how much was attributable to his ego, which had been swelling ever since the evening eight months ago when this young vixen had selected him from a crowded bar, and brazenly picked him up.

She had spent the night on that first evening, and he was smitten with her casual sexiness. She seemed to know exactly what turned him on without ever asking, and she had an innate sense of what he found sexy and exciting. She took excellent care of herself, and inevitably dressed with a flair that was either absent or undeveloped in other women Barent had known. His mind had toyed with the idea of inviting her to move in with him, but he had not yet breached the subject. He suspected she might not be as enthusiastic about the idea as he would like, and he himself remained equivocal. Was he really all that sure a live-in relationship was what he wanted? He really didn't know that much about her.

Still, she slept over two or sometimes three nights a week, and weekends when he wasn't working. She seemed to like his company, but neither had mentioned love. He wondered where it would all end up, and resolved to tolerate his fair share of the ambiguity until he could be more sure about things. His experiences with women had produced a caution of commitment that was difficult for him to overcome. In a word, he didn't understand women, and didn't trust them. His ex-wife and the State of California had collaborated to make sure that any trust that he might have salvaged when his marriage dissolved was destroyed in the divorce proceedings. He knew his distrust was an emotional dead end, but it was a friend that protected him from injury as well. Love inevitably caused pain; distance never did.

Jessica ushered him into his tiny apartment, helped him undress, and solicitously tucked him into bed, bringing him a glass of water and his pain medication. The bandaged hand lay like an eyeless, white teddy bear atop the bedspread, and Barent began to relax as the throbbing subsided.

"Mind if I stay?" asked Jessica. "That way, if you need anything, I'll be here, and I've got to be at work early. It seems kind of pointless to go home now. I'll leave early."

"Sure," agreed Barent, affably. His head was starting to fuzz out from the second dose of medication within the hour, and he was certain he could sleep. The hand, and its throbbing pain, belonged to somebody else. He watched with amusement as his conscious mind checked to see if the pain was really still there. He apologized silently to his liver.

He watched as Jessica peeled her clothes off and slipped into bed with him. He felt brief stirrings of interest at the sight of her naked body, with its small, firm, interesting breasts and slim hips, before he dropped suddenly away into a deep and dreamless sleep.

CHAPTER 8

"Had a nasty one last night," reported Aaronsen as Barent entered the office. "Say, what happened to your hand?" Barent's eyes were bleary from waking an hour ago from his drug-induced sleep, and he felt 'rode hard and put away wet', as Aaronsen was wont to say. A shower hadn't seemed to help, and washing was a real pain in the ass with the bandage on his hand. Halfway through the shower, he realized that a plastic bag and a rubber band would have kept the dressing reasonably dry, but by that time it was too late. He had rebandaged the hand with considerable effort, and it looked like the work of a rookie on the first day of his first aid training. Even dressing required extra effort. The taxicab that brought him to work had been late. His mood was black.

Aaronsen, himself in coveralls, fairly reeked of a fire scene. The unmistakable smell of a structure fire emanated from his hair and clothing. There was a smudge of soot on his face, to which Barent pointed silently, by using eye contact and touching his own face. Aaronsen pulled a handkerchief from his pocket and wiped it off.

"I cut it on a glass last night. Seven stitches. Jim, what happened last night?"

"That explains why you didn't answer your pager. I tried to call you early this morning, actually. A little after four. Three sets, in an apartment building. All in exit stairways. The fires, two of them didn't take. The third lit up and gave us a fight. Whoever made the sets could have had only one thing in mind: trapping the occupants on the second floor. Our perp is a real sicko."

"Shit. Who's on it?"

"Me. I can handle it, and you've got the Wellman fire. I've already done some of the photo work, but if you can spare Castaneda, I can use him. We've still got a bundle of cause and origin work to do. I came back to the office to get a warrant." That three separate fires had occurred in the same building at the same time was sufficient probable cause for a criminal search warrant in and of itself. The odds of such a group of fires being accidental were astronomical. Aaronsen had done the right thing. And they had another crook to look for, this one dangerous, and probably crazy.

"Castaneda's all yours. Take him. Seen Brooks yet?"

"He's upstairs, getting coffee."

"We're going over to the burn ward to talk to Sutcliffe today, after Caulkin gets here. They are shipping him to Sherman Oaks this afternoon. We'll see if he can tell us anything about the fire."

"Tell him to hang in there. We're all rooting for

him. Let us know how bad it is."
"Yeah."

* * *

It was hard to look at Sutcliffe, but necessary. Barent, Caulkin, and Brooks stood self-consciously by the hospital bed, staring at a form swaddled in bandages. Sutcliffe lay prone, on his stomach, with his face in some sort of cradle, apparently unaware as yet of their presence. Parts of the bandages were soaked through with weeping fluids from the burn injuries, and tubes with intravenous solutions entered the bandages at a number of sites. Superficially, the room smelled like a Band-Aid® factory, but underneath was the subtle sour, warm, fetid miasma of weeping flesh and plasma.

"Fifty eight percent," said the nurse, anticipating their question about the percentage of body area burned. "His chances are fairly good for survival. Infection is his biggest enemy now." She had distributed surgical masks and sterile latex gloves to all three before they had been allowed to enter the burn ward through gasket-sealed doors. "He's in for it on debridement and rehab. There will probably be major skin grafting for the next two years, and occasionally after that."

"Can he talk?"

"For a few minutes, but he won't like it much. His

face is burned except for a ring that was protected at his breathing mask seal. It hurts him to move any part of his face, and the less he does, the better, at least for now. Most of his serious burns are on his back."

Barent bent down near the silent form of Captain Sutcliffe. He looked for a place to put his hand, both for balance as he lowered himself, and to establish a reassuring contact with Sutcliffe. There was nowhere to put it, so he dropped to both knees and looked uncomfortably up at the officer's face, feeling vaguely ridiculous. "Mike," he said gently. "Mike, can you hear me?"

"Uh-huh." The voice was oddly distorted, partly from his downward-facing position, but more from his efforts to speak from his throat without moving his lips.

"Mike, we need to know what you saw on the fire. Can you help us? Can you tell us what you saw?"

"Uh-huh."

"Tell me what happened."

Mike Sutcliffe spoke, exercising care in pronouncing certain consonants that required facial movements for clear enunciation, but the story emerged.

"Looked alright goin' in. Smoke high. Small flames in the middle. Som'n happened, got real hot, real fast. Like a blast furnace. I ran. Couldn't help it.

I ran. Oh, God, I left my crew..."

"Let it go, Mike. There was nothing to be done. If you hadn't gotten out, you would have died." Barent wanted to reach out and touch him, to share the torment with the reassurance of physical contact, but there was no place within reach that would bear his touch.

"Maybe better. The kid, your nephew? I'm sorry. Jesus, I'm sorry. His gear just went to flames. Sudden bright light, white light. Hot, like nothing you've ever seen. He hit it with the hose stream, and it blew up, got hotter. Like a jet engine. Roared. J.R., I heard them scream. Nightmares. Better 'f I died. Coward."

"Bullshit!" said Barent, his voice both restrained and adamant. His eyes were watery; tears and grief lurked just below the surface. He had started his career in fire suppression, cut his professional teeth at the end of a hose line. He knew with a shared intimacy how Sutcliffe felt, not just from empathy, but from common experience. It took superhuman effort not to give his anguish voice. Hearing the details of his nephew's death from his mummified, tormented friend and co-worker wrenched him apart inside. He squirreled away from the agony by focusing on Mike. A grapefruit grew in his throat, tears edged at the corners of his eyes.

"You're alive," Barent continued, "and you've got work to do. You've got to keep it together and get better, no matter what it takes. The guys at the station know you aren't a coward. Every one of them knows he would have done the same thing, and they're happy you're alive. They're *proud* you're alive. Hang in there, and beat this thing." The knot hardened at the back of Barent's throat from swallowing his own pain without giving it voice.

Barent felt a hand gentle on his shoulder. He turned, looked up. A nurse had materialized to stand at his side.

"You've got to leave now. He's had enough for the time being. He has no stamina at all now, and he needs to rest."

"Yeah. Thanks." Barent rose, unembarassed by his tears, and gestured to Caulkin and Brooks to precede him out of the room. "Thanks, Mike. I'll be back. We need more information from you to help find out who did this." The words were a little lame, but Barent's intent was to give Sutcliffe a job to do, make him believe the investigation depended on him, and thus encourage him to fight. It was the best he could do.

"J.R." The sound was slurred, the 'R' almost a grunt. Barent turned back.

"Yeah, Mike?"

"You know what's worst?"

"What, Mike?"

"All the burns are on my back. On my friggin' back."

"Shit, Mike."

As Barent emerged with his cohorts from the hospital lobby into the sunshine, he dug out his Winstons® and realized that he had forgotten his lighter. He patted himself down, and realized that he must have left it in the office. That was O.K. He had been cutting back, and that he had forgotten his lighter was a good sign. It meant that cigarettes were losing some of their importance to him. But he really wanted one at this moment. It would ease the knot in his throat, and stop the shaking in his hands.

* * *

They decided to split up. Caulkin and Brooks would go to interview Archie Wellman, and Barent would start looking for places to buy the ingredients for thermite. He found three and drew blanks on all of them. Nobody had sold either of the ingredients to anybody in the last month or so, and a sale to an individual of sufficient quantity to construct a device would have drawn attention, and been remembered. The demand for the materials in small quantities was not that common, and they were not usually sold over the counter, but purchased in bulk from industrial suppliers.

On impulse, he drove to the nearest supplier of bulk bottled industrial gases, identified himself, and asked the counter clerk if anyone had purchased an empty pressure bottle recently.

"We sell five or six sets of acetylene welding bottles a month," the clerk told him. "We replace about a hundred others, but they are almost always empties returned for refill. We simply give them a new cylinder, and refill the old one."

"And there was nothing unusual about any of the sales? In the last month, I mean."

"No, not that I can recall."

"Acetylene welders are always sold with two bottles, one for acetylene and one for oxygen, right?"

"Yeah."

"Did anybody come in here and buy just one bottle?"

The clerk scratched his head, then looked at Barent. "Yeah, now that you mention it. A guy came in and bought a single empty oxygen bottle. About two weeks ago. I forgot."

"Can you describe him?"

"Yeah. Small guy, mid twenties, long hair. Not one of our regulars. We get a lot of long-hairs in here. They usually live out in the country, and keep a torch around for repairs. But they buy full bottles, and this guy wanted his empty. I had to unpack it special. He was about five feet four or five, moustache. Pale. He was real pale, like he hadn't been outside for a long time. It caught me funny, he wore gloves. Most guys take off their gloves when they come in, but I remember he didn't. I figured maybe something was wrong with his hands, y'know. When I brought out the bottle, the money was already on the counter, and he just scraped up the change and put it in his shirt pocket. With his gloves on."

"What was he driving?"

"I didn't see. He said he didn't need any help with the bottle, and I went into the back as soon as he went out the door."

"Did he buy anything else? Besides the bottle, I mean." Barent was beginning to think he was onto something. The behavior that the counterman described was unusual enough to pursue the investigation further.

"No, ...yeah, wait! He bought a welding rod. One welding rod. We normally sell them in boxes of two hundred and fifty, or five hundred, but this guy wanted just one. Uncommon type, at that."

"What type?" Barent's heart leapt into his throat as the counterman answered, confirming the scent.

"Magnesium. The guy bought a magnesium rod."

"Did you write out a ticket?"

"Always. We do it on computer, and use it to track inventory, and for mailing out ad specials. Might even have his address."

"Can I see it?"

"Hang on, it'll take a few minutes. I'll have to look through the tickets by hand." He retrieved a box from an office in back and placed it on the counter, stopping to sell a customer a welding helmet, then returning to his search. He fanned through several dozen invoices, then stopped. He pulled a yellow sheet out of the box.

"Here it is! I got it," he exclaimed. He handed the yellow sheet to Barent. There was the man's name, address, and his signature. The signature was oddly forced, angular and erratic. Barent had observed that criminals often wrote in elegant, flourishing penmanship; it was almost a mark of certainty, although worthless by itself. This signature looked like crazed glass.

Barent asked the man for a copy, and the man nodded and vanished into an office behind the counter. Barent heard a copier whine as it heated up, and the man returned in a moment to thrust the still-warm sheet into his waiting hands. Barent could almost smell the scent of his prey on the sheet.

"Look, it may be real important to preserve that slip," said Barent. "What do they do when they're done with it?"

"Well, this ticket was for cash. I suppose they'll pitch it. Or file it with the accountant."

"Can you have them save it? Call me when I can pick it up?"

"Sure." He reached out and accepted Barent's proffered business card.

"Listen," Barent explained, "I need your name and address. I may have to get in touch with you at a later time as part of the investigation I'm doing." The man wrote the information on the back of a business card and handed it to Barent.

"Can you tell me what this is all about?" he queried.

"Maybe nothing, yet. If it does turn out to be important, I'll get back to you. Meanwhile, it's too early to say. But, thanks, and you may have helped a lot." Barent left, and drove back to the office.

As he drove, elated at the luck of getting such a solid lead, he thanked his lucky stars that the man had bought the welding rod at the same time he bought the empty bottle. It would mean nothing to the counterman, or to the untrained mind, but to John Randolph Barent it showed sophistication, and intent. And it suggested carelessness, or arrogance; the bad guy didn't expect them to make the connection. Magnesium was one of the few materials that could be used to trigger a thermite device. The rod would have to be pounded flat in order to be ignited by a normal flame, but once lit, it would burn for several minutes at a temperature of over two thousand degrees. It would delay the ignition of the device, and provide an ignition source, all for a dollar and thirty-one cents. It cinched it for Barent. He was convinced he had his man. Now, there remained only to prove it.

He considered the name on the copied sales slip. *Well, Mr. Jason Grover,* he thought, *where were you on the night of October twelfth?*

CHAPTER 9

Marty Caulkin and Dave Brooks were waiting for Barent when he returned to the office. He held his own news until they had briefed him on their results. Archie Wellman had not cracked, but he was worried, sweating. He had asked persistently when his records would be returned, even though there was no business that could be done from the burned out shell of his workplace.

"We Mutt-and-Jeffed him," reported Brooks, referring to an interview method where one investigator took the side of the interviewee, protecting him from the ire of the other, who fumed and threatened. "We came that close to reading him his rights, but there just isn't enough, yet. He's in financial trouble with the company. Missed a payroll last month. The records don't show it, there's a good cash flow; he showed us. He's insured to the nines, and the payments are current. Kind of makes me wonder if our Mr. Wellman doesn't play the ponies, or something." Brooks paused thoughtfully a moment, then went on.

"Anyway, he knows we're interested, and we decided to let him sweat, see if he makes a bad move. If he's been skimming, he might crack. It's a lighter rap than a double murder. Then, we could offer him a deal to give up the torch."

"If you turn a single piece of additional hard evidence, I want you to read him his rights. I don't want to blow this by getting a confession before we've Mirandized him." Barent had seen investigations go down the tubes, and criminals walk free, because of overly enthusiastic interviews. He did not want that to happen here.

Marty understood this, and reassured him. "We stayed on the right side of the advisement. We didn't say anything that suggested he might be a suspect. We just went for general information incidental to the fire, and the business. Asked him about recently terminated employees who might want to get back at the company, that sort of thing."

"Do you think, then, that he might have hired the job? Gotten a pro?"

"Real possible," observed Caulkin. "The Brave New World folks would have that type of connection. Nobody has ever made them on the fires they had. And he does owe them a quarter of a million. It's in their interests for him to remain solvent. It wouldn't surprise me to find out that he got a little help from his friends."

"Well, I may have our torch," Barent announced with an unmistakable air of smugness. It was a professional indulgence that they allowed him, particularly since it made for a good piece of work if it were true. He explained the matter of the empty oxygen cylinder, and the magnesium welding rod, and showed them the sales slip.

"Lets run him!" suggested Marty. "NCIC, ICPI, CLETS, the works. Let's find out what this guy does for a living!" Caulkin referred to standard computer record searches that would give them a rap sheet on Mr. Grover. Brooks recognized two of the programs from his police work, the National Crime Information Center, and the California Law Enforcement Telecommunications System, but had never heard of the third.

"What's ICPI?"

"The Insurance Crime Prevention Institute. They keep a data base on insurance fraud, fires, that sort of thing," Marty answered, his surprised eyes looking particularly amazed as he nodded his head to affirm his own recommendation. "We'll check, but if he's a pro, he'll probably come up clean. I'll bet on it."

"And, then?"

Barent tapped the copied yellow sheet he had brought from the gas supply shop. "Then we go talk to the man," he said. Turning from his comrades, he went about making the necessary calls.

* * *

Aaronsen came into the headquarters building

just after the three other investigators left to find their Mr. Grover. He was agitated, and he reeked of smoke. He made a beeline straight for McCabe's office. There, he caught McCabe before he could go to lunch, and the two men spent the next forty-five minutes behind closed doors in McCabe's office. At the end of their discussion, McCabe made the necessary calls, and issued instructions to Aaronsen. Then, he made an appointment with the Fire Chief. He was an hour and a half late for his luncheon engagement, and he had a headache to write home about. Still, the new development that churned in his mind was extremely important. The Fire Chief must be appraised immediately of the serious nature of the information Aaronsen had brought in, and of what actions he, McCabe, had taken with regard to it.

CHAPTER 10

Jason Grover lived in a vacant lot. The address that the investigators found on the sales slip turned out to be an empty parcel of land between two apartment buildings on the south side of town, near the railroad tracks. Dry grass stubble covered the earth on the lot, and it had been cleaned recently. There was not even a refrigerator box that could be used as a domicile by a transient.

They had been particularly interested in finding Mr. Grover, and still were, but they would clearly have to look elsewhere. His rap sheet had been faxed in from the National Crime Information Center, and Marty had lost his bet. Grover had been convicted once for felony arson, once for burning the property of another, a misdemeanor, and as if that wasn't enough, he had three counts of lewd conduct on the record. He had done eight months at Camarillo for the arson. His sole punishment had been to have his freedom restricted while he had his head examined at the State Facility for the Fundamentally Bewildered and Criminally Disposed.

"Looks like our boy hangs out in the men's room at the park," commented Marty, "and likes to play

81

with fire." The inference was reasonably sound; one lewd conduct arrest could be anything, but three indicated a pattern of behavior.

"Yeah, but look at this," Barent pointed at the sheet and tapped it with the nail of his left index finger. "No activity in the last five years. Bad guys don't usually stop doing what they do, just like that," he remarked. Brooks, reading over his shoulder, pointed at the FAX sheet. "Why do you suppose he suddenly got clean, with a track record like that?"

"Maybe he turned pro and cleaned up his act," Barent speculated.

"It's possible. Maybe he just got better at his favorite things, and hasn't been caught lately." Marty scowled.

"Well, he's sure beginning to look like our perp. Last known address?"

"What else?" It would be difficult, but it could be done. The last known address was five years old.

"Where did he do his time?" queried Brooks. "Maybe they can tell us something."

"Let's find out everything we can about this guy. Maybe something will break if we know enough." Barent's basic tactic had always been to get inside the criminal's head, to think like the bad guy thought, and to do this, every scrap of information had value. Collecting the information was a dull; plodding process of phone calls and interviews—and dead ends. It took an obsessive and analytical mind to go the distance. Barent knew he had one, and knew Caulkin did, as well. It was time to find out about Brooks.

"Brooks, it's time to crack the books," Barent said.

"Books?"

"Phone books."

While returning to the office, Barent leaned over the car seat from behind and instructed Brooks as Marty drove.

"You know what we know. Now here's some background to help keep you from wasting a lot of time barking up the wrong tree. First, our guy is male. Nine out of ten fires are done by males. If a female sets a fire, it's usually on the bed where her man has taken a lover. She'll usually do his clothes, too, particularly his underwear. I'm sure you get the symbolism." Brooks smiled briefly, snorted quietly, and Barent continued.

"While our bad guy has a history of sexual deviation, or deviant behavior, it's probably not connected with the fire. What I mean is, the guy's not a pyro. Pyromaniacs, people who get a sexual charge out of setting fires, are actually quite rare—less than a tenth of a percent of convicted arsonists are actually pyromaniacs. They're usually not too sophisticated, and they're fairly easy to catch. Just look for the guy in the crowd with the wide, glassy eyes and the trenchcoat. They like to hang around and watch the fire after they've set it.

"Our perpetrator, on the other hand, is cool and very proficient at what he does. He may have chosen fire to express himself for some deep-seated psychological reason, instead of burglary or fraud, but he doesn't get a sexual charge out of it. It's business, strictly business. He's probably set several fires during the missing five years of his life, and hasn't been caught. He will be very hard to nail, because he's not stupid. He will have a good alibi when we finally find him, and he will probably not have left much, if anything, by way of evidence that connects him directly to the crime scene. He plans his work carefully, even obsessively, and has probably never been seen by the people who hired him. He's paid in cash, at a mail drop, or something. There won't be a paper trail."

"If that's the case, why wouldn't the people who hire him simply not pay?" Brooks wanted to know.

"It's simple. What he did *for* them, he could just as easily do *to* them. They know that. It's in their interests to pay, promptly, after the fire. Besides, there's a certain honor among thieves." The *non sequitur* didn't faze Brooks. The meaning was clear.

"So, how do we follow the money? Marty said to follow the money to find the crook."

"Once we get enough evidence, we search financial transaction records. First, we establish clearly that the businessman and the arsonist deny knowing each other. I'm sure Wellman will cooperate with that. Then we link them together, destroy the alibi. Maybe we find the deposit in one bank account and the debit in the other, after the fire. With luck the amounts will match, and the dates will mesh with our time-line. Our arsonist probably doesn't take money up front, and doesn't lock himself into a performance date on the 'contract', at least not without jacking up the price. If anybody knows precisely when he's going to do the job, his risks become unacceptable."

"What if the torch doesn't deposit the money? You'd never get the match then."

"His employer still has to take it out of the bank. The withdrawal alone can be evidentiary, especially if the customer can't explain what the money was used for, and it happens around the time of the fire. Sometimes that's enough circumstance to get a businessman to roll over."

"And sometimes not?"

"Sometimes not." Barent shrugged.

"So then, how do we get the fire setter?"

"Get into his head. Get into his head."

They pulled up at the headquarters building, and Barent went in to brief McCabe on the status of the investigation. After he had reported their progress to an obviously preoccupied McCabe, he asked about the progress in the apartment fire that Aaronsen was working on. Nervously, McCabe told him what Aaronsen had told Barent already, earlier in the morning.

"Listen, J.R.," he said. "Your only priority right now is the Wellman investigation. It's too important, and I don't want you doing anything else until you bring me a suspect. Aaronsen can handle the apartment fire. There's no reason to believe they're related."

Barent shrugged his shoulders and went home. Odd, he thought, that McCabe should point out that the two fires were unrelated. Unless, of course, they *were* related. But that defied the odds to the point of being absurd. The M.O.s were totally different, and the motives were, too. One was for profit, and one was for spite, or something else. McCabe was weird. That explained everything.

CHAPTER 11

Nine-year-old Jason Grover crouched in the terror of the night. In the darkest corner of his bedroom, he ground his palms desperately into his ears to keep from hearing the screams and pleas of his mother and the crash of breaking china in the kitchen below. He shook with dread at the noise, which notified his young mind of the abuse in store for him, once his drunken stepfather had finished with his mom.

He hated the man, and feared him with a blind and numbing fear born of his own powerlessness against the unpredictable violent outbreaks. The abusive behavior had started barely six months after his mother married the man, two years ago. Jason barely remembered his real father, a big and boisterous man who liked to toss him into the air while he squealed in delight. He wished fervently that his real father would come back, and save him and his mother from the terrible things that Carl did to them. Momentarily, he hated his real father for not saving them, and then felt guilty about that. A tear ran down his cheek, and his dread became all consuming as he heard his mother's screams subside to wretched sobbing. There was nowhere to run. He

87

cowered in abject apprehension. He heard the creak of a stair tread as Carl climbed the stairs toward his room.

Another tear formed on his cheek, but he did not cry out. In the months that this had been going on, he had learned to leave his body while the brutish Carl used it, and not to return until the pain subsided. He did not understand how it worked, but he felt himself leaving now, as the footsteps approached in the hallway outside his bedroom door. By the time the door opened, the mind of Jason Grover was elsewhere.

He had cried out for his mother, screaming "Mommie! Mommie! Mommie!" the first time Carl had come to his room and done the evil, unspeakable things to him. She had come to his cries then, and had been beaten savagely again for her trouble. And he had not escaped.

There, in the darkness after that first time, Carl had snarled into his ear, as he sobbed in pain and humiliation. Reeking in a cloud of whiskey breath, Carl told him that he would kill his mother if Jason breathed to anyone a word of what had happened. And Carl would know if he told. There would be no place either of them could hide.

Jason had gone to school the next day without seeing his mother. He carried his terrible secret in silence, and had avoided his friends by ducking out of sight if he saw them approach. He waited in the safety of the rest rooms until the class bells rang, and slipped into the classroom just ahead of the tardy bells. He returned home at the end of the day to find his mother uncommunicative, her lips swollen and discolored. Dark bruises on her cheek bones were barely concealed by make-up applied heavier than usual. Her eyes were swollen and puffy. He tried to speak to her, to tell her of what Carl had done, and she refused to listen. Instead, she sent him to his room abruptly. He was dismayed and confused. She was his rock, and she would not help him.

The beatings and abuse went on, sometimes worse but never predictable. They came to live in a silent apprehension, both mother and son, speaking little and watching with an all-encompassing alertness for signs that Carl was about to go off. Two months after his tenth birthday, largely ignored except for a new shirt his mother gave him before Carl came home, his life was changed forever in ways he would never come to fully understand.

He had a dinner with his mother—a special dinner of baked ham and scalloped potatoes, which was Jason's favorite. He asked her if it was a special occasion, and she had merely nodded and smiled, if grimly, for the first time in months.

"I love you, Jason," she had said. "I'm sorry, so sorry for what Carl has done. He won't do it ever again. He'll never hurt you again." She had come around the table and stroked his head, petting his fine, straight blond hair with a protective intensity that Jason found both comforting and disturbing. He hung his head. They were just empty words; her promise of rescue meant nothing. Jason had no reason to believe anything would change. He did not hate her for it. He accepted her touch, hoped it helped her feel better. Carl would be home soon, and they would see. The maternal promise of salvation held no substance for the ten-year-old boy. Life had shown him no reason why it should. He did not see the thousand-yard stare and the sheen of unshed tears in his mother's eyes.

That night, Carl had come home late, drunker than usual, and the signs were there. He entered the brightly-lit kitchen in the dark house, and bellowed "Elizabeth!" There was no answer, and a tirade of his cursing tumbled drunkenly into the unresponsive silence. There, on the kitchen table, was a bottle of his favorite that he had no recollection of having purchased, and he decided to have another drink before he hunted up his wife to beat the silence out of her. Afterwards, he thought, he would find that wretched kid of hers and have a little fun.

He poured the whiskey into a glass, spilling it in his drunkenness. Again he yelled into the darkened house, "Elizabeth! God *damn* it, Elizabeth, come here when I call you!"

He drank more, great gulps of the amber forgetfulness as he called out repeatedly. He railed and cursed a wife that failed to attend him. Elizabeth did not come, and he knew the kid was cowering in the bedroom. He went upstairs to find his wife, and teach her a lesson about coming when he called. He was madder than a nest of wet hornets, and it was Elizabeth's fault. She was really going to get it this time.

He stumbled noisily up the stairs, stomping past Jason's room, and flung open the bedroom door with a crash. A shaft of light from the hallway fell upon the empty bed, and he assumed that she was hiding in a dark corner, as well she should. As he reached for the light switch, he felt a movement behind him, and turned partially around as a heavy brass table lamp smashed into his skull.

He dropped like a stone into an unconscious heap on the floor. Jason's mother, finished with the brutality of this insidious beast, set the blooded brass lamp aside, and reached in the darkness for a tin of lighter fluid. She squirted it over the unconscious form of her tormentor, clutching the tin in both hands to still their shaking. As the stream struck his face and eyes, Carl woke from the stinging, cold wetness that his besotted brain could not identify. He turned, and faced upward, peering through the darkness at the single, wavering flame of a match. Behind the flame, the eyes of his wife held an expression of triumphant resolve that was almost, but not quite, madness.

As the match flame registered on one part of Carl's sodden brain, the smell of the lighter fluid was identified by another part of his mind. As the match dropped slowly toward him where he lay, the two parts of his mind assembled the two pieces of information into their meaning, and he cried out in rage. He reached, too late, to bat away the match. The saturated sleeve of his shirt brushed the flame. Elizabeth leaped back as his entire form flashed to flame with a whoosh.

She backed away from the screaming form, her eyes wide and fascinated as Carl batted and beat furiously at the flames that suddenly lit the bedroom like midday in hell. Shrieking in agony, and the terror of more agony to come, he rolled around on the floor, but the flames reignited the unburned drenching of lighter fluid as fast as he slapped them out. In seconds of eternity, the mortal screeching ended, and she watched, motionless, as Carl collapsed on the floor beside the bed and became still. The flames licked up the bedclothes, and climbed the draperies. The acrid smell of burning fabric nauseated her. The radiant heat from the growing blaze penetrated her fascination, and she sprang to action.

Elizabeth turned abruptly and scurried toward Jason's room. He had emerged, and stood, terrified, in the hallway in his underwear. His spindly child legs reflected the orange glow that now tinted the hall as tongues of flame licked out from the bed-room door and black smoke belched from the open-ing to slither along the ceiling in the hallway. Eyes wide in uncomprehending horror, he waited, frozen, to see what his mother would do next, and what Carl would do to them in retaliation. They were in big trouble now.

Elizabeth Potter gathered her child into her arms and fled the flames that licked out into the hallway from the bedroom where Carl lay. Holding the boy close, she went to the street, where she watched as the fire destroyed the upper floor. Bathed in the radiant, red glow of the flames she stood at the curb, clutching her boy tightly as the first fire engine arrived. In the excitement of the moment, no fire-man noticed the look of profound relief on the woman's face as she held her son and watched her house burn to the ground.

John Barent, then a rookie fire investigator, did take notice of the faint smell of lighter fluid about her person when he interviewed her twenty minutes later. As the result of the interview, John Barent placed Elizabeth Potter under arrest, and saw to it that her son, Jason, was remanded to Child Protective Services for care and temporary housing.

That night, as he shivered in the cold air and watched the flames from within the protective embrace of his mother, a demon was born in the child mind of Jason Grover. The flames of his burning house reflected in his moist but tearless eyes. He watched, mutely, as the flames wrapped themselves around the house in a purifying embrace, flowing and magical. He had no power. The power, he saw clearly in his ancient, wordless mind, was in the raging flames. And, he decided later, in the man who took his mother away.

CHAPTER 12

"You know, he didn't speak for almost a year after his mother went to prison, Father," said the elderly woman earnestly, pouring more tea into fine, rose-patterned china cups. "Now, he's talking, but there are other things he does that worry me to distraction. I'm simply at a loss. And at my age, it's difficult for me to guide him." Her transparent hands fluttered over the tea service like a pair of white doves afraid to land.

Lyda Potter was still uncomfortable having the parish priest in her own home. Priests were easier to relate to in church, where their context was clear. Nothing more nor less than a profound concern over her grandson's behavior motivated her to bring Father Timothy into her home on this Tuesday after-noon and feed him tea and sandwiches. The alterna-tive, a psychological counselor, was unthinkable. If the neighbors got wind of a head shrinker in the house, the lace curtains would wave and the air would buzz with their concerned, holier-than-thou speculations. But a priest could come and go with impunity, and none would comment on the duration of his visits or frequency of her spiritual guidance needs. And the priest didn't charge for his services, which was, unfortunately, a consideration as well.

"What gives you the most concern?" Father Timothy leaned forward earnestly, his balding pate catching the rays of the afternoon sun that streamed through the parlor window. He was an exceedingly slender man, and aquiline of feature. He had a ready sense of humor when it was appropriate, when his collar came off. He even joked occasionally that his tonsure was a God-given thing when he referred to his own premature pattern baldness. Now, however, he caught, or at least reflected, the mood of his lamb. He knitted his brows in sympathetic concern and encouraged Lyda to go on.

"He's cruel, Father. The cat won't come near him. I don't know what he's done to the poor creature, but she leaves the room when she sees him, slinks out and hides. I caught him dropping lit fire crackers into an ant hill, and lighting matches to singe the ones that were scattered when the firecrackers went off." She paused, and looked up, beseeching Father Timothy for reassurance with wide and earnest eyes.

"Go on..."

"Well, he seems to have a fascination with fire. Small wonder, I suppose, with his mother and all. I mean, all kids go through a stage, they say, but his interest seems to go beyond what's normal for a boy of fourteen. He gets a far-away look when he kindles a fire in the fireplace on cold days. He enjoys it too much. Other kids would be treating it as a chore after the novelty wore off, but he enjoys it. He's very good at it, even with wet wood. It's one of his favorite things to do, and it's almost the only time I see him smile. And, frankly, the smile frightens me."

"As you say, fascination with fire is a common thing among young children," observed Father Timothy, nodding reassurance. "Still, he *is* a little old for that. I suspect there has been some regression in his behavior level as the result of the trauma of having his mother taken away. And to prison. Do the other children know about that?" Father Timothy absently scratched what little hair remained at the back of his head with an aristocratically slender, manicured fingernail. He sipped his tea once, and saucered the china cup.

Lyda Potter cast her eyes downward in shame, patted her print dress, smoothed it in her lap. "I think so. I've heard them. Children can be so cruel."

"What do they say?"

"I've heard them refer to him as 'Jailbird Jason', and heard them call his mother a 'jailbird'. I can only imagine what they say when there are no adults within earshot. He doesn't seem to have any real friends. Sometimes he comes home all dirty, with torn clothing. He says he fell down, but I think he's telling fibs. I think he's been fighting with the other kids. He plays alone a lot." She said this last in a manner that inflated Father Timothy's scrutiny, and piqued his interest.

"What do you mean by that? What does he do?"

"It's difficult for me to express... It's just that he locks himself in his room, or in the bathroom, for long periods. I...I think he abuses himself." The words came out in a shameful, hushed tone. She immediately tried to minimize their import.

"I mean, I've never seen him or anything like that," she added hastily, clasping and unclasping her hands nervously in her lap. "It's just that he spends so long, and so often..."

"I see." Father Timothy smiled reassuringly. "You never raised any boys, did you?"

"No, there was only my Elizabeth."

"Well, let me assure you that his privacy needs are not uncommon in adolescents. The time they spend in bathrooms is legendary. It's nothing to worry about. Just let him be, let him develop through it."

"I'm still concerned about these other things, Father. What shall we do about these other things? I'm so worried that something is wrong with Jason, seriously wrong." Her eyes shone with the restrained tears of her worry.

She had lost her daughter for all practical purposes, except for a monthly visit to the Central California Women's Facility in Chowchilla. There, she would be ushered into the extremely high security of the Security Housing Unit where Elizabeth would live for the rest of her life. Stone-faced matrons would allow her to spend three hours with her daughter, but only after an embarrassing and rigorous search. The search included body cavities. The attendant humiliation caused her to miss an occasional visit at the slightest excuse. The resultant guilt would drive her to make the next one that was scheduled religiously. She knew in her heart of hearts that the humiliation would ultimately win, that the visits would become quarterly, then annually, then sporadic. Her greatest fear now was that Jason might likewise be taken from her, thus removing her indirect link with her daughter, and her last remaining family member.

"I've an idea," offered Father Timothy. "Does Jason have a job? Could he use a little extra spending money?"

"No, he doesn't work. He gets an allowance. Why?"

"Well, I would like to take a closer hand in his guidance. I think it might help to give him some responsibility. The rose garden at the parish needs some consistent attention. If Jason could be convinced to take care of it, I would be able to get to know the boy, and perhaps be of some help. He needs a male influence in his life, just now, at this stage of his development. Send him by the rectory on Thursday after school, and I'll put him to work." Father Timothy beamed his reassurances.

"Oh, thank you, Father! I'm sure that would help," Lyda exclaimed, feeling for the first time in months that the problems of raising a teenage boy were not totally overwhelming. Father Timothy's offer made sense, and relieved her of some of the monumental responsibility she felt for raising Jason properly. Here was an offer of the finest ally she could hope for in her Herculean and conscientious efforts to raise her grandson as a god-fearing, law-abiding, healthy Christian.

"Then it's settled. I'll see Jason on Thursday." Father Timothy rose to leave, and Lyda escorted him to the door, beaming with hope and gratitude at the solution he had offered. She thanked him again, profusely, and he departed.

The unresolved issues that had driven Timothy O'Shea into the priesthood in the first place were still present in his psyche. They still drove an aspect of his behavior that he went to great pains to conceal. The personal demons that haunted him and ordained his behavior were mostly effectively suppressed by his entry into the clergy. God, and his belief in God, gave him the tools to resist their importunings for the most part, and gave him also the mechanism for absolution and forgiveness when his resistance failed, as it did infrequently.

The vow of chastity weighed most heavily on Father Timothy, and the demons urged him to its repudiation on those occasions when his physical body followed their urgings. In those rare, but recurrent, instances, he sought the company of young boys.

CHAPTER 13

By the time Jason Grover was seventeen years old, Lyda Potter would have been delighted to abandon her meager family fortune and move into a rest home if it meant she could be rid of the boy. It was her turn now to cower irresolutely in her bedroom wringing her wrists as Jason rummaged noisily around in the kitchen searching for something to eat. She could hear his black engineer's boots clomping around on the shiny kitchen floor leaving hideous black scuff marks. She could see, in her mind's eye, the greasy, dirty hair falling into the wildly defiant eyes. She did not understand the 'colors' he wore, tacked to the back of a studded leather jacket, but the naked skull, with a dagger thrust through one eye socket, frightened her beyond words. She was a prisoner in her own home, afraid to leave her room on the second floor when her ears told her Jason was about in the house.

He came and went, now, at odd hours whenever he pleased, and Lyda had learned to listen for the throaty, asynchronous, throbbing gallop of the idling Harley Davidson as it coasted into the driveway. She had come to dread the silence that followed when the motorcycle's motor was shut off.

The first time it thundered into her driveway, she had confronted him. "Where did you get that awful machine?" she had demanded to know.

"I bought it with the money I made working for Father Timothy," he said, sulkily.

"You could not possibly have made enough to buy that! How much did it cost?"

"None of your business."

"It is my business!" she asserted, angrily placing her hands on her hips. "You live in this house. You eat the food. You don't have a job. It is my business to know how you managed to get enough money to buy it."

Jason's eyes narrowed in a threatening, baleful glare. His lip curled into a snarl, and he unconsciously clenched his fists. The threat was all the more intimidating, coming as it did from the smallish frame and almost effeminate features of her grandson. In that instant, Lyda Potter knew she had lost her grandson every bit as completely as she had lost her daughter half a decade past. The eyes were malicious, malevolent, mean. The voice was defiantly hostile.

"Shut up, old woman," he yelled at her, lowering his head to a predatory attitude, moving into what could only be described as an attacking crouch. "I said it was none of your business. Don't piss me off." He actually hissed the words, his lip curling in a snarl. Shocked, a profoundly appalled Lyda Potter had backed away from her erstwhile grandson, fearful for her safety. In her mind, he had become an animal.

From that time forward, neither grandmother nor grandson spoke to each other. Lyda found her home a place of fear and apprehension, even when Jason was out. She had nowhere to turn for help, nowhere to run if she were to leave. Her only comfort, however thin it proved to be, was that he had never actually laid a hand on her.

Jason had never been happier. He reveled in his newfound independence. He rolled in the dung of his unenlightened self-determination. He used alcohol when he could get it, and drugs, which were easier to get, when he couldn't. School became a place for jerks and dweebs; he would get his education on the streets. He joined a gang.

His acceptance into a gang, which called itself Satan's Spawn, was unheard of in the gang's history. Its bylaws expressly forbid the admission of anyone under legal drinking age, but Jason had managed to win their approval for membership by being meaner that any three of them, and by exercising indiscriminately but discretely certain talents that he had learned from Father Timothy in the potting shed behind the rectory. For the former he was respected; as for the latter, well, it was utilitarian.

The gang leader, a ne'er-do-well named Rowley Skefich with a long history of petty crime, had decided one day that this young punk hanging around the gang members would attract unwanted attention from the police sooner or later. Moving directly to action, he ordered two of his cronies to throw the youthful Jason out of the run down house that the gang used as a flop. The kid put up a tremendous fight, lashing out viciously at Spur and Hairy, the two unlucky minions who had been assigned the job of ejecting the boy. He made no outward sound beyond the grunts of effort during his physical resistance, and the two thugs finally got their hands firmly on him and threw him bodily out the front door. He was light, small of build, and their coordinated throw propelled him in an ungainly arch over the front steps. He tumbled onto the dry, dusty lawn, unhurt but rabidly furious.

Satisfied, the two goons sauntered back into the house to go about their business. They clapped each other on the back, laughing boisterously, and made jokes about how far either one of them could throw the little faggot. Moments later, Jason slipped back into the house, this time clutching a two by four he had scrounged from an adjoining vacant lot. With his first swing, he caught Hairy full across the forehead with the flat of the board as Hairy tried to rise from the ratty old sofa in the living room. Hairy sank back onto the cushions, stunned, bleeding from a gash above his right eye.

Rowley, sprawled in a chair across the room,

yelled for Spur, who had gone into the kitchen for beer. As Spur came back through the door in answer to Rowley's call, Jason let him have it with another roundhouse swing of the two by four, like Babe Ruth with three on base. Spur had a can of beer in each hand, and moved, too late, to protect himself. The blow sent the beer cans flying, spewing foam. It broke his left hand. Spur roared in pain and rage, dancing out of the way of a second blow as he clutched his injured hand with his good one.

Jason felt strong arms encircle him from behind, restraining his attack. Thus immobilized, he was unprotected when Spur hit him in the solar plexus with his remaining good hand. Spur drew back to hit him again when Rowley said "No!"

Jason had drawn up his knees involuntarily as the result of the first blow and now was held, helpless, entirely off the floor by the arms around him in a bear hug. He retched and vomited, trying to double over, but restrained by Rowley.

"Calm fucking down, both of you!" Rowley ordered.

"I want a piece of that little asshole," Spur growled. "Let the little fairy sonofabitch go!"

"Chill out! Cool it, or you'll be getting a piece of *me*!" Rowley's voice was calm, in control, and its low tone carried the seriousness of his intent. Spur backed away, nursing his swelling left hand, muttering imprecations to himself.

"Kid, let go of the board," ordered Rowley.

"Fuck you!" hissed Jason from between clenched teeth. With a burst of renewed fury, he struggled to break the encircling arm lock.

"Kid, I can hold you like this until Hairy wakes up, and *he* can ask you to drop the board. Or you can do it now, and we can talk." Jason hesitated, then let go his hold on the two by four. Cautiously, Rowley eased his bear hug, and loosed his grip. He took a step back as Jason broke free of the diminishing restraint and whirled to face him, crouched and glared with wildcat eyes. The room had filled with a half dozen other bikers, attracted by the melee from their activities in other parts of the house.

"Whoa, kid! Party's over," he said, placating with outstretched palms. "No more trouble. Tell me what you want."

Slowly, Jason rose from his crouch, regained his composure. He looked at them quietly, calming himself from his rage. After a few moments, he spoke.

"I want to join."

"You want to join." Rowley echoed. He concealed his amusement, remembering what had just happened to his cohorts.

"Yeah. I want to join."

CHAPTER 14

Monday morning rolled around with its usual, if unwelcome, regularity. John Randolph Barent felt rested and mellow, having spent Saturday with Jessica at the beach, and Sunday watching pro football and drinking beer with her, curled up on the sofa of the tiny apartment.

Saturday had been marvelous. They packed a picnic lunch with cold chicken and a bottle of cheap Chardonnay and driven to Montana de Oro State Park, where they hiked into the dunes along a deserted stretch of coastline and spread a blanket for their picnic. They combed the beach, finding a number of Pacific sand dollars and miscellaneous shells and driftwood cast up the previous night at high tide by the storm surf from a hurricane that was still over twelve hundred miles to the southwest.

Returning to the blanket, they had lunched in a fashion reminiscent of a scene from *Tom Jones*, exploiting and amplifying almost comically the sensuality of that cinematic repast. They wound up making love repeatedly on the sand, out of the wind behind a sand dune. Jessica seemed insatiable that day and coaxed from him new heights in perfor-

107

mance. Spent, satiated, they had napped naked in the afternoon sun.

They watched the sun go down in a blaze of crimson glory, tingeing the clouds sent forward by the distant storm with the color of fresh blood. The low rays from the setting sun reflected in the still slickness of the wet sand at the water's edge. They paved a sparkling, golden path across the water to the dropping orb in the west. Pelicans floated by in an undulating row as if suspended on guides from piano wire. A lone sea otter broke the surface of molten gold not a hundred feet from them, and proceeded to smash apart an abalone shell for the meat inside, using a rock for a hammer and its belly for a work bench. They watched in wordless fascination, their arms casually around each other, as the creature finished its meal and dove again beneath the waves for another tasty mollusk. They shared a sense of awe and of privilege at having been allowed by circumstance to witness the wild thing in its environment. They felt connected, to nature and to each other, as they turned away from the darkening shore and gathered their gear to trudge arm in arm across the soft dune sand, back to the car.

They ate dinner that night in Morro Bay, in a restaurant overlooking the small boat harbor. Jessica coaxed from him the details of his erstwhile marriage to Kathleen, over more than three years now. She had met his children, Anthony and John, Junior, and spent an occasional weekend with them when John had custody. Kathleen always bristled at her presence and made life even more difficult for John when this happened. Quickly, by a mutual and silent agreement between John and Jessica, the visits were limited to John and the children only, every other week.

It was transparently clear to Jessica that John doted on the children. He always planned special activities for each bi-weekly visit with the boys. Jessica understood how Kathleen resented his ability to wow the kids on their magic weekends with him while she continued the thankless day-to-day work of raising two young boys without a father. Kathleen resented his relationship with the new woman, more because she couldn't have a similar one for herself than from any jealousy of the woman Jessica. An unspoken resentment simmered quietly inside her; secretly she wished her former husband's new lover was more beautiful than she actually was. It would have made the rejection implicit in the divorce more acceptable. As it was, the suggestion that he had left her for something less rankled.

Kathleen had simply stated one day that she wanted a divorce, one day after almost seven years together. John knew her well enough to realize that if she said it, her mind was firmly made up. It wasn't a fishing expedition to see if the marriage was worth saving. There had been no fighting, and no resistance from John. She resented him for not fighting it.

The split was as cold and dispassionate as any John had ever heard about. A glacier lived where there should have been a volcano. Ice existed where there should have been fire. Both partners had come to realize that the flame that originally had drawn them together had been doused by the routine of rearing the boys, and by the demands of maintaining a household. Kathleen had wanted more, and John Barent had no more left to give her.

The State, however, had decided that John had a lot more to give her. It had awarded her custody of the boys, had given him weekend visitation rights, and had laid upon him spousal support payments and child maintenance payments that totaled over two-thirds of his after-tax income. John had moved into a rat hole of an apartment, and had dug in with macaroni and cheese for dinner and holes in his socks to try to bear the burden.

When he missed a payment after the first, guilt-driven, expensive Christmas, Kathleen was relentless in her pressure, and when he was short on a second payment, she loosed the legal hounds. She felt that it was no skin off her nose if John had to spend what little time and money he had left to defend himself against the lawsuit. It was a matter of California law that when she prevailed in court, he paid for her attorney, as well as his own, and thus it cost her nothing to bring the action. If he failed to pay the attorney promptly, he found himself back in court again, sued for recovery of fees. He was dropping into a quicksand of debt slowly, inexorably, but Kathleen refused stubbornly and adamantly to discuss anything monetary without her attorney present.

Only a depth of credit, which remained from his more stable family days, and the acceptance of overtime work with the department whenever it was offered, allowed him to keep his head marginally above water. The relative abundance of the coming overtime check for his work on the Wellman fire funded the dinner he now enjoyed with Jessica. John wondered that this young woman deigned to remain with him. Such dinners were rare under his current financial burden, and she could certainly do better in that regard with virtually any other man. Jack had become a very dull boy.

Sunday had found him still with Jessica, who wore only a T-shirt the entire day, her cuter-than-a-button bare bottom peeking out at him as she rose to fetch an occasional fresh beer. They watched the Raiders kick the stuffing out of the Patriots, and sipped generic beer, the cheapest available brew, on the tattered sofa in front of the television. An unseasonable thunderstorm raged outside the little apartment during the afternoon. From a sheltered open window, they watched the lightening and absorbed the thunder like a drug. They drew deep breaths of the storm-tinged air that were somehow more profoundly satisfying than regular air. The weekend had been as close to a melancholy heaven as it ever got, these days.

Monday was bright and clear, the air scrubbed clean by the rain. The sun dazzled in a cloudless sky. There was an autumn bite in the air John sucked in deeply through the open window of the Alfa as he drove to the office. It would be his last good weekend for a while, but at that moment he did not have a clue that his world was about to come apart thanks to Jason Grover.

His quietly happy frame of mind didn't last thirty seconds through the door. As he breezed by the Bureau secretary on his way to his office, she flagged him down.

"McCabe want's to see you in his office, right away." Her eyes did not meet his, and her voice was flat and noncommittal. McCabe's secretary was inevitably friendly and outgoing towards Barent. But not today.

"What's it about?" he asked, innocently, not catching the full dimensions of her tone or demeanor in his mellow state.

"He just said he wants to see you, pronto." She turned coldly away, back to her computer screen, tacitly dismissing him. Barent shrugged, and did as she instructed. Women were so damned unpredictable.

McCabe's office door was closed, which was highly unusual. He knocked.

"Come!"

Barent opened the door to find Aaronsen and two cops that Barent knew from the detective division waiting in McCabe's office. McCabe was behind the desk, seated, and immaculately dressed from the pages of *Gentleman's Quarterly*. McCabe looked uncomfortable.

"You wanted to see me?"

McCabe rose, not meeting his eyes. "Sit down, John." The words were heavy, ponderous. Barent flopped casually in a chair, but not too casually. He looked around the room and leaned forward expectantly, his elbows on his knees and his hands clasped between them. Maybe something big was breaking on the Wellman Fire investigation. But, if that were so, Marty would be here, and Brooks. They were not.

"What's up?"

"John, you know Detective Sylva and Sergeant Lindenthaler."

"Bud, Jack. What brings you guys over here so early on a Monday morning?"

"We need to ask you some questions. Where were you last Thursday night?" It was Bud speaking.

"Home."

"All night?"

"Yes, all night." Faint impatience crept into his

voice. "What's this all about?" A caution sign was flashing in Barent's brain, but he needed to know more before it became an alarm. Their manner was too professional for their relationship to Barent, and it made him edgy.

Bud ignored the question. "Was anybody with you?"

"Yeah. Jessica was there."

"Who's Jessica?"

"My girl friend. She stayed over."

"All night?"

"Yes, all night! Why don't you guys just come out and ask me what you want to know?" Barent was growing irritable, defensive in spite of himself. These guys were professional friends of his, brothers under the badge. Their distant, clinically professional behavior was disquieting.

"And you didn't go out?"

"No." His voice carried a hint of the restrained impatience that was growing within him. He would play their silly game, but not much longer.

"Wasn't that the night you cut your hand?" The detective nodded at the bandage that swaddled Barent's hand.

"Yeah, come to think of it, it was. I went to the hospital. Seven stitches. Jessica brought me home. My girlfriend."

"Where was your car?"

"I left it at the hospital. My hand was too sore to

drive, and I was on meds for the pain. Bud, what in the hell is this all about?"

Bud Sylva reached into a pocket of his sport coat, pulled something out, and tossed it to Barent, who caught it with a single hand.

"Ever seen that before?"

Barent opened his hand. He looked down at his father's Zippo lighter, with the enameled Seabees crest on it. It was faintly warm to the touch, from Sylva's body heat.

"Where'd you get this?" he asked suspiciously. His hackles rose as he began to believe what his senses told him. In an overwhelming wave of what could only be described as shock, he realized that he was being questioned as a suspect, not as an associate. He made to rise, shot to his feet in indignation.

"What in the hell is going on here?" he demanded to know. Pointedly ignoring Sylva and Lindenthaler, he bored his glare directly into McCabe. "You want to let me in on the rules of your little game?"

"Sit down, John!" It was as close to a commanding tone as Barent had ever heard from McCabe's lips. Barent sat, watching the room with indignant, dangerous eyes.

Lindenthaler spoke for the first time. "One last question. Did you ever find your pocketknife? The one like Aaronsen here found on the Wellman fire?"

"No. I haven't even looked."

"John," Lindenthaler continued in an explanatory mode, "witnesses to the apartment fire Aaronsen is working on saw a car —a green Alfa convertible that matches yours —leaving the fire scene at around four in the morning. Aaronsen found this lighter, which he recognized as yours, on the lawn in front of the fire building."

"Christ, it's been missing for days..."

"John, we also found blood on a towel at the fire scene from a cut that the perpetrator must have received on his hand from a piece of broken glass in the window where he forced entry. It matches your blood type as it's on file with the department. You have a cut on your hand."

Barent looked dumbly at the bandage on his left hand, then back at Jack Lindenthaler. Jack had too many hairs in his nostrils. Barent wondered that he'd never noticed before, ordered his mind away from denial and back to the issues at hand. The game was hardball, and he needed every mental tool he could muster to protect himself. Denial wouldn't help. It was a dangerous self-indulgence.

"John, can you tell me that when we draw blood, and send it to a lab, it won't match in more ways than just the type?" Lindenthaler asked bluntly.

Barent had seen this tactic before, indeed, he had used it himself in interviewing suspects. He wondered why he hadn't snapped to the technique sooner. They believed they had him. If they could extract a confession, an admission of guilt, their job would become vastly easier. Slowly, clearly, with dread at what he knew must come, he looked up at his co-workers in the room.

"I think I need an attorney," he said, quietly but distinctly.

Bud Sylva nodded. "O.K. 'You have the right to remain silent. Anything you say can and will be used against you in a court of law. Should you desire and not be able to afford an attorney, one will be appointed...'" Bud concluded the litany by rote.

"Do you wish to speak to us at this time?" he finished.

"No. Fuck you. At this time."

"You're under arrest for the crimes of murder and arson. I'm sorry, John."

Barent exploded. "Are you fucking nuts? Murder? Of who? Who did I murder?"

"John, we're charging you with the Wellman fire, as well as the apartment fire," McCabe informed him.

"Andy, that's crazy! You know Larry was my nephew. You really think I'd do my own nephew? You fucking prick!" Unable to restrain himself, Barent lunged toward McCabe, and felt Lindenthaler and Sylva seize him roughly. Deftly, they established physical control of Barent and snapped handcuffs in place. Barent bridled, fuming silently, then relaxed and accepted the cuffs. He was amazed at how powerless the handcuffs made him feel. He would never take satisfaction in installing them on a bad guy again. It was a horrible feeling to be restrained thus.

"You didn't kill him intentionally, John," McCabe told him with a semblance of compassion. "You didn't mean for it to happen. But you did set the fire, and he *is* dead. Under California law, that's murder, every bit as much as if you'd put a gun to his head and pulled the trigger. I personally don't know how you can live with yourself."

"Horseshit."

"Also, I must notify you that you are suspended from duty. Here's the documentation." He handed an internal memo to Sylva, who, in turn, held it up for Barent to read, then folded it and stuffed it into Barent's pocket. Sylva removed his badge and weapon from him and placed the items on McCabe's desk. The humiliation was overwhelming. He had been denied even the scrap of honor he would have retained if he had been allowed to hand them over himself.

"Let's go," said Sylva.

"Where?" Barent still couldn't believe what was happening. The answer was obvious.

"County jail."

CHAPTER 15

"Bill, it's Johnny." Barent had used his one allowed phone call from the jail to call his brother. Johnny was the family's name for him; John or J.R. were the names the rest of the world used. His brother, Bill, sounded tired.

"Listen, Bill. You're not going to believe this. I'm in jail up here. They charged me with murder and arson. They're saying I set the fire that killed Larry."

"Jesus, Johnny! What can I do?" There was no hesitation in Bill's voice, and he had suddenly become more alert.

"I need bail. I don't even know how much yet. They won't arraign me until tomorrow."

"Larry's funeral is tomorrow..."

"I know...I know. I'm sorry. I'm sorry I won't be there. Even if I make bail, it'll be too late."

"Listen, Johnny. How can they arrest you if there's no evidence? I mean, how could there be evidence if you didn't do it?"

"They've got some circumstantial stuff. Where they got it is a big mystery. Bill, arson is different than other crimes. The courts recognize that it is an essentially clandestine crime, and admit circumstantial evidence a lot more easily than they do for

119

other felonies. All they have is circumstantial stuff, but it could be enough to create a threat of conviction. We won't know until I get an attorney, and he files discovery motions."

"You mean you could get convicted on this? Even if you didn't actually do it?"

"It doesn't require witnesses, only motive and opportunity. Physical evidence usually cinches the conviction, and they seem to think they have some, or they wouldn't have arrested me."

"But what you need right now is bail?"

"Yeah. I'm poor as a church mouse, what with paying Kathleen and supporting the kids. If I don't get out of here, I'll never have a chance. Since they think they've got their perpetrator, they'll stop looking elsewhere. Even though my investigation has developed a suspect, it kind of loses its shine when they've already got the investigating officer in jail for the crime. Frankly, if I can't find a way to bust the real perpetrator, I might wind up in prison."

"Jesus, Mary and Joseph, Johnny! I'll get together with the family after Larry's funeral, and we'll come up with something. Do you need anything else?"

"Only if I don't qualify for a public defender. I think I do, but I'm not sure. Incidentally, I've been suspended from the department, and I don't know when I'll be getting another paycheck. I'm not sure if Skelley applies once I've been charged. It only requires them to continue my pay during the investigation, and the investigation is over for Skelley purposes." Barent referred to case law which forbade the suspension of peace officers without pay during the investigation of complaints of misconduct. The legislation was in place because a false charge of misconduct could ruin a peace officer's life, even if it was later disproven.

"Shit falls in piles," he concluded. "I don't know where else to turn."

"Family is right, Johnny. Family is right. We'll be there for you."

"Thanks, Bill. Give my best to mom and dad. See you soon."

"Bye, Johnny. Hang in there."

CHAPTER 16

Lincoln McPike was doing time. It was more or less obligatory. As an aspiring prosecutor, recently out of an obscure law school, the job of Public Defender was a planned part of his career track on his way to the goal of a job with the District Attorney. The pay was in the basement, and his off-the-rack business suit barely managed to make the category of presentable. The tie he wore was off the rack as well, loosely knotted, of unconvincing pattern. One more year, maybe two, and he would be on to bigger and better things. The current tenure was ignominious but necessary.

Public Defender McPike secretly detested the kind of people he was forced to work with. If they weren't guilty, they probably wouldn't have been charged. He looked forward to working on the other side of the fence at the earliest possible date, making the world safe by locking up the people he was now charged to defend. At this moment, however, he focused his non-committal, washed out blue eyes on murder suspect John Randolph Barent, who was seated across from him on the other side of a barren wasteland of Formica™ in a guarded interview room in the bowels of the County Courthouse.

123

Early Monday afternoon the court had laid this case on him, and he had an arraignment and bail hearing in the matter of the People of the State of California versus John Randolph Barent in less than an hour in Superior Court, Division Two. The charges were murder, two counts, and felony arson, two counts, and attempted arson, two counts stemming from the fires Aaronsen investigated in the apartment complex that didn't catch.

McPike looked in appraisal at a wild-haired man of maybe thirty five or forty years of age, of clean jaw line, intense blue eyes peering out from underneath the black mop. The man didn't look like a murderer, but if the reports were right, the murder had been incidental to the crime of arson. A death — two, actually, with a third fireman still not out of the woods —occurring as the result of the commission of another felony was triable under the laws of the sovereign State of California as murder, a crime of intent, since the fire was intentional. The man wore orange County Jail coveralls, looked to be in good physical shape. He was an investigator, the file said. He was the worst kind of client; he'd know just enough about the system to screw himself.

"You seem to like leaving personal property at fire scenes," McPike tossed the statement onto the barren table between them like a dead mackerel, watching for the reaction. The man looked at him, directly, unflinching, and did not avert his electric blue eyes. He, too, was making assessments. He stared at a younger, shorter man who wore a three-piece suit of indistinct origin, not at all tailored. Slender, manicured, and new to the game. The man's manner was cavalier, dispassionate. Barent didn't like him.

"I've been set up. That's all it could be."

"Why would anybody set you up?"

"Beats me." The blue eyes flashed. The fullish, sensual lips remained grimly pinched into a frown.

"You're going to have to be more help than that, Mr. Barent. I can argue the physical evidence on the first fire. You were there legitimately, in the course of your duties, and you lost your knife in the debris. A stretch, but we could create a reasonable doubt. The second fire makes the first more difficult. If you weren't there, why was your car seen, and why was your lighter found, and why was your blood present? Give me something I can work with."

"Did they get a license number? Without a license number, it only looked like my car. The keys were in my pants pocket when I woke up and came to work. Nobody borrowed it. My lighter had been missing for a few days. I don't know where I lost it. Somebody put it at the fire scene. Come to think of it, I don't even know where the apartment fire was."

McPike scanned the report in his file. "Falwell Street. 1763 Falwell." He looked up, over his glasses, at Barent.

"Shit! You're kidding." Amazement flashed across the triangular face. It was replaced rapidly with concern.

"Go on, Mr. Barent. Why should I be kidding?"

Barent hesitated, then spoke. "That's my girl-friend's apartment house. Used to be. I mean, we're broken up. Months ago. Maybe a year."

"Does the prosecution know that?"

"I don't know. It sure looks bad if they do."

"It looks worse if they don't. They'll find out, I can guarantee it. And the blood? What about the blood they found there?"

"It's not my blood."

"Well, the tests aren't back. We'll have to see what they show."

"It's not my blood," Barent repeated, adamantly.

"O.K. I'll buy that, for now. What about the ten thousand dollars in your bank account?"

"What?! What are you taking about?" Barent was flabbergasted. He looked at McPike in absolute bewilderment, his eyes wide and his jaw on his chest.

McPike read from the report. The he interpreted. "Based on statements received from Archie Wellman, he paid ten thousand dollars by wire transfer into your account. He's turned state's evidence to beat the accessory to murder rap that they hung over his head. They made him a talk-and-walk deal."

Barent's jaw snapped shut, and his eyes reassumed their normal dimensions. "I don't know Wellman. I don't have that kind of money. It's got to be a mistake. Let me see!"

McPike shoved the file across the table. Barent read the statement, found and mentally confirmed his own account number. Attached was a photocopy of a bank statement he had not yet seen, showing the deposits of paychecks in amounts he remembered, and a credit entry for ten thousand dollars. The information had been obtained by warrant, signed by a judge, and executed by Aaronsen. That explained where Aaronsen had been Friday afternoon; getting the warrant. Visibly, the starch went out of him. He slumped, putting his head in his hands, shaking it slowly to and fro in puzzlement. He took a deep breath, and returned his gaze to McPike, who was waiting expectantly.

"Somebody's gone to a lot of trouble to set me up," Barent said slowly in a low voice, pinching the bridge of his nose with a thumb and forefinger. "I have no idea who it could be, but they're good, real good, and they're playing for keeps. I didn't do the crimes. I just didn't. That's that."

"The prisons are full of guys in on a bum rap. Ask any con. Why would somebody go to ten thousand dollars worth of trouble just to set you up? If I read your financial records right, you could use ten grand, couldn't you?" The question was legitimate, but it ignited a match in the powder keg of Barent's threatened mind.

"Whose fucking side are you on, McPike?" he hissed. The eyes flashed in restrained rage, stemming more from the acute frustration and the dawning understanding of the depth of his predicament than McPike's words, but directed in response to the words, nonetheless. He'd been done, and done well. The total body of evidence was compelling, and the conclusion was obvious, even to him. A jury wouldn't hesitate a heartbeat to put him away for life if he couldn't refute the circumstantial evidence. The reality of his shrinking options, and the seriousness of his situation registered, finally. His worry began to show. He chewed a thumbnail, fidgeting nervously, feeling lost and beaten. He looked down, numbly, at the Formica™ tabletop.

"What about bail? Can you get me out of here?"

"Got any money? They'll never let you use your bank account. It's been frozen as evidence."

"I'll get the money. How much?"

McPike looked at his watch. "Let's go find out," he said.

CHAPTER 17

Jason Grover had been allowed to join the Satan's Spawn due largely to Rowley Skefich's support. Rowley insisted that he stay clear alcohol and drugs. The gang didn't need a 'contributing to the delinquency of a minor' rap. Jason agreed to stay clean.

He moved out of the house with Lyda Potter and into the gang's flop, reserving the right by force to return occasionally to his grandmother's house for any depredations that might be necessary to his lifestyle. She had stopped changing the locks after he splintered the kitchen door to gain entry the first time he returned. His depredations so far cost less than the replacement of the door, and still, he had not harmed her. It was simple economics.

Rowley Skefich had some unusual connections even for a gang leader of a motorcycle club. Friends of his in high places called upon him for an occasional favor. He was always happy to oblige them, for they called not frequently, and they paid well. There was little risk, and the gang was not driven to fund itself with drug sales or other, high-profile criminal mechanisms that attracted the scrutiny of the law. Thus, they never had serious trouble with the cops; at least nothing more serious than moving traffic violations and disturbing the peace charges, which meant nothing in the big picture. The gang would have engendered even greater suspicion if its members hadn't had an occasional run-in with the authorities. The arrangement suited both Rowley and his unusual friends well. Their relationship had continued to their mutual benefit for several years.

Rowley Skefich had also been remarkably lucky his entire life, and he knew it. The new kid, the one that had fought his way into the gang by bashing Hairy in the noggin with a two by four, turned out to have talents that were specifically aligned with his needs and the needs of his friends. "Pretty Boy", as the gang had nicknamed Jason Grover because of his diminutive size and effeminacy, was an asset beyond Rowley's wildest dreams. In another context, in another life, Rowley could have gone into business with the kid exclusively. They'd have made a bundle from Rowley's connections and the kid's skills. As things were, the gang was solvent. There was always money for beer, drugs, and motorcycle repair parts.

"8923 Industrial Place, San Mateo, after May tenth, ten thousand." Click. Rowley jotted down the information while it was fresh in his mind.

It had started this time, as it always did, with an anonymous phone call during which the unidentified caller gave an address, the name of a city, a date, and a number, which was in reality a dollar amount. A second call, precisely twenty four hours later, repeated the same information in the same order, and then paused. Rowley would then agree, or decline, with a single word, depending on the information, and the gang's disposition toward the job. A counter offer was out of the question. It would show disrespect for his friends.

In this case, he had agreed. After a planning session, three members of the gang had departed on a road trip to the named city with two five-gallon jerry cans of Jason's special accelerant mix strapped under garbage bags to their sissy bars. Pretty Boy was traveling with Spur and Hairy. There was no bad blood between them despite the scar Hairy now sported above his eye, and the healed broken hand of Spur. Jason's talents would be instrumental in performance of the contract; the other two were along to learn the fine points of arson. Jason knew a lot about fire. He had already made improvements in the gang's contract performance that had impressed its employers.

For example, the gang had been using gasoline as an accelerant to set their contract fires. Pretty Boy had pointed out early on his first foray that a mixture of twenty percent gasoline and eighty percent diesel fuel would do the job better and more safely. The gasoline would increase the ignitibility of the diesel fuel, and the diesel fuel would release more heat in a shorter time than gasoline could. It was safer, and substantially more effective. The destruction was more complete because the fire was hotter, harder to stop.

Pretty Boy had also solved the problem of alarm systems for them. He taught them to defeat the tamper switches, so that they could close the valves that supplied water to the fire sprinklers. He taught them how to sabotage the water flow alarms so that the fire department didn't receive notice of the fire until a random passer-by noticed smoke issuing from the building and phoned it in. The additional burn time they achieved by delaying or defeating the electronic notification provided by the alarm systems virtually assured complete destruction of their target. Their employers, Rowley's friends, were appreciative, and more business was being sent their way.

The target in San Mateo was a vending machine parts outlet, selling repair parts for coin operated washing machines, cigarette machines, and candy dispensers. At three in the morning, there was nobody around to hear the wrenching creak of tearing metal as Hairy forced the side door of the warehouse with a crowbar.

The three men entered a large concrete block building with rows of shelving stuffed with inventory. They went straight to the fire sprinkler control. Pretty Boy fished a pocket knife and a screw driver from his jacket and went to work on the alarm system as his apprentice, Spur, held a flashlight on the work.

"You see that red wire?" he asked rhetorically. "It's hot. Red, hot. Get it? The control box imposes a current in the alarm sending circuit that cannot flow as long as that leg is hot. If you just cut the wire, the imposed current flows, and the fire department gets an alarm." Jason spoke as he worked, twisting the screwdriver to remove screws securing a cover plate. He set the cover aside. The beam from Spur's flashlight revealed a tangle of wiring inside. Scraping insulation carefully from a wire with the pocket knife, Jason continued his instruction.

"What we've got to do is fool the alarm sending circuit into thinking the red wire still has current. We clean off the insulation, and bridge the circuits here...and here. See that?"

From another pocket, Jason took a short wire lead with an alligator clip soldered to each end.

"Before you do this part, you've got to know that there is a small delay, usually around a second or two, built into a relay at the fire alarm control panel. Its function is to correct for variations in voltage in the line, so that the system doesn't send false alarms if the commercial voltage fluctuates. This operation has to be quick. You can't let that relay trip."

In the eerie light of Spur's torch, Jason connected one of the jaws of the alligator clip to the exposed spot on the wiring. He reached into his hip pocket and retrieved a pair of insulated wire cutters, which he held on the red wire above the bare spot he had scraped. Spur watched, impressed with the kid's knowledge, as Jason, the tip of his tongue exposed at the corner of his mouth, connected the second alligator end of the bridgework and deftly snipped the red lead, almost in a single action.

"There." He pocketed the wire cutters. A red pilot light extinguished on the control panel, indicating loss of power, but no alarm sounded. Jason closed the wheel valve that controlled the water supply to the sprinkler system. The building was now at the fire's mercy. "It's done. Let's burn this baby!"

As they emerged from the confines of the sprinkler riser room, the smell of spilled flammable liquids assailed them. While they had been engaged in defeating the fire sprinkler system, Hairy had perforated the tops and bases of a number of cans he had found on the stock shelves with a switchblade. The contents were leaking freely onto the floor, running under the stock shelves. Now, the three men grabbed up the five-gallon Jerry cans filled with their special mixture of diesel fuel and gasoline. They splashed it liberally around the large room, covering as wide an area as possible. They set down the empties and met at the door they had forced earlier.

"Who wants to do the honors?" asked Jason as he produced a highway fusee from somewhere on his person. It had been stuffed into the top of his engineer's boot, covered by his pantleg.

"Hey, man, let me!" Spur was enthusiastic, the model apprentice. Jason struck the fusee. With a loud "pop" it ignited. Quantities of acrid smoke billowed into their eyes. The fusee glowed red in the darkness. He handed the flare to Spur, who smiled insanely like a child. He pitched the fusee into the darkness of the warehouse interior. There was a momentary pause when nothing happened, and then the entire area flashed into flame with a muffled "whoosh!"

"Wow!" Spur stood, awed by the force of the ignition, fascinated by the feeling of power the simple act had given him. "Wow!" He began an impromptu jig, dancing around in his excitement.

"Let's get out of here!" Jason urged them. Hairy and Spur ran to their motorcycles, kicked them to life. Jason stood transfixed for a few moments, gazing hypnotically into the flames, into the very throat of the Beast. Carl's body writhed there, in flames on the floor, and the echoes of Carl's screams rang in his head. The demon, born in the dim past of Jason's life, fed upon the flames. Satisfied, Jason closed the door, turned from his burning house, and walked calmly to his motorcycle to join his comrades.

A roving security patrol guard hired by the area businesses turned the corner just in time to see three motorcycles pull into the street in front of

Biondi's Service Center. He copied the license number of the last bike onto a scrap of paper before it could fade from his memory, but made no pursuit. It wasn't in his job description. He left his pick-up truck cursing the pre-dawn cold and made a quick check of the building from whence they had come. There, he discovered the jimmied door, and the fire rolling inside the windowless warehouse. He made three calls from his cellular phone in the pick-up truck. His first call was to his supervisor, his second to the fire department, and his third to the police, to whom he provided the plate number of the motorcycle.

The three bikers were pulled over by a brace of police cruisers before they reached the city limits. The guard was thankful when he heard they had been arrested, smelling of diesel fuel, and carrying a few important and incriminating tools. If they hadn't been caught, he himself would have been the prime suspect. He didn't need the hassles.

* * *

Jason was tried and convicted as an adult. His fingerprints were not on the recovered jerry cans, but his license number had been the one the security guard copied. The judge, made aware of his troubled childhood, sentenced him to Camarillo for psychological evaluation and treatment. He was out in eight months, instead of the three-to-five years of hard time he had expected on a first conviction.

Jason emerged from the State's psychiatric care facility with a sense of purpose, and an uncompromising conviction of what he must do with his life to be happy. He had responded appropriately to treatment, demonstrated appropriate remorse for his crime of arson, and behaved himself. He had also expanded his criminal contacts, apprenticed with some of the best crooks the state could provide, and read insatiably to improve his skills in his chosen profession. He traded his skills for knowledge, and thanked Father Timothy for the currency of exchange he used. Father Timothy had given him gold, and Camarillo was in a recession.

He did not share with his counselors the conclusion he had reached during the course of his therapeutic treatment. He did not discuss the course of action upon which he decided. It would take money, lots of money, and it would alter his life irrevocably forever.

* * *

The money part was easy. Back with the gang after his release, he intercepted a call from Rowley Skefich's anonymous friends, made them an offer and went into business for himself. He quit the gang, just faded from view, and quietly broke his contact with them. They were no longer necessary to his master plan. The money came quickly. There was a real recession on, and demand for his services was high. In less than a year, working occasional nights and rat-holing every dime, he had saved enough to implement his plan. He made a final, coat-and-tie visit to his incarcerated mother Elizabeth in Madera County, and at the age of nineteen, dropped off the face of the earth.

CHAPTER 18

"The Court finds that there is sufficient cause to bind the defendant, John Randolph Barent, over for trial on all counts of arson, attempted arson, and murder as charged. Trial in the matter of the People versus John Randolph Barent is set for thirty days hence, on November twentieth, in Superior Court, Division Four. The defendant will remain confined without bail in the County Jail until the time of trial."

Judge Gerald Hammer closed a file on his bench with finality and directed his bailiff to bring in counsel for the parties to the next case on his docket. The Barent arraignment proceedings had gone on for two-and-a-half hours. Aaronsen had testified as the investigating officer, looking sternly at Barent as infrequently as possible. The court heard damning testimony from an accounts clerk at Barent's bank. Archie Wellman testified to the transfer of funds by wire into a specific account number, but stated that he could not identify the defendant as the party who had contracted to set the fire.

"What about bail? You never even asked for bail!" Barent snarled in disgust at McPike. Barent was in a panic, and he was livid with rage at the Public

Defender.

"When we spoke earlier, you were a suspect. Now you're a defendant. The State doesn't allow bail in murder cases."

Barent stared at him in stark disbelief, which gave way quickly to a black and awesome rage at the betrayal. "You could have told me!" he hissed, fulminating through clenched teeth, gesturing wildly in emphasis. "I asked you, and you shined me on, you sonofabitch!"

McPike's eyes narrowed, and his hands froze in the act of replacing papers into his open briefcase. Barent's agitation was attracting the attention of the bailiff, who moved quietly into position to assist the attorney should it become necessary.

Underneath the fury at McPike's betrayal, a part of Barent's mind whirled in desperate analysis. No bail meant that he would not be able to go after the real perpetrator, and he was the only one inclined to do so. The evidence presented at the hearing was damning. Barent would have convicted himself on its strength if he didn't know better. And there would never be a better opportunity for escape than now. The handcuffs would be back on in moments for the trip back to the County Jail. With a cry of despair that would later be described by bystanders as the roar of an animal, Barent leaped the balustrade and sprinted out of the courtroom.

The carpeted halls of the courthouse were nearly empty this late in the day. A few stragglers with late court times salted the corridor, looking up wide-eyed in surprise and fear from their personal preoccupations as Barent blazed by them in an orange blur. He managed to turn a corner as the older, slower bailiff emerged from the courtroom in pursuit.

"Stop! Stop that man!" he yelled ineffectually as Barent turned the corner, now out of his sight.

Barent had a plan, knew where he was going. Nearly a decade earlier, he had been assigned to perform the Fire Safety Compliance Inspections for the construction of this building and had monitored progress and the installation of fire safety systems throughout all phases of its construction. He knew the building literally from the inside out. He hoped he knew it better than his pursuers.

He bolted through a doorway, passed through a building maintenance office, and found a remembered access door that lead to the air conditioning mechanical area. He entered. The hum of the machinery masked the sounds of his footsteps on the hard plywood floors as he searched for a hiding place. Breathless and panting, he opened an access cover and climbed inside a room-sized air conditioning unit that was not operating. He pulled the cover back into place behind him, holding it determinedly with great difficulty since he had no way to latch it into position. There, silent but for attempts to control his ragged and noisy breathing, he waited for the searchers to pass him.

Moments later, the bailiff entered, winded and puffing like a steam engine under load, but intent on his duty. A Sheriff's deputy had joined him, and both men clomped around noisily, searching the room carefully but quickly. They peered behind machinery, looked into exposed duct grills. Satisfied, they radioed a report to whoever was coordinating the search and left the mechanical area to continue the hunt elsewhere. Barent heard the door close as they departed.

Carefully, Barent set aside the access cover and rubbed his fingers and wrists, which were sore from holding it in place. He curled his fingers a few times to work out the stiffness. His breathing came easier now. He forced his mind to calm itself while he tried to comprehend the enormity of what he had just done. It was important, he knew, to remember his status. He was a defendant in a solid murder case who had escaped from under the noses of the authorities, in front of a judge. If there had been any questions in their minds of his guilt, his behavior now would resolve them, and not in his favor. Moreover, they —that vast amorphous 'they' that covered everybody who was not 'me' —would be extremely pissed at him for giving them the slip, making them look bad. He was irretrievably committed to a course of action that held his only hope of avoiding a life in prison.

Mentally, he assessed his resources and found them dangerously deficient. He had no money. His bank account was doubtlessly frozen solid by the court. He had only the clothes on his back, orange coveralls stenciled 'County Jail' front and back These were definitely not suitable for wear on the street. He dared not go home, and he dared not contact friends. There would most certainly be a bench warrant out for his arrest. To enlist the aid of anyone he could count on would put them at risk of being charged with harboring a fugitive, at the very least. He dared not move from his hiding place for several hours, and he needed to figure out a way to leave the building unobserved when the time came that it was safe to do so.

"Not a bright picture, Johnny Boy," he mused wryly aloud to himself in a low voice. "From law-abiding citizen to felony fugitive in one easy step..." The air conditioners hummed mindlessly, filling his head with their noise. Actually, leaving the building would be easy, he thought to himself as he began to make plans. He would not leave *this* building, but would depart from the Courthouse Annex, a completely different structure. A utility tunnel connected the two buildings. He had used it numerous times in the course of his inspections during construction. Courthouse employees used it now, mostly on rainy days, as a dry route between the two buildings.

Finding clothes was a thornier problem. Even if

he left the building safely, he wouldn't last long on the street in his current garb. He might be able to find a judge's robes hanging in a closet somewhere, but going abroad in judges' robes would attract almost as much attention as his orange jail outfit. If he waited to slip away until the wee hours of the morning, after the bars closed and the town was asleep, his chances were better of escaping unseen. But then, where was he to go?

The hours passed. Barent had no watch, but he could look through the louvered air intakes to the streets intersecting below. He found he could approximate time of day by the traffic activity levels. The streets were crowded for the hour after most offices closed at five p.m., then traffic lightened while most people were at their evening meals. Then it picked up again at seven or so: early birds going out on the town. Another pick up in traffic occurred at around eleven o'clock when the theaters let out, and a final surge swelled the streets as the bars closed at two in the morning. Time seeped past like cold oil dripping through a pinhole, and Barent was able to make some tentative plans and fine tune his escape route. He grew increasingly hungry and thirsty as the oily hours dripped past. He peed in the farthest corner of the space.

Jessica was his only option. Most of his friends were fire department members. They all knew his fugitive status, and wouldn't dare to help him because of repercussions in their jobs if they were found out, and he would not place them in such a vulnerable position anyway. But his relationship with Jessica was largely unknown to the department. He had not spoken of it and hadn't intended to until he was reasonably certain it would endure. They did not yet know of her, and she knew none of them.

The disinterested public defender had not summoned her to testify in Barent's defense. He said the alibi she could provide was too flimsy in light of the physical evidence in the DA's hands. It would be a waste of time at this juncture. Better to save it for the actual trial, he'd said during the pre-arraignment conference.

His years with the city fire department had taught Barent the locations of every back alley and cubbyhole in the city. At what must have been three in the morning, Barent slipped from the mechanical room into the silent, deserted corridors of the courthouse. His first stop was at a drinking fountain, where he quenched his driving thirst on the chilled water. He drank so fast it gave him a headache. He drank greedily until he could drink no more, in spite of the lancing pain over his eyes from the cold liquid.

With caution, he moved to the stair tower, descended four floors into the basement and found the tunnel, not having encountered any of the janitors he knew must be about. He left the annex build-ing by a sub-grade utility exit. It dumped onto a stair-way, which ascended into the alley between the courthouse and the annex. A bitter cold cut him sud-denly with its edge as he moved outside. In the dim alley, he did up his coveralls against the knife-like chill.

Sliding from shadow to doorway recess, sprint-ing across brightly lit streets after carefully watching for signs of distant but approaching traffic, he made his way cautiously out of the deserted downtown district toward Jessica's place.

He arrived after two hours of apprehensive trav-el, exhausted, shivering with cold, and desperately hungry, at the back door to Jessica's ground floor apartment. It was dark inside; no light showed. He tried the sliding glass door; found it locked as he'd expected. He knocked quietly. There was no response. Moving to what he believed to be the bed-room window, he knocked again, louder. Again, there was no response. The room remained dark, but he thought he heard movement.

"Jessica!" he said aloud, urgently controlling the volume of his voice. "Jessica, it's John!" There was no response from within.

Then, a drawn blind parted in a horizontal slit and he heard Jessica's gravelly voice: "John, is that you?" she asked incredulously.

"Jessica! Let me in!" His tone was something both

a demand and a plea. The blinds closed again and a light came on, then more light poured onto the patio from the sliding glass door. He heard the movement of the latch, and went to the door. Jessica slid open the door, and Barent nearly fell through it. She hugged him, kissed his cheek demurely. He felt her svelte body beneath the terry robe she had thrown on, and wondered that he could respond so strongly in his present straights.

She put him at arm's length. "I thought you were in jail," she said. "What are you doing here?"

"I escaped. Have you got anything to eat?" The relative warmth of the apartment began to heat Barent's cold body and triggered a fit of shivering.

"You're freezing! Let me get a blanket." She vanished, looking in puzzlement over her shoulder as she left the room, and returned in seconds with a furry, warm blanket. She spread it on Barent's shoulders. Leading him into the kitchen, she pulled the cold remnants of a half-eaten pizza from the refrigerator and stuck it in the microwave. She tapped out the time setting and pressed a button. The microwave hummed. While Barent shivered at the kitchen table, wrapped in the blanket, wordlessly she put water on to boil, and assembled the makings for coffee.

The bell rang on the microwave, and she delivered the pizza to the table in front of him. He ate ravenously, burning his mouth with the pizza, which had not heated uniformly. He jumped up and drew himself a glass of water from the kitchen tap, cooling the burn in his mouth and slaking his thirst in the same act. By the time he was back at the table, Jessica had set a cup of steaming coffee at his place for him, and brought one for herself. She sat across from him, looked at him appraisingly. She smoothed her hair, tousled from sleep, with her left hand and spoke. Her right hand clutched the lapels of her terry robe together modestly.

"Tell me everything," she invited. Cupping her coffee in both hands, she peered over the rising steam expectantly, inviting his speech by her silence.

Barent told her of his escape, triggered by his outrage at the duplicity of the public defender, and of his plans for locating the person who had actually done the crime. He would contact his brother, get a car and money, and catch the sonofabitch himself. Meanwhile, he needed a hot shower, some clothes, and a few dollars in traveling money. Jessica agreed to help him with the last three items.

Barent paused, feeling the exhaustion of his flight and the late hour creep into his body. "I really need to sleep," he said. The shivering had stopped. He looked over his empty coffee cup with half-lidded eyes at Jessica, who regarded him with a curious intensity. Her terry robe had fallen open, revealing most of her right breast. It was small, well shaped.

She caught his eye with her own, and smiled.

"What is it?"

"I've heard," she murmured coyly, raising an eyebrow, "that it can be particularly exciting to make love when people are at different skin temperatures. One really cold, the other all warm and cuddly. Like us." She rose, and came around the table to stand in front of him, allowing her robe to fall open. "We'd better hurry if we're going to find out for ourselves."

John Barent discovered in that moment that he really didn't need sleep as badly as he thought.

CHAPTER 19

When Barent awoke, Jessica was gone. He felt groggy. A splitting headache pounded away behind his eyes like John Henry's own hammer. His temples drummed with a Buddy Rich solo as he swung his feet to the floor. For a few moments he sat very still, his throbbing head cradled in his hands. Finally, he lifted his head and allowed his eyes to stagger about the room. Daylight slithered into the space around the edges of the window coverings. The night was gone.

Laying on a chair were a pair of men's blue jeans and a faded blue sweatshirt. He wondered with a transient flicker of jealousy where Jessica could have gotten her hands on male clothing so quickly, but decided what he didn't know couldn't hurt him. There must have been other men in her life before him, and he really didn't want the details. It was so typical. The clothes were a little on the tight side, but serviceable. He wadded up the orange coveralls he had been wearing and stuffed them into a paper bag he found in the kitchen.

He found freshly brewed coffee in the kitchen, too, and a mushy note from Jessica wishing him luck and urging him to keep her posted. It sat weighted with a salt shaker on the kitchen table. Clipped to it were five twenty-dollar bills.

As he sat toying with the note and drinking his coffee, it struck him that there was something wrong with the apartment. He had only been there once before, on the night when he had first met Jessica. Since that time, their meetings had been mostly at his place. He hadn't noticed anything amiss back then. But now something nagged at him, tugged at his unconscious, made him uncomfortable. He couldn't figure it out. He shrugged off the uneasy feeling, chalking it up to the justifiable paranoia of his circumstances.

He had to get out of town, and he wasn't at all sure how to go about it. The police would be checking the obvious ways. They would certainly have his photo distributed to the patrol watch by now. They would be watching the bus station, the airport, and his car. Besides, most of the local cops knew him on sight. If it were he doing the looking, he would be sure to leave the fugitive's car handy where it was, in hopes that the fugitive would try to recover it for a getaway. He had to figure out something else.

He stared out the window, spreading the drawn blinds with his fingertips. It was a Chamber of Commerce brochure kind of day. Sunlight splashed all over the vacant parking lot like liquid sparks from a cosmic welding torch. The air was clear and clean, invigorating. All the apartment dwellers were at work, if the empty parking lot was any indicator. He went to the back door, out onto the patio where he had entered in the early morning hours, and found his salvation. Jessica had a bicycle there.

He jotted a brief note to her, but he left it unsigned. He wheeled the ten-speed out the front door into the empty parking lot. He climbed on. It had literally been years since he had been on a bicycle. The politically correct fitness hysteria that encouraged people to bicycle to work had passed through him like an x-ray, without apparent effect. There in the parking lot, he discovered that the old saw about never forgetting how to ride a bicycle wasn't exactly true. On wobbly wheels, feeling like he was going to spill any instant, he pedaled off clumsily down the road, headed out of town.

Barent wheeled into a Pismo Beach Stop-and-Rob an hour later, seeking an anonymous microwave breakfast. He possessed two new convictions about his life. The first was, cars are good. The second was, he was out of shape. His thighs ached from the pedaling, and his wind had failed him on two occasions, necessitating a breather under a freeway overpass at the Avila Beach exit, and again at the top of the Ontario Grade. He could feel the lactic acid building up in the muscles of his thighs, and he knew that tomorrow they would be sore. Most of all, his butt was excruciatingly painful and tender from the bicycle's hard seat.

Still, cycling had its redeeming merit. He found the smells and textures of nature were available to him for savoring on a bicycle in ways that travel at sixty miles per hour in an air-conditioned automobile—or even his *al fresco* Alfa—prevented. Dry, golden grass covered the hillsides and filled the air with the sweet and dusty smell of fall in central California. The ubiquitous oaks were heavily burdened with ripening acorns. Leaves on the willows that clogged the roadside swales were tinged with yellow. Their musty, sweet smell spilled out onto the roadway, spreading in the still air. There was life along the road verge, scuffling in the drainage ditches and flitting about in the trees, that he had forgotten was there. The fall migration of tarantulas was on. Flying along at sixty miles per hour in a steel and glass bubble, he would have never noticed. But on the bicycle, he had noted in passing three of the huge, furry spiders as they slowly crossed the frontage road, purposefully on their way to wherever they went during the rainy season, which was still a month off. They all moved in the same direction, as if responding to a common call. They were moving to higher ground.

His fear of being recognized and recaptured faded with each mile and each minute that he put between himself and home. He bought Gatorade and microwaved a couple of unimaginative salt-and-cardboard breakfast sandwiches. He bought a pack of cigarettes, and got matches from the clerk, and a Styrofoam® cup of black coffee with a lid. Everything went into a paper bag, and he pedaled south with the bag dangling from the handlebars to a tiny park, where he sat in the sunshine and ate.

The flavor of the cardboard food was unexpectedly intense, and the Gatorade® quenched a thirst at the molecular level. He uncapped the steaming coffee. He lit a cigarette. He inhaled deeply and felt the dizzying rush of the nicotine as it intoxicated his system. He savored each drag on the cigarette, and enjoyed each sip of the coffee to a profundity that made him wonder if he had somehow forgotten until now the basic principles of enjoyment.

A monarch butterfly floated by, on its way to nowhere. Signs in the park told him that this was a stopping point on the monarch migration. Pictures in the kiosk showed the branches and leaves of the eucalyptus trees in the park grove as they would be in February, covered densely with thousands of the orange and black butterflies. Barent promised himself he would return and see it one day.

Barent lit another cigarette and thought about his current situation. It seemed that everything he counted on for his sense of security was gone. He felt naked, alone. He could not contact friends; it would place them in jeopardy. His wallet, with its credit cards and identification, was in the hands of the county jailers, so he couldn't rent a car. To return for his own Alfa was out of the question if he valued his liberty. His capital consisted of ninety-two dollars and eleven cents of borrowed money. Even if he spent it carefully, it wouldn't last long, especially at convenience store prices. He had no shelter, and only the ill-fitting clothes on his back. The penetrating cold of another October night was mere hours away.

Momentarily, a feeling of hopelessness overwhelmed him, washed over him like a breaking wave. How, in heaven's name, would he manage to see to his basic needs, elude the cops, and still find the wherewithal to hunt down Jason Grover and prove that Grover had done the fire that killed Larry? The simple things stymied him; food, clothing, shelter, and transportation. He had none of them. Well, he though wryly to himself, there was the bicycle...

His brother, Bill, was his best chance of obtaining some resources, but Bill was three hundred miles away in Blythe. He pedaled back to the minimart and found a pay phone, then thought better of it. Instead, he rinsed the plastic Gatorade bottle, and filled it with tepid water from a hose bibb on the side of the building. He climbed on the bicycle and set a goal: Santa Barbara by nightfall. There was a homeless shelter there. He could do it by nightfall if he could average ten miles an hour.

* * *

Lofty, unrealistic goals have been the disappointment of many a man, and John Randolph Barent was no exception. Ten miles an hour for eight hours proved to be substantially easier in the saying than in the doing. He wheeled into Gaviota State Beach in late afternoon, his muscles sore and aching, fatigued beyond belief, forty miles short of his destination. The last several miles of his ride were mostly downhill, or he would not have made it that far. Rather than enter the campground, he searched and found a clearing in the willows along the creek. There, he collapsed on the dry grass in a spot of sunshine after hiding the bicycle out of sight.

CHAPTER 20

He came awake with a start sometime after nightfall, having slept the sleep of the dead while the sun slipped into the Pacific Ocean. The still, chill air in the little arroyo where he had dropped off on the grass to sleep, exhausted, just before sunset had coated everything with a saturating dew. He forced his stiffened muscles into service. He rose from the damp ground and began to jump up and down in the tiny clearing. He beat his shoulders with his arms and puffed like a locomotive between chattering teeth. A few hundred feet away, traffic hissed by sporadically on the Coast Highway. On his opposite side, he could hear the hiss and muffled crash of waves breaking along the shore in the State Park. He was amazed at the noise that overlaid the silence.

Every movement was painful. He had clearly overdone it yesterday. It occurred to him that his reintroduction to bicycling should have been a gradual thing, more cordial, more incremental than it had been. Now, he paid for his haste in forming an intense relationship with a ten-speed mountain bike absent the convention of a formal, phased introduction. It felt as if his legs would never work again, as if his shoulders had been used to build the great pyramids at Giza. Warmed slightly by his calisthenics, he sat down again. He leaned against a small oak at the edge of the clearing, begging respite from his miserable muscles. As he lowered himself, he emitted a sub-human groan at the pain of the motion.

He shivered until exhaustion forced sleep, then dozed fitfully until cold drove the sleep away. He spent interminable hours of acute discomfort in this half-waking wretchedness, waiting for the sun's return. No night could ever be so long, and in his waking moments, he clutched his knees to draw himself into a ball against the penetrating damp. Hunger and thirst arrived during the night, but he had nothing to give them. They hung around and complained like visiting in-laws about the poor quality of the fare. Barent thought that dawn would never come.

The smell of wood smoke awakened him as the eastern sky began to lighten. Then, the unmistakable and nearly orgasmic smell of fresh coffee came to him on the still air. He rose to his feet. His body ached from the cramped position it had held all night; to move was to waste the little heat he generated in heating a new position. The damp earth had sucked heat from him like a cold bath. He staggered stiffly but single-mindedly toward the smell, drawn like a bee to a flower. Shuddering, stumbling and grunting with the effort of moving his complaining limbs, he staggered toward the enticing odor. He burst precipitously from the willows into a campsite.

Its occupant uttered a startled squeak, and turned to face him, crouched, holding a frying pan like a baseball bat at the ready. The woman's dark eyes were wide but determined, and she did not back away even an inch as the apparition that was John Randolph Barent lurched from the undergrowth. Leaves and grass festooned his ratted hair. The specter that loomed before her looked most nearly like an out-take from The Return of the Swamp Creature. It stumbled on a root and fell to its knees, looked up in chagrin at the poised frying pan.

"I smelled the coffee," Barent croaked, still on all fours, as if it explained everything. Nearly feral eyes gazed upward from under a wild halo of disheveled black hair. He bared his chattering teeth in an attempt at a smile. It came off as a grimace, and he gave it up. "I'm sorry if I frightened you. I'm harmless, really. Really. I must look like hell...I spent the night in the bushes."

The woman held her stance, saying nothing. She was small, dark of feature, but pretty. Short black hair framed an almost pixyish face; in its center was a nose that harkened back four generations to the Irish moorlands. Her blue eyes regarded him without blinking. She wore bluejeans and ankle-high laced hiking boots. A cream colored turtleneck climbed almost to her chin under a navy blue, quilted down jacket. Between her and Barent, a fire crackled happily in the fire ring. As the heat radiated into Barent, warming him even at his distance, he shivered violently, uncontrollably, and nearly fell on his face.

"Please, lady? I'm really cold. I won't hurt you. I just need to get warm," The plea in his voice could only be sincere. He shivered involuntarily again, his entire body wriggling like a Rottweiler happy to see its master.

The woman lowered the frying pan slightly, stopped, and then dropped it to her side. Still she said nothing. Barent moved tentatively toward the fire, and when she did not react, he scrambled clumsily over to the ring and sat as close to the flames as he could, shaking like San Francisco in 1906. The heat consumed his attention. While he struggled with a single-minded evaluation of whether it was warmer to put his hands in his armpits or extend them over the flames, he forgot for a moment that the woman was even there.

He was reminded when she set a cup of steaming black coffee cautiously in front of him, and backed away, still watching. He glanced gratefully at the woman. He reached to pick up the coffee, but his shivering made it impossible to lift the cup without splashing its contents all over himself. He sat it down without drinking, to wait for the spasms to subside.

"You've been out there all night?" It was the first time he had heard her speak. She had a pleasant, vaguely exotic voice. Her tone was one of confirmation rather than disbelief. Barent nodded mutely and glanced at her. Then he went back to his shivering.

"I heard you. You sounded like an animal. Why were you grunting like that?"

"Cold. I was cold and stiff, and I couldn't sleep." Barent's eyes confirmed this statement; the upper lids were puffy and drooped, the eyes themselves were black, pitted olives, sunken into their sockets.

"What's your name?"

"John. Most people call me J.R. Friends, anyway."

"It seems like you don't have many of those right now. What are you doing here? Where is your camping gear? Where is your car? Were you mugged?"

"It's a long story." He reached now for the coffee, his muscles finally under control enough to hold it without spilling.

"Are you homeless?" The question sounded odd. Barent hadn't thought of himself as homeless, but, in fact, he was for all practical purposes. He certainly couldn't go back to his apartment in the converted garage behind Mrs. Forrester's house.

"I guess you could say that," he offered lamely.

"Well, you're not very good at it, are you? I mean, you don't even have a jacket. It got cold last night."

"I know," said Barent, trying to keep the sarcasm

out of his voice. He knew all about how cold it had been.

"Would you like something to eat? I was just about to cook breakfast when you stumbled out of the bushes." The first rays of sunlight reached the campsite. It felt good on Barent's back. The shivering, painful as it had been with his stiff muscles, was finally beginning to subside.

"Anything. Yes, please."

She went to the tailgate of a white Range Rover and fumbled around in a box, returning with a plastic bowl and two packages of instant oatmeal. From the fire she took a pot of heated water, and poured some into the dry oatmeal, stirring it with a spoon. She handed the bowl to Barent, who ate ravenously. He had never even liked oatmeal, but this stuff was fantastic.

"Do you live here? In the campground?" she asked as he ate.

"No...no. I'm just passing through. I'm on my way to see my brother, get some help." Barent spoke between mouthfuls of oatmeal, which was heating him now from the inside. He knew it sounded lame, but he didn't care.

"Where is he?"

"Blythe. Down near the Colorado River." It wouldn't hurt to reveal his destination to her. Barent felt reasonably safe from pursuit.

"Well, I'm going that way. When you've finished,

get your stuff, and you can ride with me if you like. If you'll clean yourself up before we leave, that is. You're really a mess."

"I don't have any stuff." The bicycle could remain stashed where it was. He could buy Jessica another when this was all over. This woman's unexpected offer of help was a godsend. The thought of getting on the bicycle for another day and another night like the one he had just spent was an anathema.

The woman was incredulous. "No sleeping bag?"

Barent shook his head.

"You could have died out there."

"From what? There aren't any wild animals, and there aren't any mosquitoes. It's too cold for rattlesnakes. How could I have died? Killer racoons?" Barent scoffed.

"Exposure. Hypothermia. You were pretty bad when you came into my camp. You could have died from exposure."

"Well, I didn't. I'm O.K." Barent realized she was right. He felt a little stupid; he should have known better. But then, what had his choices been? "How is it you know so much about hypothermia?" he asked her, trying to lead the conversation away from himself.

"I'm a nurse. I work in a clinic in San Jose."

"What's your name? I haven't even asked you your name. Or thanked you, for that matter. Thanks." Barent gestured to the fire ring, and the empty oatmeal bowl.

"Ardi Powell." She went back to her vehicle, and returned with a towel and a bar of soap. "Go clean up," she instructed. "There's a restroom about two hundred feet over that way." She pointed.

"What kind of a name is R.D.? What's it stand for?"

"It doesn't stand for anything. It's short for Ardath. A - R - D - I."

"Oh. Nice name." Barent rose stiffly and shambled slowly off in the direction she had indicated. He found the restroom easily enough, and stripped to his waist. He lathered up with the soap Ardi had given him. He winced and puffed through pursed lips as the cold water chilled him all over again.

The sheet of polished steel that served as a mirror reflected an appalling sight. He fished the leaves out of his rebellious hair, and wet it well without using the soap. There was nothing to be done for the blue mask of unshaven stubble that peered back at him from the metal mirror. He dried himself with Ardi's towel, and stepped out into the sunshine to warm up after his icy ablutions. He was beginning to feel human again. The air was still cold, but the warm rays of the sun were a gift from heaven itself. He turned slowly to allow them to warm every side of him.

He pulled his cigarettes from his pocket, fished around for matches. When he removed the first smoke from the pack, he found it had been broken in two. His pants were just a shade too tight, and his balled up position had broken most of the smokes in the pack. He found one that was only bent and wrinkled, and carefully smoothed it between his fingers. He applied the flame and took a deep draw. It tasted like hell. He took another drag, just to be sure, and then pitched the entire pack into a nearby garbage can.

When he returned to the campsite, Ardi had the fire cold out, the Rover packed up. She was waiting patiently for him. He was reassured. If she had been gone, he wouldn't have been too surprised. The price of a towel and a bar of soap was a small tithe to pay if she had just wanted to be rid of him. A lot of people would have done just that.

"So how close are you going to Blythe?" Barent asked after they had turned onto the highway and the tires whirred contentedly under them, moving southward along the coast. Sunlight radiated warmly through the windshield. The ocean, visible now below them, faded from a crisp azure to Prussian blue on the distant horizon. Oil platforms dotted the channel, islands of industrial activity in a tranquil sea. One platform in particular jetted a horizontal flame that must have extended out over the ocean at least forty feet. The air was clear, and the first of the Channel Islands was visible to the south. Barent couldn't remember its name.

"I'll take you all the way. I'm going camping in the desert, and Blythe is as good a place to start as any. We'll be there in about seven hours."

"You're going camping alone?"

"Yes." She said the single word defensively, in a way that discouraged Barent's further inquiry, and a cloud passed almost imperceptibly across her countenance. She was actually quite attractive, Barent reflected. She was small, slender, and svelte, leggy and long-waisted at the same time. Her complexion was remarkably smooth and light; her lips were full without being excessive. Dark, large blue eyes glanced occasionally at Barent during their conversation, appraisingly, then darted back to the roadway. Her hair was the color of a raven's wing, but fine of texture. It contrasted almost starkly with her pale skin in a striking way. Barent had not yet seen her smile.

The warmth and vibration of the car combined with Barent's fatigue from his restless night. Ardi's last response had blocked further conversation in a way he did not quite understand, and in his silence and relative comfort, his eyelids began to droop. He dozed, drifting pleasantly in the sunshine and the hum of the tires on the roadway.

CHAPTER 21

The long, monotonous ride across the open desert finally softened her up. They had fueled the Rover in Indio, and Barent insisted on paying for the gas. They had a wordless burger in a Denny's at the freeway ramp, which he also paid for. He ruefully watched his cash reserves drop to a little over half of their initial amount. No matter; after eating he had phoned his brother at work, making arrangements to meet at a truck stop near the Arizona border. Barent had not wanted to visit Bill at home. It was a place that might be watched. He would have watched it, if he had been trying to catch himself.

The dull, treeless monotony of the Chocolate Mountains as the road rose up from the Coachella Valley worked on her, and then the tedium of innumerable creosote bushes vanishing into the flat distance of the open desert ultimately broke her resolve. They finally began to talk, with Ardi actually breaking the ice.

"So," she began conversationally but cautiously, "do you have a home? What are you doing traveling about without a suitcase or a change of clothes? I mean, if it's none of my business, you don't have to answer, but I was curious." She stared intently down the highway, superficially occupied with her driving.

"I'm going to see my brother. I had —no, I *have*— some difficulties and he's agreed to help me."

"So, what do you do? Do you work, or do you just stumble out of the bushes at public campgrounds? I mean, I see a lot of homeless folks, and you're not. You don't fit the pattern."

"How can you be so sure?" Barent was curious. She had been so definitive, with apparently so little information about him, that he was interested in how she had arrived at her conclusions.

"Lots of ways. For example, homeless people show more wear, on their hands particularly. Your hands are smooth and not callused. You haven't been gathering wood and building fires under bridges and in culverts. You've had a shower in the last three days, and a haircut less than two weeks ago. You aren't alert to exploit opportunities like the homeless people are. And you expect to be seen."

"What?" Her last comment was puzzling to Barent. "What does *that* mean?"

"Homeless people, no matter where they came from originally, quickly learn that they are invisible. Other people don't look at them, don't relate to them. It's almost as if they are afraid that if they acknowledge a homeless person, they will become one. The homeless people I've seen have come to expect this, and they learn unconsciously not to expect to be noticed. It imparts an unmistakable aura to their demeanor, and you don't have it. You still expect the world to notice you."

"I'd as soon it didn't, for a while."

"That begs an explanation." The question, for it *was* a question, lay between them like an invitation, and a challenge. Barent sensed that his answer would determine what directions their future relationship would take, and he liked this woman's matter-of-fact approach to things. She held the potential of becoming a friend, and he was loathe to let the opportunity slip by without at least trying. He decided to tell her the truth. He could use a friend just now.

He looked at her directly, his eyes without artifice. "O.K. But you must hear the whole story, and please don't be alarmed by what I tell you first. I'm an investigator for the Fire Department in my home town. An arson investigator. I wear a badge, protect lives and property, that sort of thing. I've been at it for fifteen years."

"I know some firemen, paramedics actually. Nice guys."

"Well, I'm a nice guy, too. So what was I doing at the campground, in the bushes? I was arrested for a fire I didn't set —two fires, actually. One of them killed my nephew. He was a firefighter, too. I got away at my arraignment, jumped the railing in the courtroom and ran. I made it to Gaviota on my girlfriend's bike, and spent the night in the bushes because I didn't have any place else to go."

Ardi said nothing, but Barent could tell that her mind was grinding out a risk evaluation. Here she was with a fugitive from the law, and she was obviously wondering if she was in any danger. Barent took steps to reassure her.

"I've got a lead on the guy who did the fire. For some reason, I've been set up. I know it sounds fishy, but it's the truth. Anyway, they have enough circumstantial evidence to convict me. My only hope is to find the real bad guy, and bring him in. I couldn't do that from inside a jail cell, so I escaped."

They were in the middle of the open desert, halfway between Blythe and Indio. That Ardi was now very apprehensive was obvious. Barent decided to take a chance.

"Look. If you're worried about what I might do, pull over at the next ramp, or right here, even, and let me out. I'm not dangerous, but if you have any misgivings, just pull over and let me out."

"If you wanted to hurt me, you would have tried something by now. I'm more worried about what might happen if the police find you and I'm helping you. That's illegal, isn't it?"

"Only if you know you're doing it. I won't tell."

Ardi was thoughtful a moment. She had been cruising along at seventy-five miles per hour, and slowed now to a more reasonable sixty. The desert seemed to creep by at the reduced speed. At last she spoke.

"Tell me the whole story."

CHAPTER 22

They found the truck stop Bill had suggested, on the outskirts of Blythe. It was actually little more than a service station and restaurant with a very large parking lot. There were dozens of trucks parked about. That usually meant good food.

They ordered, and talked across an unhurried meal. Ardi enthusiastically examined the information Barent had given her as they drove across the open desert. She analyzed it, looking for the glue that would hold it all together. Barent answered her questions patiently, waiting for Bill to show up after work.

"You say your father gave you the Zippo that was found at the second fire scene, and that it was your knife under the debris at the first one? Who had access to both those items besides yourself?"

"Nobody. Anybody. Hell, it could have been anyone. I may have dropped the knife. I just don't know."

"Nonsense. Most of the people in the world don't have ready access to your personal possessions. We can rule out about four and a half billion people on that basis alone! So who did? It would have to be somebody close to you, somebody you know. A co-worker? A room-mate?"

"I live alone. I leave stuff in my desk at work from time to time. It could have been a co-worker, I suppose. Everybody on the department knows about that cigarette lighter. It's politically incorrect that I smoke, and they rarely miss a chance to rag me about it."

"You smoke? I've been with you all day, and you haven't smoked anything. You really smoke?"

"I guess I forgot to today. I didn't even miss it, until now." Barent looked absently for cigarettes, patting his pockets in the characteristic order of a smoker searching for a pack, then remembered he had thrown his cigarettes out at the Gaviota Campground. "That's funny," he said, bemused. "I haven't even missed it."

"You're on a roll," encouraged Ardi. "Stay with it. Now, what about the car and the blood at the second fire scene? I mean, your hand is bandaged. How do you explain all that?"

"Well, I figured the car was just a look-alike. But that doesn't work; there aren't many cars around like mine. It's pretty unmistakable."

"So, where was your car when it was supposed to have been seen?"

"At the hospital parking lot. My girlfriend took me home after I cut my hand."

"Where were the car keys?"

"I don't remember. I was pretty dopey after the

drinking and the pain pills I took. No, wait, they were with me, at home. I remember, because I went to work the next day, and I had them."

"Is there a spare set of keys to the car?"

"No. I meant to have one made, but I never got around to it."

"So, either your car was hot-wired, or somebody slipped into your house while you were sleeping and took the keys. If somebody hot-wired it, you would have seen the damage when you took it to work the following morning. So somebody must have taken the keys."

"No. That's just not possible. Jessica was with me all night. I may have been down for the count, but she would have heard anybody that came in during the night. She's a real light sleeper."

"And that doesn't suggest anything to you?"

He thought for a second, then explained. "The guy I'm looking for has enough electrical knowledge to hot-wire a car without messing it up. I know for a fact he understands how electronic alarm systems work, and how to defeat them. He did it on the fire that killed Larry." He paused thoughtfully for a moment, then went on.

"Look, Ardi, this isn't getting us anywhere. We can speculate all day, but the guy who did the fire bought the stuff to make his device at a local welding company. I've got his name, Jason Grover, and I just have to track him down. He's probably gay—if his rap sheet is any indication—which makes it easier. There aren't that many gay hangouts on the Central Coast, and he may frequent one. We know he lives in the area. I've got motive, which was arson for hire. He got ten thousand dollars for it. We know that because the guy who hired him took that amount of money out of his bank before the fire occurred. The fact that ten thousand dollars showed up in my bank account just goes to prove that somebody wanted to frame me for the fire, and was willing to spend ten thousand dollars to do it."

"You didn't tell me about that."

"I forgot."

Ardi looked at him skeptically. She cocked her head and raised an eyebrow. "You forgot?"

"I forgot."

At that moment, his brother Bill came through the doorway, paused, and scanned the seating area. He spied John, smiled tightly and waved as he made for their booth. Barent got to his feet and met his brother. They hugged, longer than a simple greeting between sensitive men of the nineties. Their contact transmitted volumes about their feelings of loss of Barent's nephew, Larry, Bill's son. Finally, they parted.

"I'm sorry, I'm so sorry about Larry. Bill, he was a great kid. I'm sorry."

"We missed you at the services," said Bill. His eyes glistened with the nearly unendurable barrage of emotions that seeing his younger brother stirred to the surface. Not only was relief emerging at J.R.'s arrival, but the reactivated memories of Larry showed through as well. His grief was too recent, and was controlled in its expression only by a colossal effort of will. He masked it by turning his attention to his brother's companion.

"Who's this?" he inquired, nodding at Ardi, who remained seated in the booth.

"This is Ardi. She gave me a ride here. Ardi, this is my big brother, Bill."

Ardi smiled, struck by the family resemblance.

Bill acknowledged her greeting. "Pleased to meet you. Thanks for helping my little brother find his way here." He turned back to Johnny.

"We've got to talk..." Bill's suggestion was clear, and Ardi made as if to rise.

"Ardi, you don't have to go. Bill, she knows. She's cool. She helped even after she knew."

Bill looked at Ardi dubiously.

"I can leave..." Ardi volunteered.

"No, please, Ardi. Please stay. For Pete's sake, finish your meal at least."

Ardi's suggestion, her offer to depart, created in Barent a sudden wave of —what? Fear? Apprehension? Regret? It didn't fit in any pigeonhole, but it emerged surprisingly strong. He did not want her to leave; he did not want her to leave *him*. The feeling was absurd. How could he have formed an attachment to her in the short time they had traveled together? Besides, she would be leaving soon, anyway, for her sojourn in the desert, and to return to her everyday life. That life did not include him.

He turned his attention back to Bill, and they sat down. John told his brother the whole story as they finished eating, including details on both of the fires of which he stood accused. The waitress allowed them to continue over repeated refreshers of after-dinner coffee, as the dinner trade tapered off.

"So you think you can get this guy?" Bill asked, finally. "And make it stick?"

"Yes. I'm not sure how I'm going to prove it yet, but the proof is there. I just have to find it."

"What if you're caught in the meantime? I mean, before you've got a case built."

"Then, I'll probably go to jail. They're certainly not going to let me escape again. I'll probably get some extra time coming for unlawful flight to avoid prosecution. I've got to nail this guy, and do it right. Unless I can get him dead to rights, there's no reason they won't convict me. No reason at all. Perry Mason doesn't work here anymore. The idea of proving somebody else's guilt to prove my own innocence in open court is sheer Hollywood. In reality, it just doesn't happen."

"So, what can I do to help? What do you need to pull it off?"

"Shit, Bill. I've got nothing. It's been amazing

how quickly all of my resources were stripped away. I need a car. I need a place to stay, close to the suspect. I need clothes. I will need more food soon. I need a job; I didn't tell you I've been suspended without pay."

"You need money," said Bill succinctly. He reached into his hip pocket and brought forth a folded number ten envelope. "I figured you would. After all that business with Kathleen and the kids, I can't imagine you'd have a bank account. It's got to be costing you a fortune. Vicious little bitch..."

"She's not a vicious little bitch," Barent found himself defending his ex-wife. "Things just didn't work out. I think she gave it her best shot; I'm not an easy guy to live with. Don't blame her, Bill. Don't blame anybody." He wondered at his sudden defense of Kathleen. He himself, did, in fact, blame her for his economic woes, and for leaving him in the first place. He blamed himself for trusting her, on the intellectual side of his mind.

"Sorry, Johnny. Sorry," Bill said placatingly. He changed the subject. "Listen, Elaine wanted you to come by the house, but there have been cruisers up and down the street for the last few hours, and I don't think it's a good idea. I think they're driving by every couple of hours looking for a new car in the driveway, or something. It's better to wait until this is all cleared up before you try to come by..."

"Makes sense. It's what I would have done if my

bird had flown. FAX the local fuzz a picture and ask them to check his brother's house. They'd be stoked to get the collar; cops think differently than we do. They would love to have one-up on the boys up north, and they would rub their noses in it."

Bill smiled, then frowned abruptly. Barent turned around to see what had caught his brother's eye. Two city police officers had entered the restaurant and were taking seats at the counter.

"I think it's time to leave," Barent said under his breath. "Ardi, you might want to stay here until we've gone. No point in taking any chances. Thanks for everything, and if you'll jot down your address, I'll take you to dinner again when this is all over."

"I'm staying with you. Bill can't drive you out of here, and they won't be looking for three people together. Once we get clear of here, then we can make some decisions. Meanwhile, you need me."

"O.K. O.K. Let's just keep it casual. Bill, can you get the check? We'll wait for you outside." Barent was elated and relieved that Ardi was not staying behind, but concealed it behind a final swig from his coffee mug. He looked up, meeting her eyes. He was not sure what he saw there as she met his gaze.

"Let's go," said Bill. As he rose from the booth, casually he tossed a five-dollar bill on the table. "I'll get the check." J.R. looked at the fiver with a wistfulness that surprised him.

Outside, darkness had fallen, and then been driven back by the fluorescent lights of the truck stop. They bathed everything in a greenish, eerie light. Moths fluttered noisily against the light covers. Lepidopteran kamikazes, they fried themselves against the hot lights for reasons they could not examine. Their bodies littered the ground below the lights like fallen soldiers on a medieval battle-ground. The brothers embraced, with much back patting, and then broke apart.

"Where too now, Johnny?" Bill wanted to know.

"Camarillo."

"Good luck."

"Give the rug rats a hug from their 'Onca Johnny'." Elaine had had two more kids fifteen years after Larry was born. Barent knew it was a source of great joy to them that they now raised, in effect, a second family. It was also a bond that would help them survive Larry's death with their marriage intact.

"You bet. Be careful."

CHAPTER 23

"Why?" Barent wanted to know.

After leaving Bill at the restaurant, they had stopped by a large discount store where Ardi had taken some of his money and gone inside alone to buy Barent a change of clothing and an inexpensive sleeping bag. She also bought a razor, shaving cream, deodorant, a toothbrush, and a small tube of toothpaste. They had looked at Barent's hand, unraveling the dirty, tattered rags that remained of his original bandage, and decided that no new bandage was needed. It was healing nicely. Ardi promised to pull the stitches in the morning, when the light returned.

While she was inside, Barent examined the contents of the open envelope his brother had given him. It contained two thousand dollars in twenties, minus what Ardi was using inside now, and a credit card. A note attached instructed Barent to use the card whenever he could, and save the cash for the times he couldn't. Bill said in the note that he would pay the billings without question, and instructed his brother to stay under the two thousand dollar limit. Barent felt a tear come to his eye, and he bit his lip.

Family. Bill had come through beyond Barent's wildest expectations, and in the midst of his own fresh grief at the loss of his son.

Barent mused that there had been no discussion, no real reminiscence of Larry, during their meeting. He felt as if they had unconsciously avoided the subject —as if they knew intuitively that when the grief finally emerged, it would incapacitate them both. It had not been the time.

Ardi and Barent had left Blythe then, traveling north on Highway 95, on the California side of the Colorado River border with Arizona. After about an hour's drive northward Ardi had pulled the Rover off the road and into the dense willow and cottonwood brakes along the banks of the river. Without words, the two travelers shook out sleeping bags in the light of a battery lamp that Ardi placed on the hood of the Rover. The bottomland along the river here was flat, and they had no trouble locating a small clearing to lay out the bags. Barent had climbed into his and Ardi brought the light, a jug of water, and a roll of toilet paper. She placed these things on the ground at their heads, between them.

"Just in case..." she said softly, flashing the light on the pile of conveniences. Then she crawled into her sleeping bag and killed the light.

The blackness was intense, relieved only by starlight which seemed in contrast to blaze from the velvet heavens. Barent was amazed. It had been a long time since he had seen the stars as only the desert could show them. It reminded him of Larry, and he grew thoughtful, introspective. As he lay on the hard ground looking up, an orbiting satellite passed across the seemingly stationary field of stars.

Still staring upward, fingers laced behind his neck, his hands cradling his head, Barent had asked "Why? Why are you helping me?"

Ardi was silent a moment, then she spoke.

"I'm not real sure," she told him. "I guess I have some sort of rescue need that you're triggering. I'm a nurse, remember. Nurses like to save people; it's an occupational hazard. They like to make things better, make the hurt go away. Besides, I needed an adventure, and the universe seems to have provided me with one. This has definitely been more interesting than what I had planned."

"It doesn't make sense. Why would you go out of your way to help me? The state says I'm a murderer, and they can prove it. How can you be so trusting?"

"You're not a murderer, J.R. Your eyes give you away; they're free of subterfuge; they're innocent, caring eyes. And I saw you with your brother. There's too much warmth, too much sincerity there, and too much grief for me to believe you're guilty of what you've been charged with."

"Even so, why would you alter your own plans to help me? I mean, this is your vacation isn't it?" An owl glided across their little clearing, a dark shadow against the stars, deadly on silent wings, hunting. It swerved at the sound of Barent's voice, and vanished. After a pause, Ardi spoke.

"I think I finally decided when you defended your ex-wife to your brother. You were loyal to both of them. Most men would have let it ride, what he said. Up until then, it was only an idea in the back of my head."

"So, uh...what is the history of Ardath Powell that she should be traveling alone into the desert? Do you seek a vision?" Barent asked tentatively, changing the subject, but not really. He allowed the sudden silence between them to run its course. Finally, Ardi spoke.

"It's kind of complicated. I guess, in a sense, I'm using you. To do a reality check about men in general." Again she paused, then continued after a time.

"I broke up with a man two, nearly three, months ago, and I thought I was going to die. I really loved the bastard. Everything was going along fine until I came home early from work one day and found him pounding away at some little bimbo he picked up God knows where. In my own damned bed," she added venomously.

Her voice leveled out. "Anyway, it shook up my world. I was like a zombie at work. My social life dried up. I didn't know who I was anymore. I finally had to get away, and took vacation time. I had a lot of time on the books, and I thought if I did something different, it might help. I packed up and headed south. My only destination was 'away', and it wasn't until last night, while you were moaning and crashing about in the bushes, that I decided to go to the desert. You know, I barely slept, with all the racket you made."

"So...is it helping?" Barent ignored the indictment.

"We'll see." She sighed. "We'll see."

Barent heard a rustling of adjustment and glanced toward Ardi in the starlight. She had rolled to face away from him, telegraphing a tacit message that the conversation was over. In a calm voice, he heard her say "Good night."

He returned his gaze to the velvet sky, blazing with diamonds, while his ears absorbed the cacophony of wild noises—frogs croaking, crickets chirping, rodents rustling through the dry willow duff, and the cottonwoods sibilating in the night wind—that civilized men call silence.

CHAPTER 24

Camarillo was potentially a problem. Jason Grover had done time there for psychiatric evaluation, and there were records, including the address destination of his release, but they were available only through official channels. Barent knew his status was anything but official. He didn't even have his driver's license, let alone his official I.D. and badge, which they would surely ask to see before they gave him any information. His clothing, while suitable for camping in the desert, was not going to lend him credibility at the state facility. He would have to dump three or four hundred dollars of his limited funds into presentable clothing, even if he could solve the identification difficulty. Whatever ploy he might choose would carry risk, for if he were discovered, he would find himself in effect already in custody. Despite its medical and psychiatric long suit, Camarillo remained, in fact, a prison. He might get in, and never get out.

Marty Caulkin might help. He was just unconventional enough, and they were old friends. Barent decided that contact was a necessary risk, and had Ardi stop at the next public phone they came upon to make the call.

Marty answered on the second ring. The State Fire Marshal's office wasn't very well funded, and there was no intermediate secretary at the regional field office.

"State Fire Marshal's Office, Deputy Caulkin speaking."

"Where are the best chili dogs in the galaxy?" asked Barent in his best quiz show baritone.

"J.R.! Where the hell are you?"

"Answer the question." The question was designed to remind Caulkin of their personal relationship without actually bringing it up.

"Frank's Fabulous Foot Long Hot Dogs. Now tell me where you are!"

"In a minute. Listen, Marty, do you think I'm guilty of the fires?"

"It doesn't matter what I think. You're in deep shit."

"Well, I'm not. I'm innocent. I had nothing to do with it. We have a suspect; Jason Grover. When I was arrested, everybody stopped looking for him."

"Not everybody."

"What do you mean?"

"I mean, I didn't even know you were arrested until just before the arraignment. That asshole McCabe didn't bother to clue me in. Anyway, I kept on following the leads we developed together. It's interesting, as far as I got. I can't do it openly now, of course; the boss would nail me to the wall. We don't have money to investigate crimes where the suspect is already in custody. But I've found out some interesting stuff."

"Such as...?"

"If I help you, I'm an accessory after the fact. To murder, J.R. And, there's the aiding-a-fugitive charges that would be filed. And, of course, I'd be divulging confidential information relevant to an investigation to the suspect in that investigation. I'm pretty sure that's a crime."

Barent knew then that Caulkin was going to help him; the intent nestled there in the tone and the enumeration of the crimes he would be committing in doing so. Barent smiled to himself. Marty was setting himself up for a lifetime supply of free chili dogs, and wanted Barent to know it.

"If I'm innocent, there *is* no fact. Cut the crap, Marty, and help me get off the hook. If I can't find this guy, I'll be doing time, either in a State Prison, or in South America. My life's on the line, here, buddy."

"Prison would not be good. You're still cute enough to cause fist fights in the inmate population." In his mind's eye, Barent could see Marty's bulging eyes twinkle over an obscene smirk.

The operator cut in and demanded another eighty-five cents. Barent fished frantically in his pocket, and came up with the change, dropped it into the coin slot.

"Ah!" observed Caulkin. "Calling from a pay phone."

"Gold star, Sherlock," said Barent in a tone of friendly sarcasm. "C'mon, Marty. Give!"

"Well, I called Camarillo for starters. I got them to FAX me Grover's file, minus the medical records, of course. Doctor/client privelege. And I talked to the head bull on Grover's cellblock while he was in. They remember him. Studious, kept to himself, but he was suspected of homosexual activity while he was there. Unofficially, of course. The bull said he was banging anybody who could do him some good. The bull also said he was mean, bitter about something. It didn't click until I read his file." Caulkin paused.

"And?"

"And, you busted his mama, fourteen years ago. Remember the Potter case? Elizabeth Potter did her husband with lighter fluid and a brass lamp? She's in Chowchilla, for life, premeditated murder and arson. It was your first major investigation. It was good work. I pulled the case from the city files."

"I remember. She's Potter, he's Grover. How come?"

"The kid was from a previous marriage, and Grover was the father's name. I guess she took back her maiden name after the divorce. Remember Potter's defense? She plead self defense against the old man's drunken brutality and abuse. It might have flown today, in the sensitive nineties, but not back then. Back then, there was *no* excuse for killing somebody. I think the old man may have been abusing the kid, too. Child Protective Services vanished him before the trial, and it never came out, but the pattern is there. He was ten years old then; he'd be twenty-four or twenty-five now."

"So, what was his release address? Where did he go from Camarillo?"

"Just a second. I've got it here somewhere..."

"Marty, I'm out of change," warned Barent in a near panic, patting his clothing, then gesturing frantically for Ardi to come over to the phone booth from where she waited in the Land Rover. She didn't see him, and he did not call out, for it would have told Caulkin he was with somebody. "Hurry up!" he breathed into the receiver.

"Got it! 2119 Cypress Street. In Atascadero."

"Thanks, Marty! I owe you a big one." He repeated the address to himself, trying to cement it into his memory until he could write it down.

"What are you...", Marty began, but never finished The operator cut back onto the line, demanding another eighty-five cents.

"Marty, I'm out of change. Thanks. See ya!"

CHAPTER 25

Rowley Skefich tilted back in his chair and propped his feet on the front porch railing at 2119 Cypress Street, careful not to spill his beer as he shifted his position. Through the "V" of his crossed, grease-covered black engineer's boots, he watched a slender, dark man with unruly hair leave the passenger side of a white British Land Rover. The man looked appraisingly at him and at the house, and walked across the dry and battered lawn towards him. An indistinguishable figure remained in the driver's seat, a shadow behind tinted glass.

The guy needed a shave. The blue shadow of a three-day beard was visible even from a distance. Rowley smelled cop, but not the garden variety. There was something different about this one. He was dressed wrong, too casually. There was no tie, no sport coat. There were no bulges. Cops who dressed in civvies almost always wore ties and sport coats, unless they were undercover. And they always had bulges. If this guy were undercover, he'd have never approached in this way. The self-assurance of authority was absent from his gait, the watchfulness of a man used to working in a hostile environment was not so pronounced. The man

195

moved like a cat, but not like a lion. Presently, the man stopped in front of him, at the base of the dilapidated porch steps, and regarded him thoughtfully in silence.

Finally, Rowley surrendered to the silence and to his curiosity. "What the fuck do you want?" The voice was hostile, challenging, but the eyes remained flat. It sounded like footsteps on a gravel driveway. He tilted the beer can to his lips and drained the remaining contents. Belching, he crushed the can and pitched it carelessly into the corner of the porch where a pile of its brethren lay, likewise crushed and used up. The allegory was lost on Rowley, but the dark man made the metaphorical connection without expressing it.

"A trip down memory lane. I'm looking for somebody." There was just enough response to Rowley's challenge to keep him interested. This wasn't a shakedown, or it would have started by now.

"Nobody here. Get lost." The gravel crunched, the eyes stayed flat.

"I'm looking for Jason Grover."

Rowley hadn't heard Pretty Boy's real name in half a decade. The little punk had screwed them good when he got out of jail, weaseling away the gang's best clients. Rowley was tempted to rat the little punk on general principles, but refrained for the moment. He wanted to see what was behind the inquiry.

"You're a cop." It came as a statement, not a question. Barent responded by seating himself on a step and leaning casually against a pillar. It placed his head below Rowley's, and answered the accusation more eloquently than any verbal response could have. He was not here as a cop.

"I've got fifty bucks. Help me, and it's yours."

The loss of business from Rowley's 'friends' when Pretty Boy stole the contracts had hit the Satan's Spawn hard in the treasury. The beer parties were now of the 'bring your own' variety, and the gang had been deteriorating ever since. Some of the guys had even taken straight jobs. There just wasn't the money in the petty burglaries and enforcement contracts that there had been in arson. During the last few years, Rowley had come to find himself increasingly a gang leader without much of a gang. The dead soldiers in the pile in the corner of the porch were mostly chain store generic beer, the cheapest available. They were symptomatic of hard times for Rowley Skefich. He scratched his bare belly, where it hung obscenely over his belt-buckle as his filthy undershirt had ridden up.

"Make it a hundred." Fifty would have been enough; Rowley wouldn't mind seeing the source of his headaches come to grief. Still, a hundred was better. It was ballsey, but the world wasn't giving Rowley an abundance of opportunities to exploit these days. He would exploit this one to the limit.

"O.K. Fifty if you talk to me. A hundred if you tell me anything I don't already know."

"Let's see it. This is a cash and carry deal."

Barent pulled a pair of fifties from his shirt pocket. He thumbed one of them to Skefich, who leaned forward to snatch it, and held on to the other. He met Rowley's eye and cocked an eyebrow in invitation to speak.

"What do you want to know? I ain't seen the little punk in years."

"Where is he now?"

"If I knew that, I'd activate his fucking dental plan. He landed here when he got out of the joint and hit the ground running. He took some stuff with him. *My* stuff."

"What does he look like? Can you describe him for me? I've never seen him."

"Why do you want to find him?"

"It's personal. He did a number on me, and I want his ass."

Rowley chuckled obscenely. "Everybody wanted his ass. And most everybody who did got it at one time or another. We called him 'Pretty Boy'. He was short, maybe five-five, and skinny. Dishwater hair. Pretty, like a girl. But mean. Jesus, was that kid mean! The first day he came here, he took out two of my lieutenants with a two-by-four. Nasty little shit. He didn't have an ounce of loyalty in him."

"He came back here when he got out of jail,"

Barent observed.

"He wanted money. He said he needed lots of money. He ripped off our business contacts, and took them for himself."

"Did he say what for?"

"Nah. For the first month or two after he came back, he got a lot of letters here from a medical clinic. I figured he had some sort of health problem that needed fixing. Or, maybe AIDS. It wouldn't surprise me if he'd got AIDS, the way he fucked around. If he was a girl, he'd have been a real slut. But always for something. He used it to get what he wanted."

"Do you remember the name of the clinic? I know it's been a while, but can you remember it"

"Yeah, matter of fact I do. This one will cost you the other fifty."

Barent handed it over.

"I remember because it was such a weird name for a clinic. Usually they're Professional this or Medical that. This one was 'New Horizon'. Just that. New Horizon. Sounds like a fucking rehab clinic, but the kid never touched drugs or booze. At least, they weren't a problem."

"Where?"

"How the fuck should I know? San Diego, somewhere."

"So what happened to him?"

"He vanished. One day he was here, and the next day he was gone. He never came back. But we knew he was around. He was still working our contracts. We never saw him, but we saw his work."

"What did he do? What was the work that you saw?"

"Now that, my friend, is none of your fucking business. Time for a beer." Rowley grunted to his feet, and turned toward the doorway. He was done. He had his money, and the questions were swinging dangerously close to his own past crimes. He turned in the doorway, leaned against the grimy jamb. He belched and squinted at Barent.

"Just what did the little bastard do to you, anyway?"

"He killed my nephew. In a fire."

"Figures," said Rowley, and he ambled inside to find another can of beer, leaving open the door behind him.

Barent went to the open door. "Where can I find him?" he called into the dim interior.

"I haven't got a fucking clue, I already told you," Skefich hollered back. "He used to hang out in that fag bar on Price Street, but nobody's seen him for years."

"Thanks. I may be back, if I've forgotten anything."

"Bring money."

* * *

Barent hung up the telephone, more puzzled than ever. The call had been to New Horizon, the clinic in San Diego that Rowley Skefich had mentioned. He had hoped to get some clue as to possible medical requirements of Jason Grover that might lead him to the man, possibly confirmation that Jason had AIDS, and would be therefore might be associated with a local support network. Instead, he was politely stonewalled.

"Well?" Back in the Rover, Ardi looked at him questioningly.

"You feel like driving to San Diego?"

"What's there?"

"Maybe an answer. Maybe nothing."

CHAPTER 26

They stopped by the bar on Price Street before leaving town. It was a dismal place in daylight. Its dark interior walls stood now devoid of romantic secrecy in the stark light, like the wrinkles of a dowager after a sleepless night.

It catered to the black-leather-and-chains crowd. It was nearly empty now, just after opening at noon. Two men in black leather jackets nursed beers at the darkest end of the bar. They were sitting too close together, Barent thought. He turned his attention to the blond-haired, dark-eyed man behind the bar counter.

He wore a black leather vest that revealed an expanse of hairless chest and bare muscular arms that were tanned beyond perfection. The man polished a glass casually with a towel, obviously turning the glass and manipulating the bar rag in a way that showed his musculature to its best advantage. Ardi hovered unobtrusively behind Barent as they approached him with their questions.

Barent caught the bartender's eye, and the man began to dry the glass *obscenely*. Barent wouldn't have believed it could be done, but it was there before his eyes. He snorted to himself, and asked the man about Jason Grover.

The bartender had never heard of Jason Grover, or of 'Pretty Boy'. Barent found himself wishing he had a picture to flash; names were seldom known in places like the Back Door. He made a mental note to try to get his hands on Marty's file when he returned from San Diego. He had no idea how he would go about this, but he knew it might be possible. Marty kept files, he knew, files independent of the official reports in the office. Maintaining independent files of criminal investigations was an illegal practice, and the existence of the unofficial files would be cause for Marty's termination if their existence were ever discovered. But the practice gave him an investigative edge, and he had more convictions under his belt than any other investigator in the state. And it would also enable him to provide Barent with information independently of any agency contact. The burning question lay in the balance of his loyalty to Barent against his sense of duty, which would require him to take Barent into custody if he could.

As they drove south, Ardi turned to him briefly, her hands still on the wheel.

"You don't like gays much, do you?"

"I don't care for them one way or the other."

"You might have gotten more out of the bartender if your face hadn't shown such disdain. Couldn't you tell he was put-off?"

"Come on," he scoffed. "It couldn't have been

that bad. He was put off because he thought he was talking to a cop. Besides, did you see what he was doing to that glass?"

"It was that bad."

"I've got nothing against gays," Barent asserted defensively. "They are an evolutionary dead end. If everybody was gay, that'd be the end of the species. Ergo, it's not right. At a very basic level, it doesn't perpetuate the species." The flaws in the argument clearly were not apparent to Barent.

"Whatever you say." Ardi frowned, shook her head slowly from side to side. She concentrated her attention on the white lines on the pavement that rushed at her like tracer bullets from an unseen paint gun. She gripped the steering wheel at ten and two. *There are none so blind as those who do not wish to see,* she thought to herself.

After a time, Ardi suddenly asked without preface, "Why would anybody want you to go to jail? Who has it in for you badly enough to set you up so well?"

Barent turned toward her, cocked his left leg onto the seat, and stretched his right arm along the window. "Remember that call I made from Camarillo? Well, I called a buddy of mine in the State Fire Marshal's Office who was helping me with the investigation. Marty Caulkin. He got the files from Camarillo, which is why I didn't have to go in myself. He says that I busted Jason Grover's mother for murder and arson fifteen years ago. She doused her husband with lighter fluid and lit him off. She's still in jail. I remember her, but I don't remember the kid. He was only about ten years old. I felt real bad about sending her up, the mother, and I've felt guilty ever since. I think the old man was abusing her. I've even felt guilty about feeling proud that I'd made a bust stick on my first solo investigation."

"Lots of guilt," Ardi nodded, as if to herself. Then she glanced at Barent. "Why do you give it space in your head? It was fifteen years ago."

"It's an old friend. I'd miss it if it didn't come and visit every now and then."

"It's such a waste."

"It's mine to waste. Isn't my five cents almost used up, Lucy Brown?" There was a faint peevishness in his voice which Ardi's ears caught.

"I suppose. I'm sorry to be such a nag. It's your business. You know, I really hate it when I do that. I hate it when I nag."

"Forget it."

* * *

The waiting room at New Horizon was done in the non-committal pastels and putty grays that were setting interior designers on fire half a decade ago. The walls were oddly barren, and relieved only by subtle color changes in the ubiquitous pastel motif. Upbeat Muzak wallpaper music trickled into the room from unseen speakers, barely detectable at the threshold of conscious hearing, like the meaningless hum of chorusing insects on a warm spring afternoon. A single man, small and oddly effeminate, cowered behind a magazine in a corner chair. Surreptitiously, he eyed Barent and Ardi with what Barent thought was undue suspicion as they approached the receptionist. The young man never met their eyes directly as they crossed the room.

The receptionist acknowledged them with a subtle mixture of studied indifference and aplomb. Without any overt hostility, she managed to convey the idea that they were not welcome without an appointment, regardless of their business. There was no overt clue as to what the specialty of the office was. There were no telltale brochures arrayed on an end table, no trade magazines fanned in the magazine rack. There was no emergent clue about what the purpose the office actually served, or the medical specialty it represented.

Admittedly, Barent had no hope of obtaining specific information about Grover as a patient, but the obscurantism that met his initial phone call had triggered his sense of inquest. He was sure, without a cognitive reason to *be* sure, that there was more to be discovered. He could practically smell it.

"I'm sorry," apologized the receptionist, smiling

stiffly with mendacious politeness, "but Doctor Lindquist doesn't see any patients without a referral from another physician."

"Can you tell me what specialty he practices?" Barent wanted to know.

"The Doctor's specialty is referrals."

The answer was circular, transparently canned. Barent decided to take the final shot. "Does he treat AIDS patients?"

"No, he does not." The receptionist looked directly at him. "I'll have to ask you to leave now. The doctor will be happy to see you when you have a proper referral." Her tone, while it fell well short of overt enmity, left no doubt that she intended to provide no further assistance. Barent thanked her with matching insincerity, and they left.

"Looks like a dead end," Ardi observed as they walked back to the car. "What a cold fish!"

"*Au contraire, mon cher'*," Barent responded in ratty, Anglicized French. "There's something there. Something that will tell us about Jason Grover if we can figure out what it is."

"So, how do we do that? She didn't tell us anything. We don't know anything more than we did before. I think we've wasted a trip."

"She did tell us something we didn't know. We know the doctor's name. Let's find out what we can about Dr. Lindquist."

It was late afternoon, and there were not many

campgrounds in the city of San Diego. "Let's get a room," Barent suggested, "and we can make some calls tomorrow morning after we've rested."

"Suits me," said Ardi. "A hot bath would be a dream come true."

"Uh...I haven't got a lot of extra money, just now. Would you mind paying for your own room?"

"Why don't we get one room and split the cost?"

Barent looked at Ardi, raising an eyebrow. Ardi caught the question.

"That's not what I had in mind! We're adults. We can share a room without creating a situation. Besides, you have other loyalties. I'm not going to compromise your virtue, if that's what's worrying you. It's just a way of saving money."

"You're right. Sorry, it just surprised me." Barent felt sheepish, as if he had made an indecent suggestion, when in fact that had been the farthest thing from his mind. Still, from time to time, he found it difficult not to consider his options with regard to his new ally and traveling companion, but indulged his thoughts only after recognizing his general state of mind. He was alone. Her companionship was an island of reassurance in a sea of doubt, and her presence was a bulwark against feeling the fear of his predicament. Never did he consider seriously breaching his commitment to Jessica, unstated as it was.

They left the central business district, and got

directions from a gas station attendant to the lodging district. Eschewing the pricey lodging in Old Town, and the costly downtown hotels that catered to business conventions and expense accounts, they found a relatively inexpensive motel in Mission Valley with a bathtub in the room, and checked in. Ardi handled the registration while Barent waited in the Rover. Ardi lead the way to the ground-floor accommodations. Barent was still looking around the room when he heard the first splashes of water filling the tub.

CHAPTER 27

Check-out time was eleven a.m. Barent made his calls beginning at nine thirty, feeling remarkably refreshed after a stinging shower and a shave. His first tries were non-productive. The world of medical referrals wasn't open for business until ten.

There were a number of medical referral services in the phone book, but he met with difficulty in his approach. They were used to recommending specialists for specific illnesses, and their data bases did not respond well to matching a type of care to a specific physician's name by searching for the physician.

On his fourth call after ten a.m., he hit pay dirt. A friendly voice with a Georgia accent answered the phone, and Barent bantered before asking his question. The voice, whose name was Andrea, knew of Lindquist, indirectly through a friend of a friend. She would not discuss the matter over the phone, but agreed to meet for lunch and other consideration at a restaurant that she named.

Ardi had listened to the entire conversation mutely, but was dazzled by Barent's artificial charm.

"You really can turn it on when you want to, can't you?" The question's tone was somewhere between

211

bemused and accusatory.

Barent ignored the question. "We've got a luncheon date," he said. "Get a move on!"

Ardi raised an eyebrow in inquiry.

"A Georgia peach. Says she knows Lindquist, but wouldn't talk over the phone. She wants lunch, and an engraved portrait of Ben Franklin."

* * *

The Georgia peach's eyes fell, and the corners of her mouth turned down wryly when she saw the handsome, resonant voice she had agreed to meet was in the company of another woman. Barent missed it, but Ardi caught the shadow of disappointment that moved fleetingly across Andrea's face during the introductions like a bat across the moon's full face. There had been another agenda.

They were shown to a table. After some ill-concealed fishing as to the nature of Barent's relationship to his companion, the peach ordered salad and fried prawns. Barent and Ardi ordered coffee. The significance of that was not lost on Andrea. Mentally, she shrugged and decided to settle for cash.

They made small talk as Barent sipped his coffee. Andrea Massey was new to California, transplanted less than a year from her native Georgia. She was, she rattled on, tired of the south, and wanted to meet a different type of men than the type she complained was endemic in her native state. Living on slave wages, Sunday football, and cheap beer wasn't her idea of a rosy future. What she really wanted was to meet a doctor, marry, and raise babies in an eight bedroom house, but it wasn't as easy as it might sound, she explained as she consumed the prawns with a ravenous concentration born at least partly of real hunger. She had taken this job just to make ends meet, and it didn't pay very much. She glanced at Barent significantly as she said this, and Barent, as if on cue, slid a folded fifty dollar bill across the table to her. It vanished below the table, and the peach blushed ever so briefly.

"He's a psychiatrist," she disclosed finally, over pecan pie á la mode. "He specializes in sexual dysfunction. He's not listed with the agency. I just happen to know of him because a friend of mine went to him once." She continued eating, concentrating on the nearly surgical removal of a bite of pecan pie from the wedge. She would not meet Barent's eyes.

"That's it?" Barent asked incredulously. "That's all you can tell me?" He looked at the edge of the table, where he had seen the fifty disappear. "Look, Andrea, that's not a fifty dollar piece of information."

"Yes, it is."

"Andrea, it's a rip-off."

"So? What can you do about it? It's more than

you had when you came in here."

Barent sighed and shot a glance at the ceiling. She was right, and a part of him nagged. If she was willing to do the song and dance he had just seen, she probably needed the money more than he did. He frowned, unwilling to make a scene, but not satisfied with the transaction. He frowned again.

"You pay for the lunch. C'mon, Ardi. Let's get out of here."

CHAPTER 28

There was no reason to remain longer in San Diego. They headed back up the coast. While she drove, Ardi questioned Barent pointedly about the difference in his negotiations with Rowley Skefich, which she had observed from the Rover at the curb, and his less successful interchange with the woman at the restaurant. It was the same situation, but the outcomes were vastly different. The only variable Ardi saw was the gender of the person Barent was dealing with.

"You've got a problem with women, don't you?" she asked after she pointed this out to him.

"Yeah. They always leave when the going gets tough." Barent referred to Kathleen, primarily, and Ardi picked up on it.

"You're projecting one woman's behavior onto all women. Why do you defend her so if you hate her so much?"

"I don't. It's just that she must have had her reasons."

"Well, I know it's a radical idea, but was the option of staying and working things out ever considered? I mean, there was a lot there, wasn't there? Not to mention the kids."

215

"I considered it. It takes two." Barent was grim, his tones clipped and bordering on sarcastic.

"It may take two, but it begins with one. Did you ever talk to her? Did you ever tell her how you felt?"

"She knew. She knew how I felt. She left anyway. What was I supposed to do?" Barent was beset by a nagging feeling that there was, in fact, more that he might have done. Ardi was nudging him toward the idea that it was better to stay married and work things out than to go straight to dissolution. It tweaked his guilt, and he got defensive. "Look," he said, bristling. "You weren't there. It's none of your business. Leave it alone."

"I'm just suggesting that it makes more sense to work things out than to split. Splitting is the coward's way out, and I think it's not really the solution in most cases. The price is too great."

"I said leave it alone," Barent snapped. He regretted it instantly, but not enough to continue the discussion, or to apologize. Ardi withdrew, concentrated on her driving. A cold and awkward silence saw them both to the end of the day's drive.

* * *

They were waiting in the parking lot for Jessica when she got home from work. Barent had carefully cased the area for surveillance during the hour before she arrived home. He found nothing, and directed Ardi to enter the parking lot and park facing out. They waited in the Rover for Jessica to show.

Her car appeared, a few minutes after five. As she fumbled with the key to her apartment, they walked up behind her. She sensed the motion and turned toward them. Her face registered brief surprise, then a probative concern. Then she went to Barent and embraced him.

"I wondered if I'd ever see you again," she breathed. "The police have been here. Where have you been? Who's this?" She nodded toward Ardi with a curious gesture as she broke the embrace. Ardi found the gesture oddly disquieting.

"Jessica, this is Ardi Campbell. She's been helping me. Ardi, this is Jessica." The women shook hands in a peculiarly stilted manner. Volumes of information were transmitted between the two women by that brief contact, although Barent saw only a cordial handshake.

"Come in, come in. You must have a lot to tell me."

Ardi sat quietly observing as Barent told Jessica of the past days' activities. He felt he was very close to getting his man, and to clearing himself of the charges. Some key part of the puzzle was still missing, but they would find it. It might be in the files on the investigation, and he thought he had devised a plan to acquire them.

This woman of Barent's was a strange bird, Ardi

mused to herself as the two talked. She couldn't quite put her finger on it, but her sense was that there was more to their relationship than either one of them acknowledged. Ardi sobered as a nagging disquiet moved into her mind and set up camp like a visiting aunt.

Ardi had expected Jessica to be some color of jealous that she had spent so much private time alone in lonesome places with her boyfriend. If she was, she showed no sign of it. Jessica was cordial as she invited the two into her apartment. Jessica did not bristle, or spike an occasional word with a double meaning to warn Ardi off her man, as Ardi expected—hell, as she would probably have done herself in a similar situation. Even the apartment itself bothered Ardi, although she was at a loss to say why. Something was wrong. Something just didn't fit, but she couldn't put her finger on it.

She began to wonder what in Heaven's name she was doing in this place. Why had she gotten involved with a total stranger who stumbled out of the bushes into her campsite a week ago? What had she been thinking as she ferried him from place to place, drawn inexorably into the web of his personal life? No, she corrected her thought, *allowing* herself to be drawn in. She could have said no at any instant, but she hadn't. Well, it still wasn't too late to back out. She would say her goodbye, and move on down the road. Hanging around like a third wheel on a bicycle —a *tertium quid*— wouldn't do. It just wouldn't do.

Still, she enjoyed him. He was good company, and her adventures with him had taken her mind off her own pain and her anger and grief that were at the root of this trip.

It suddenly struck her with an awesome clarity that she was defeating her own healing pilgrimage by helping him. She was using him to escape the grieving and growth that was the core purpose of her travels. She realized that she hadn't thought of her recently failed relationship with Jerry in the days she had been with Barent. She vowed that she would return to the process that she had started when she drove south out of San Jose over a week ago. She forgave herself the lapse, but admonished herself that it was time to get back in harness and go to work on her issues.

Wryly, she admitted to an attraction for the man that had been growing in her during their odyssey together. He was interesting and intelligent, if somewhat tangled up in his confusion regarding women and their place in his life. He exuded a boyish charm while at the same time making her feel safe and protected as she had not for some time now. And the hair! He had the most unruly hair she had ever seen. She found it endearing, and not just a little amusing. She wondered if he hadn't triggered in her some immature urge toward mothering, the cousin of the care-giving behavior that was the source and sustenance of her career as a nurse.

Ardi started as she was yanked from her thoughts by the touch of Barent's hand on her shoulder.

"C'mon. It's time to go," he told her. Noticing the expression on her face he asked, "Is anything wrong?"

"No. No. I was just thinking. I'm tired." She shook off her thoughts like a wet raincoat.

"I can't imagine why," said Barent facetiously. "Let's go get a couple of rooms." He turned to Jessica. "I'll see you in a while," he promised.

CHAPTER 29

"I can think of only one other person in the world who would be interested in that file." Marty Caulkin steepled his fingers thoughtfully and leaned back in his chair. The springs croaked in protest. They had not been oiled in a decade, and they had been supporting Atlas' own load of Marty Caulkin for longer than that. It didn't take a gigantic leap of deductive reasoning to know who was behind this visit.

He regarded with his perennially surprised eyes the tiny, slender dark-haired woman seated across the desk from him. She didn't smile, and didn't answer. She had been coached to play it close to the belt, and to let Marty do most of the talking after asking him for his file on the Wellman Fire Investigation. He had not yet even asked a question, and she ignored his veiled invitation to disclose her agency.

He leaned forward, placing his pudgy hands flat on the desk top. Late afternoon sun backlighted him, making it difficult for the woman to read his facial expressions.

"Are you familiar with the term 'accessory after the fact'?" he inquired casually. "It is the crime you commit when you knowingly help a criminal get away with his crime. It carries a jail term."

Still, the woman said nothing. Her hands lay quietly in her lap; her face remained calm, demure, and expressionless. She had already forgiven herself for acquiescing to this final task on behalf of John Barent, and had told him as much. One more favor, and she was 'outta here'. Besides, the cat of curiosity still scratched at the post of her mind. It was like watching a movie, this whole Barent thing, and she couldn't bring herself to leave the theatre before the final curtain.

Marty Caulkin let his own silence burrow into her mind. Most people in such a situation would become uncomfortable, and volunteer information just to water the wordless desert created by the lull in the interchange. Not this one. She held her ground and sat quietly.

"How is he?" Marty went straight to the issue of what they both knew, but neither could say. Having failed by subterfuge, he tried frankness.

"He's fine. He needs the information you have. He needs a picture." Her voice was easy, yet restrained. It's pitch was pleasantly low, but not gravelly. Ardi Powell had been relieved of her illusions, and was fully appraised of the risk she was taking. It was a gamble, a calculated risk, and it could cost her dearly if Caulkin's sense of duty won out over his curiosity.

Barent had been convinced that Caulkin would be too curious to detain her. Barent knew he dared not visit in person. Marty would have no choice but to take him into custody. Ardi, however, might surprise him just enough to make him wonder what was going on, just enough to cause him to defer his duty until he knew more.

Ardi, for her part, had been coached not to be shocked by the speed at which Caulkin snapped to the implications of her presence. "Don't try to play cat and mouse with Marty. You'll be the mouse," he had warned her.

"Where is he?" Caulkin asked point blank, with just the right amount of forcefulness to get an answer if one was to be given.

"He told me that if you ask that question, I am to tell you that the chili dogs are on you next time, for 'felony stupidity', was what he said."

Caulkin chuckled. "You realize I cannot give you any official files. What we *can* do, however, do, however, is to meet again, after lunch, and I will discuss further the details of his surrender into custody."

"He said that would be fine." Ardi had been briefed on this aspect of the transaction as well. It gave her no pause; everything was going as Barent had said it would.

"Say four-thirty?"

"I'll be here. Thank you." The woman got up and

left the office, with Marty rising and moving around his desk to escort her to the door. As soon as she was gone, Marty's stubby fingers busied themselves punching the buttons of the phone. He would need help to put his plan into effect—help he could trust.

* * *

Ardi was back in Caulkin's office promptly at four-thirty.

"Will he come in?" asked Caulkin. "Will you tell me where he is?"

"I don't know where he is."

"Well, you must realize I cannot give you any records of the investigation, even though I have a complete copy of all the information we have in the manila envelope right here on my desk." Marty gestured at a fat yellow nine by twelve envelope that sat casually at the corner of his desk. It displayed no markings.

"Yes, he told me the last time I saw him that you would not be able to give me anything. He's not willing to give himself up, just yet. He said you'd understand."

"I do. Now, please excuse me. I have a matter of pressing urgency I must attend to. It shouldn't take more than a couple of minutes. I'll be right back." Marty rose and left the room. She watched as he turned down the hallway, away from the front door.

Ardi shook her head in amazement. Barent had described the ritual right down to its nuance. Her part now was to simply steal the file, to just put it under her arm and walk out the door. The machination was designed and choreographed so that the worst Marty Caulkin could be accused of was stupidity in leaving her alone with it. Stupidity was not a criminal offense. Providing investigation files to a charged felon was. Ardi scooped up the file and walked quickly out of the office. Her heart was in her mouth, and her skin was a whiter shade than pale.

As she pulled away from the curb in the Rover, she watched the rear view mirror. Sure enough, a nondescript sedan with black-wall tires eased quietly into the traffic stream behind her. Everything transpired as Barent had said it would.

Following the plan, she headed for the central business district. There, she parked the Rover on a side street and walked to a sidewalk cafe with the envelope under her arm. She took a table and ordered a cup of coffee. She pretended not to notice as the sedan took up a parking space at some distance, but still in view. Nobody left the sedan, and Ardi stopped watching. The coffee was served. Ardi sat in the open air, watching the people go by, and sipped the coffee.

The manila envelope sat on the table, within arm's reach. She eyed it, wondering what new light its contents would shed on search for Jason Grover. Curiosity triumphed, and she reached for the envelope. She opened it. Barent owed her that much, she told herself.

She read the investigation report by Inspector Aaronsen that described the two fires and clearly established their connection. There followed a form documenting Barent's arrest. There were a number of pages titled "Evidence Log", forms that documented the physical evidence that had been taken in the course of the investigation. There was a blood analysis of blood found on the second fire scene, and a copy of the departmental report showing Barent's blood type, and reporting a positive DNA match. Following that, a series of narrative reports told of interviews with witnesses who saw Barent's car at the second fire, and documented the medical care he had received for a cut on his hand.

The evidence and the reports were so convincing and compelling that Ardi began to wonder if Barent had lied to her, and was actually guilty of the crimes. The thought nagged at her as she began to read the next page, an old parole report pertaining to Jason Grover. There was a letter of permission from the parole board for Mr. Grover to leave the state temporarily to complete elective surgery at Johns Hopkins Hospital.

She read with interest the full investigative file of Elizabeth Potter, dragged by Caulkin from the archives, as her waiter refilled her coffee. Potter had been arrested, tried and convicted of homicide. She had murdered her husband by dousing him with lighter fluid and setting fire to him. Ardi shivered involuntarily. What a horrible way to die!

The woman's son, Jason Grover, age ten, had been remanded to Child Protective Services. It was a fascinating and tragic case. The file material on Jason Grover followed. She read the rap sheet that Barent had told her about during their long hours on the road. A history of arson and lewd conduct was confirmed there.

Then she turned a page, and her heart nearly stopped.

A rude, copied, photographic image, reproduced too many times, was recognizable on the page. The face was younger, the hair was shorter and lighter in color, and the context was absent. But there, unmistakably, the features of Jason Grover were depicted on the page. The haunting eyes of Jessica stared back at her.

Her mind reeled as the connections were made. They had been there in abeyance, awaiting only this final piece of the puzzle to fall together in dizzying clarity. The permission letter for elective surgery at Johns Hopkins suddenly fit. It was one of only three hospitals in the United States that performed transsexual surgery. She had read about it during the course of her medical training.

She now knew why she had found Jessica's body language so disquieting. The messages were conflicting, as if the gender identity was confused. Jessica's gestures were the gestures of a man made by the body of a woman. They did not flow. The grace of her movements was artless, contrived. In the absence of the explanation, she had been unable to pinpoint it.

And her unease about the apartment where Jessica lived suddenly became crystal clear. There was no *history* in the apartment. Jessica had no past displayed there. There were no high school yearbooks, no photos of friends, none of the usual knick-knacks and family junk that people inevitably dragged around with them as mementos of earlier times. Jessica's memories, whatever they might be, could not be displayed without divulging her secret.

Ardi tried to still the shaking in her hands, and calm her reeling mind. John must know what she knew as soon as possible. If Jessica were behind the fatal fire, he would be in danger beyond his wildest suspicions and from a quarter where he would not be expecting danger.

The nurse Ardi realized that there would be problems as well with John Randolph Barent as he was forced to assimilate her new information. His homophobia, which she had seen manifest in his treatment of the bartender in the bar on Price Street, would exacerbate his shock when he realized the

implications of his relationship with Jessica. Ardi
could only pray that the shock did not immobilize
him. He would need to function well and compe-
tently now. Ardi remembered his statements to
Jessica about being close to catching the culprit.
He'd told her virtually everything. If Jessica believed
him, as she must, she would be forced take precipi-
tous action to stop him before his knowledge jelled
into a certainty that pointed directly to her.

The Ardi who was not a nurse drew away from
the implications of her discovery in distaste. She
was unsure how she felt about this strange and interesting man who had invited himself into her life.
She thanked god in relief that there had been no further intimacy than they had, traveling together.
Physical involvement would have created a much
stronger reaction, and she was in no state to deal
with it. How could he not have known? How could
he have ignored the signs that she had snapped to
immediately, and which she found so disquieting?
She returned to her nursing mind, to concern for
another and for John Barent in particular, as a
refuge from her own feelings.

She had no idea where John was. He had anticipated her being followed when she picked up the
files from Caulkin's office, just as he had anticipated
the fact that Caulkin would allow her to steal them
rather than give them to her overtly. He had
instructed her to lead them on a merry, innocent

chase. Take in a movie, go window-shopping, daw-dle and drive them nuts with the waiting for her to go to ground. After dark, she was to park the car with the valet at the biggest hotel in town, then slip out through a back door on foot to walk the few blocks back to the room they had actually rented elsewhere. The watchers would be spread too thin to follow, and would watch the car and the hotel lobby, maybe check the registration. He would come by her room at the motel when it was safe, later in the evening. Until he did so, she had no means of contacting him.

CHAPTER 30

John Barent rolled away from Jessica and uttered a contented sigh, fighting an overwhelming desire to drift away into sleep. She had been even more passionate than usual after their separation of several days, and she coaxed from him one of his finest and most energetic performances. Now, spent from his efforts and sapped by his release, fatigued from days of flight, he found a place that felt safe. The relaxation crept over him like a warm and liquid blanket.

"What time is it?" he murmured from within his fading consciousness. He was too comfortably drowsy to turn and look at the clock on the nightstand.

"Late. It's late," answered Jessica.

"I've got to meet Ardi at the motel," he sighed.

"It's late. She's probably asleep."

"She's got the case documents. She's got a picture of the suspect. She's got the key to my freedom."

"Why don't you wait until tomorrow?' Jessica coaxed him, purring. "She'll still be there. Let her sleep. You can rest for now. 'Knit up the rav'led sleeve of care'," Jessica stroked his bare chest gently, encouraging him to relax, to rest.

The logic was immutable, and the invitation was

231

what Barent's fatigued mind wanted to hear. It sounded like a good idea—no, a *marvelous* idea. And, it considered Ardi. Surely she must be tired as well.

"Ummmmh," was the last noise he made as he dropped away to the warm and beckoning darkness of Morpheus.

When his breathing deepened, Jessica eased herself out of his limp embrace and dressed quietly. She had miles to go before she slept, and promises to keep.

* * *

Streetlights glowed with haloes through an unseasonable misty fog as a dark figure quietly mounted the stairs that lead to room 235 at the Homestead Motel. The room's window, fronting on the exterior exit balcony, was lightless. Directly below the room the white Range Rover sat parked, beaded with drops of condensed mist that caught and reflected the diffuse light like a field of rhinestones.

The figure set down a large carbon dioxide fire extinguisher in front of the door to room 235 and peered carefully around the parking area. Satisfied, it bent over the steel bottle and unscrewed the valve cap. It removed the expansion cone assembly. The two pieces were only hand tight, and would never have held the nearly two thousand pounds of pressure that would have been present if the steel bottle had in fact held a charge of gas.

The gas had been discharged, and the empty bottle was filled with a precisely measured and proportioned mixture of powdered metals. The army called it Thermite. The recipe was easily available to anyone who wanted it, and was willing to do the necessary research in the right books. Jason Grover had done his homework, and the mixture was correct. He reached into his pocket and extracted a twelve-inch strip of magnesium ribbon. He inserted the ribbon into the open mouth of the steel bottle and forced the ribbon well onto the powdered metals. Once again, he scanned the empty parking lot, looking for signs he had been observed. Nothing moved.

He placed the bottle directly in front of the door to room 235. From his pocket, he retrieved a butane cigarette lighter and lit the magnesium ribbon. It popped, sputtered, and burned with a flickering, bouncing, blinding white light. Dense white smoke roiled upward under the balcony roof. Jason Grover retreated toward the stairs, his shadow dancing eerily, cast before him in the quavering, flickering white light from the burning magnesium.

He stopped, breathless, at a public phone across the street from the Homestead Motel and collected himself. He dialed 911. It rang twice.

"911 Emergency. What is your emergency?" A clear and alert voice queried him with brusque politeness.

"I want to report an escaped prisoner, a fugitive." Jessica gave John Barent's name, and her own address. "He's there now."

"And the number you are calling from?"

"Forget that. You have the information you need."

"But, we need..." began the dispatcher. The line went dead as Jason hung up. Across the street, the magnesium fuse ignited the thermite and the steel bottle shot a column of bluish-white light into the balcony roof with the sound of an F-15 climbing out on afterburners.

The dispatcher shrugged her shoulders and hung up. At that moment, the bells, buzzers and whistles of the Consolidated Police/Fire Dispatch Center all seemed to go off at once. Stacey Kraft was thankful that she was not alone on the boards. While she dispatched police units to the reported fugitive, her partner began picking up numerous 911 calls that suddenly lit up the console. The automatic alarm system reported a fire condition at the Homestead Motel, and confirmation was received by telephone from numerous callers. As soon as two cruisers had been dispatched to her police call, Stacey turned her attention to assisting her partner, and rang down a first alarm assignment for the fire department. The units reported their response in under a minute, and there was a brief respite in radio traffic while they were enroute, and before their arrival on the scene.

On the arrival of the first fire units on scene, Stacey assisted with the dispatch of the third alarm that was ordered immediately by the Officer in Charge. Even from the windowless bowels of the Police Department basement where the dispatch center operated, it was clear that they had a working fire with a major rescue problem; a nasty fire in a building full of sleeping people. It was evident in the immediate call for a third alarm, skipping over second alarm status, and it pervaded in the controlled professional voice of the Officer in Charge as he ordered additional resources. The situation was going to hell, and would continue on its way there until the third-alarm resources could arrive. There was a special call for an ambulance. Stacey Kraft would earn her pay tonight.

* * *

Distant, insistent pounding awakened John Randolph Barent from a deep and drifting sleep. As his mind clawed its way to consciousness, the pounding became louder. For a panicky instant, he did not know where he was; then he remembered. He realized that someone was at the door, and was determined that it should be answered. Where in the hell was Jessica? He reached across the bed for her. The sheets were cool.

He slid into his pants, and went to the front door, which shook in its jambs from the blows. Then he remembered his fugitive status, and peered through the blinds before answering the door.

His heart leaped with an adrenaline surge as he identified Terry Benson, a patrol officer he knew, standing at one side of the door, his weapon drawn and ready. He turned and fled toward the back door. He unlatched the lock and slid it open, and stepped directly into the waiting arms of two more officers who were stationed there against precisely this eventuality. He was tackled and handcuffed face down on the patio slab before he even saw who they were. He was yanked unceremoniously to his feet, and found himself staring at two more of his erstwhile friends.

"You don't do the fugitive thing very well, John." Officer Dale Kennedy put away his revolver, snapped the holster catch, and brushed himself off. "You embarrassed the shit out of us when you got out of town. Welcome home, asshole."

A fine mist that was not quite fog and not quite rain landed on John Barent's naked back with the cold prickling of a thousand needles as he was hustled to a squad car by an officer at each elbow.

CHAPTER 31

Homestead Command, the motel fire Command Post, needed more police officers for traffic and crowd control. The formation of Homestead Command, thus officially naming the incident, told Stacey Kraft that there was now a senior command officer in charge of the fire at the Homestead Motel. She could breathe a little easier. She keyed a microphone and hailed the patrol cars she had earlier dispatched to the fugitive call. They were the last uncommitted police resources in the city.

"One Adam twenty-seven, One Adam twenty-nine, respond to Homestead Motel for traffic and crowd control. Report to Homestead Command."

"Control, One Adam twenty-seven. I have a prisoner on board."

"Your discretion, twenty-seven."

Patrol Officer Dale Kennedy was surprised. If they were giving him a choice between responding to the fire scene and booking his prisoner, the situation must be bad. The patrol car would hold the prisoner. He could be handcuffed to the wire cage between the front and back seats, which made the car a sort of mobile jail. Without a further thought, Kennedy committed to the fire scene. It offered more excitement than the booking process for his prisoner, and it sounded like he was needed.

* * *

Captain Gary Trish leaped from the cab of his fire engine as it came to a halt in front of the burning motel. He had left the sirens on until the last possible moment to alert the sleeping occupants. He immediately contacted his dispatch center and ordered a third alarm. As he looked upward at the heart of the fire, he heard and felt the pump of the fire engine engage. The characteristic whine and rumble of the turning centrifugal pump added its own noise to the din.

A column of bluish-white light issued from an indeterminable point on the second floor balcony. It flared too bright to look at directly, and Trish got his information from peripheral evidence. The heat had ignited the entire exit area. The radiant heat was an order of magnitude greater than he expected, greater than normal combustibles could produce, and he fell back behind the fire engine, using it as a shield. He was pretty certain that the paint was being blistered on the exposed side of the engine, and his engineer would have to abandon the control panel if no protection could be provided. He had seen the white light before, and he had heard the jet-engine noise. The Wellman Fire! This stuff, whatever was burning, ate water for breakfast.

His instincts and training went into high gear. He formed a plan of attack and ordered the next due engine to provide him with a water supply. His primary problem was rescue, but he was not certain that a direct attack on the fire would best serve that purpose. Rather, he would get hose streams between the fire and the occupants, and commit to a holding action until more units could arrive.

As he turned to issue the appropriate orders, he saw in horror that his fireman had climbed atop the engine and was rotating the deck gun into position to hit the fire. The pumps were running. In seconds, the man would throw a valve and dump water on the white light at over a thousand gallons per minute.

"Ruiz!" Trish screamed with tremendous effort to be heard over the din. His fireman turned to look at him.

"No water!" he yelled, making a cut-off gesture at his throat to reinforce the message. He doubted that Ruiz could make out a word over the roar of the fire and the howling of the pumps.

Ruiz raised his hand as a shield in front of his face and eyes, palm open towards the fire. The gesture told Trish that the radiant heat was intense. Ruiz then threw the valve at the base of the deck gun. A tremendous blast of high pressure water shot from the nozzle directly toward the whitest part of the fire. Trish had no choice: he hit the deck behind the engine without time for a prayer.

The water in the stream was ripped into its component molecules by the tremendous heat of the thermite reaction, and the hydrogen and oxygen recombined instantly in a colossal explosion. The shock wave caught Ruiz and propelled him off the top of the fire engine in a flailing arc of thirty feet. In horror, Trish watched him fly through the air. It appeared unsurvivable.

With a sinking feeling, Trish rose from his prone position and started around the engine in search of his pump operator, who would have been as exposed to the blast as Ruiz had been while operating the control panel. He ran directly into the man, who had abandoned the panel and sought protection from the radiant heat by moving behind the fire engine. He, too, had been knocked to the ground by the force of the explosion, and rose only to be bowled over again by Trish rushing to find him. They went down in a heap.

Numb and a little dopey from the explosive percussion, they staggered to their feet, each using the other as a prop to assist in rising. Trish put his hands on the man's shoulders and yelled at him over the noise "Ruiz got blown off the top!"

They turned in the direction Ruiz must have flown, and began moving in that direction. The pavement was covered with debris from the explosion, but no piece of it was large enough to be Ruiz. Unexpectedly, and to their great relief, a charred and blackened Ruiz stumbled almost comically toward them through the smoke. Water streamed from his protective clothing in torrents as he staggered toward them. The three men met in the middle of the space in a shoulder to shoulder embrace.

Trish was overcome. For one horrible, soul-wrenching moment in time, he had believed that he had lost his entire crew. Now, they were together. Now they were alive.

"I'm O.K.," said Ruiz, grinning insanely. "I landed in the swimming pool."

CHAPTER 32

Ardi had gone to the late matinee at the Fremont Theater. The file, in its manila envelope, lay safely in her lap as she watched *Kiss of the Spider Woman* on the big screen.

Her tail, aware of the multiple fire exits from the theater, had no choice but to abandon his vehicle and follow on foot. He flashed his badge to the ticket-taker, who did not know what to do. The ticket-taker called a supervisor over, and the tail was detained a moment while he explained that he was with the State Fire Marshal's Office, there on official business. The supervisor immediately assumed that the deputy was there to conduct a fire inspection, and was hesitant to let him into the theater without an escort.

The seconds ticked by while the deputy patiently explained that no, this was not a fire inspection, and no, he did not require an escort, and would the staff and management please ignore his presence. Finally, the theater manager agreed to let him in, insisting that he sign a ledger before entering the loges.

Two or three minutes had passed during the dialogue, and the deputy was concerned that his target might have given him the slip by using one of the fire exits. His first scan of the occupants of the darkened theater, before his eyes adjusted fully to the dim light, seemed to confirm that probability as fact, and he cursed under his breath. His eyes grew accustomed to the light conditions. He scanned the audience again, slowly. There she was!

He breathed a sigh of relief, and quickly sat down where he could watch her. It occurred to him that the darkened theater would be an ideal place to pass the envelope, and he carefully examined every theatergoer who even remotely approached his quarry. Nothing happened.

Ardi left the movie house with the crowd. She was surprised to find it dark outside, somehow unconsciously assuming that no time had passed while she had been watching the movie. The streets were wet, and a heavy mist obscured all but the nearest buildings. Conversations and random comments she heard among the departing moviegoers suggested that, for the most part, they couldn't figure out what the movie had been about. Ardi knew what the movie had been about. It was about the betrayal of love to self-interest. There were no surprises there.

Something about that thesis, and the emotions it stirred in Ardi, combined with the weather to trigger a change in her. She walked to the Rover, aware of but unconcerned about her tail. The misting rain dusted her hair with diamonds that reflected the neon lights of the bars and restaurants along the sidewalk. She inhaled the moist air like a swallowed sob. A great sadness welled up in her, a grief tinged with frustration at what might have been and was not, and could not be. A tear grew at the corner of her eye, then lost itself in the wetness of the night rain.

Ignoring Barent's careful plan, she drove the Range Rover straight back to the Homestead Motel. There, in the darkness of her room, she lay face down on her bed. She allowed the feelings to come. The tears followed in a torrent as she went about the work of grieving for the lost love that had driven her on this pilgrimage. Deep and cathartic sobs racked her, and these she muffled by burying her face into the bedclothes. She had done the disbelief, then the anger, and the bargaining without any clear sense of process. Now, she was done with the denial. After a time, the sobbing subsided in the darkness. Fully clothed, she fell into a deep and dreamless sleep that was no longer escape.

* * *

Outside the Homestead Motel, on the street, Marty Caulkin watched the door of room 235 from an unmarked government sedan. He had relieved his deputy, sending the man home after a briefing with a promise of remembrance and six hours of overtime. He was prepared to spend the night watching the door and the white Rover against the likelihood that John Barent would show up. He opened a bag he had brought along, and unwrapped a cold cardboard hamburger, and soggy, limp fries. He poured a cup of coffee for himself from an oversized thermos, and set the cup on the dashboard, where it instantly fogged the windshield.

Hours passed. The coffee grew cool, and the night cold. He fired the engine, ran the heater to take off the chill. As the car warmed, his inactivity and the primitive forces of warmth and late hour began to act upon him. He grew drowsy, and caught himself, as if from a fall, when he began to drift off. He rolled down the window and sucked in a great breath of cold, moist air. He shut down the engine, vowing to himself to freeze to death before allowing himself to fall asleep. He glanced at his watch. It was almost three-thirty in the morning. Barent hadn't shown himself.

He came instantly alert as he noticed a small, dark figure walking toward him, nearly half a block away and away from the lighted areas of the street. The figure turned and entered the motel parking lot, and in the improved light, Caulkin could see that the person was carrying, of all things, a carbon dioxide fire extinguisher.

Puzzled and curious, Caulkin watched the figure

move carefully up the stairs and down the balcony corridor. It stopped in front of room 235, looked suspiciously around and began fiddling with the extinguisher. The shadowy figure then stood upright, seeming to go through its pockets, then bent once again over the fire extinguisher.

A flame appeared, and suddenly there was a bright, white light, like burning magnesium. The figure darted away. Marty sat immobile for just a second as the enormity of what he had just witnessed struck him. Commonly, arson investigators spent their entire careers without ever having witnessed the actual commission of the crimes they investigated. He had just seen the perpetrator do the crime! Now, if he could identify the perp, he could get a conviction on direct testimony! It was incredible, unheard of!

He sprang into motion, leapt from the car, and ran toward the suspect. His mind was moving at the speed of a bullet train. He thought about running up and immediately and snuffing the white flame that burned on top of the fire extinguisher, then realized if he did that, there would be no crime. California law required that structural damage must occur before arson was chargeable as a felony. Unless structural damage occurred, the best he could hope for would be misdemeanor charges for kindling a fire on the property of another; the illegal campfire statute. That wasn't nearly stiff enough, given the transparent intent of this act. He had to let it burn, just for a minute.

Suddenly, his mind snapped to the fact that he didn't *have* a minute! This was the thermite suspect! The blinding white light was nothing more than a fuse! He must get the fuse snuffed before it could trigger the devastating reaction of the thermite. But how long was the fuse's burn time, and how much remained? He broke off his pursuit of the suspect, and turned for the stairwell. Then, he slowed, and stopped. He didn't dare mess with the fuse. If it triggered the thermite while he was anywhere close enough to snuff the fuse, he would be killed nearly instantly, and his body would be vaporized during the course of the reaction. Vaporized. The option was unacceptable. His only choice was to call the fire department, then go after the suspect. He certainly couldn't handle the fire alone, without equipment.

At that instant, there was a startling pop from the set in front of room 235, and Marty Caulkin had no more options, no more decisions to make. The thermite ignited with the noise of a jumbo jet on take off, and a blinding bluish-white column of fire vaporized the roof overhang above it. Marty realized that his only recourse was to alert as many of the sleeping occupants as possible, and get them out of the building. Pursuit of the suspect would have to wait.

CHAPTER 33

Ardi was awakened suddenly by the pop of a champagne cork outside the door of her room. She realized that while she had dropped off into a deep sleep after her crying jag, a part of her remained alert for sounds that would tell her J.R. had arrived. Why would he bring champagne? she wondered.

She sat upright in the darkness, rubbing the sand of dried tears from her eyes. Her mouth felt dry. She must look a sight. There had been no knock, as yet, and she wondered if she had time for a trip to the bathroom sink for a quick damp cloth. She felt for the switch on the night stand lamp, found it, and turned it on. She looked toward the bathroom door, then her eyes snapped back to the balcony door in bewilderment as an immense roaring assailed her ears. Her only thought was that a jet was crashing into the motel. That's all it could be.

Frozen she sat, mesmerized by a light of such brightness that it penetrated the lined draperies drawn at the window. Before she could move, the draperies burst into angry flame, and spot on the wooden door began smoking, charred into a widening black stain, and melted away in an expanding ring of intense heat that was beyond combustion.

249

In less than the space of a breath, the door burned through. A surreal, unworldly shaft of brilliant white light thrust through the widening hole, and the room heated to intolerable levels.

Ardi screamed in terror. She scrambled across the floor in a blind and frenzied flight of panic to the bathroom. She felt on her skin an unbearable, fiendish heat of the monster's breath, and slammed the bathroom door in the face of the demon flames that had suddenly invaded her room. Her mind noted with puzzlement the acrid and nauseating smell of burning hair.

Uttering little whimpering noises of abject terror unconsciously, she stumbled into the tub and hit the shower control. A cold spray hit her, cooling her skin, and damping the clothes that were smoking on her back. She felt the cold, and not the pain, and the analytical side of her nurse's mind told her that she had escaped being burned only by the narrowest of margins. If she could feel the cold, and not just a reduction in pain, she wasn't burned. She couldn't be burned.

With renewed horror, she watched from the spray of water cascading around her as the monster's breath blackened the inside of the bathroom door. She screamed. The sound was simultaneously hopeless and defiant.

CHAPTER 34

Officer Dale Kennedy had acquiesced to Barent's plea to move his handcuffs to the front, rather than behind Barent's back where they had originally been installed while he was face down on Jessica's patio. It was a small concession, but he would not have made it under normal circumstances. It was driven both by the fact that Barent was a long-time acquaintance and a brother under the badge, and by the probability that Barent would be spending a lot of time in the back of the cruiser while he, Kennedy, assisted on the fire scene.

"Holy shit!" exclaimed Kennedy under his breath as the burning motel came into view. "Look at that!"

A fire engine stood in front of the motel in the parking court, engulfed in flames, billowing great roils of black smoke. Dozens of people in various states of undress stood dumbly around the scene in clusters, watching, shivering in the misting damp of the night. They flinched, crouching ineffectually as one of the flaming tires on the fire engine exploded, and the apparatus dropped onto its naked wheel like a shot elephant dropping to its knees.

Three or four rooms in the center of the balcony were on fire, and the rooms below them were beginning to ignite as well. In the middle of it all, a white-hot star burned unimpeded at a temperature of over half that of the surface of the sun.

Kennedy pulled the patrol car to the curb well away from the area of operations. He shut down his rotating beacons, killed the engine and turned over his shoulder to speak to Barent.

"Stay put." he said. "I'll be a while." He swung himself out of the car and loped off toward the fire to find the command post.

Barent took in the scene through the cage grating with a mounting dread and frustration. This was the motel where he had installed Ardi before she went to pick up Marty Caulkin's files. The blazing star seemed to be at precisely the point of the entrance to her room where they had done their planning. It could only mean that, somehow, Jason Grover had found her and Ardi was in trouble, if not dead. But Jason Grover didn't even know she existed! It wasn't possible. It didn't make any kind of sense. Coincidence? Barent, a firm believer in coincidence, doubted that it operated here. Further analysis could wait. Ardi was in that room, and Barent had to act!

There were no door handles on the inside of the patrol car. He would have to break something to get out. The side windows were high strength tempered glass, strong enough to remain intact with a direct hit from a sledgehammer, he knew from his early career training. Any blow he could give them with his hands or bare feet would be ineffectual. His only remaining option was the rear windshield. The glass there was of a different type, with laminated plastic sandwiched invisibly in the center of the panel. It would be strong, and even if he could fracture it, he would still have to clean the broken glass from the opening before he could get out. Without gloves, his hands would be cut to ribbons.

He swung around, positioning his bare feet for a kick at the rear window, with his back on the bench of the seat. The seat back interrupted the full swing of the kick, and the angle of the window deflected most of the energy that remained in the kick. He hurt his feet, bruising his heels, and produced no result.

In rage and frustration, he turned his energy to the side windows. A spring-loaded center punch would take them out with a flick of the wrist, but he had no such tool. He repositioned the handcuffs on his wrist, turning the sharpest point to use the fullest force of his swing, and struck the glass. The point slipped during the swing, and his hands bounced ineffectually off the window. The handcuffs bit into his wrists with excruciating pain.

He used the pain, and the rage at the pain, and the panic, and the feelings of hopeless frustration, and his fear for Ardi's safety. He wound them all together into a mighty blow that drove a point of the handcuffs into the tempered glass with a force he would not have been able to generate without the emotions. The window disintegrated as he punched 'through the temper'. He yowled with pain as the nerves from his handcuffed wrists telegraphed a numbing, tingling pain through his elbows and up his arms.

Wincing, he thrust his hands outside and pressed the latch on the outside door handle. In an instant, he was out of the patrol car and running, clad only in the jeans he had donned to answer the door when the cops had knocked. Adrenaline masked the pain in his tender feet as he sprinted to the back of the motel. The front was fully involved in flame. It was further blocked by a burning fire engine. It would afford no access, and no way out.

He rounded the corner. The back of the motel was still cool. No flames were yet visible at the windows. The windows themselves were set high and small on both floors. They were the small postage stamp lights that were commonly installed in motel bathrooms.

A fire crew worked there, a truck company. They were setting up an aerial platform that would provide access to the upper floor and to the roof. Although the front of the motel was only two floors, the back side was nearly three stories. The natural grade of the lot fell away at the rear, and the motel foundation sat atop a retaining wall. The aerial platform had plenty of reach; the additional height was not a factor.

The crew had the outriggers extended, and over the thundering engine Barent could hear the hydraulics cycling through the relief valve. The ladder crew was less than a minute from elevating the boom. The water supply was in place. Barent knew from that observation that they were not concerned with rescue. Rather, they intended to use the apparatus to place an elevated water stream over the fire. It wouldn't do. Barent needed the apparatus for rescue.

He slipped unseen into the cab of the unit, fumbled for the radio microphone with both hands. He found it, and keyed the mike.

"Truck Two, this is I.C. Leave your equipment in place and report with crew to the Command Post at Side One for assignment to rescue."

Puzzled, the officer coordinating the deployment of the aerial platform stopped mid-stride and dug his portable radio from the shoulder pocket on his bunker gear. An order to a rescue assignment was perhaps the only order the officer would accept without questioning instructions to leave his equipment in place. Rescue of human life had an unequivocal priority. Barent couldn't see him, but heard his radio transmission response.

"Truck Two, copy. On our way!" It was the last transmission that the aerial crew would make for a few minutes. Budget cuts in a troubled economy had caused the deferment of several purchases incidental to normal operations of the fire department. Among these was the scheduled purchase of replacement radio batteries, which cost something in the neighborhood of three hundred dollars each. Stretching their use beyond their recommended useful life had saved the department several thousand dollars. It was why, after the truck officer's acknowledgment transmission, the battery in his radio went quietly, silently, irretrievably dead.

The entire crew formed up with the officer, and they left at a dog-trot for the other side of the building.

* * *

At the Command Post, Battalion Chief Albert Digby heard an order transmitted over the radio that he had not given. Someone was redeploying manpower from one of his units, Truck Two. He had deployed the unit to the rear of the motel with an assignment to get a fire stream above the fire. Even a rookie firefighter knew that all orders cleared through his command post. It was the cornerstone of the Incident Command System; *nobody* freelanced. He'd have somebody's ass for this.

It fell to the various officers to request resources in support of their operations, not simply appropriate them. There were never enough resources. Digby's job, and his alone as the Incident Commander, was to prioritize their deployment for the best effect. When the command chain fell apart, people died, usually firefighters. He keyed his portable radio to transmit.

"Truck Two, I.C. Continue your original assignment! Acknowledge! Truck Two, acknowledge!" There was no answer as Digby waited an appropriate time to allow the officer to return the radio call. It didn't happen, and at the moment Digby was about to transmit a second time, the roof fell in over a part of the motel.

Flames and billowing clouds of smoke boiled up through the new opening. The fire had created its own chimney. It would be almost impossible to stop without the elevated stream from Truck Two.

* * *

Barent cleared the cab of Truck Two with a great leap. He glanced after the crew from Truck Two as they vanished around the corner of the building toward their new, bogus assignment. He went to the forcible entry compartment, and took out a set of thirty-six inch bolt cutters. Crouching by the side if the fire apparatus, he fumbled with the tool, trying to keep the cutting jaws on the case-hardened chain of the handcuffs while applying sufficient leverage at the handles to cut through the chains. He couldn't use his hands for this; they had to stay at the jaw end of the tool. He tried several positions, none of which afforded him enough leverage to make the cut. He was going to have to do his work handcuffed.

"Need some help with that?" asked a familiar voice. Startled, Barent looked up from his frustrated efforts to the serious face of Marty Caulkin. For a motionless instant, his eyes met Marty's. He was not sure what he saw there.

"Would you?" he asked, extending his wrists. "Ardi's in there! I've got to get her out!"

Without further comment, and much to Barent's surprise, Caulkin took the bolt cutters. He engaged the jaws on the handcuff chain, and applied all his strength. The chain parted with a snap. The bolt cutters were ruined as the case-hardened handcuff chain destroyed the jaws, but the chain was severed by the sheer dint of Marty's leveraged strength.

"Thanks." Barent looked quizzically at Caulkin, wondering why he had helped. Marty nodded silently, and stepped back. Barent was puzzled, but didn't ask. Would Marty try to stop him? There was a way to find out.

At that moment, the lid of a toilet tank came smashing through a second floor window, and fell to the ground, where it shattered with explosive force, casting porcelain shrapnel like a ceramic hand grenade. Barent looked upward toward the high, small window. Ardi's face, soot covered and blackened, appeared at the window, and she began screaming wildly for help. Her eyes showed almost comically wide and white from her blackened face. The terror in her voice was unmistakable.

Barent ripped open a Blue Bag, extracted a Nomex coat and pants, and a hard-hat, and quickly donned them. Every man on a fire suppression crew carried a Blue Bag. It contained lightweight fire resistive gear for fighting wild land fires. The gear was substantially different from structural fire fighting gear. It sacrificed some thermal protection for lighter weight and mobility. Barent's only justification for using it was that it was better than his bare skin.

No boots were carried in the Blue Bag. Barent scrambled barefooted up to the platform and threw the switch that powered up the hydraulics. It had been years since he had operated a platform. The knowledge was still there, but the technique was rusty. The boom surged violently upward from its cradle with his first application of power from the joystick. Still lifting on the joystick, he pressed it forward more gently. The boom began to telescope out from its mounting on the pedestal, extending the platform basket toward the building.

When he judged he had sufficient height to reach the window where Ardi was screaming, he pushed the joystick gently to the side, eased back on the forward pressure. The basket arm rotated on its geared turntable, swinging toward the building.

He glanced toward the window, adjusting his control, and was amazed to see that Ardi had somehow climbed out of the window, and was hanging with both hands from the window ledge thirty feet above the ground. A tongue of flame shot out the window above her and blowtorched up the side of the building.

"Ardi! Hang on! I'll be under you in a few seconds!" Barent yelled above the roar of the flames. He was trying not to fight the control stick, and trying to fight his own urge to come in faster. If he slammed into the building, her tenuous grip might be dislodged by the shock. Gentle was the ticket...gentle...

"My hands are burning!" Ardi wailed. "Hurry! Oh, God! Hurry!"

CHAPTER 35

Jason Grover hung up the phone at the pay booth, and turned to watch as the tremendous heat from the thermite ignited the front of the motel. He knew he should run, knew he should leave the scene, but was unable to tear himself away. It was foolish to remain, but he could not help himself.

He stared at the growing fire with wide, unblinking lemur eyes. The dancing flames, reflected in the moisture of their lenses, danced there as barriers to what lay within. Nothing could pass the wall of raging flames in those eyes and enter the mind of Jason Grover. The flames were wall and fortress, moat and keep.

From somewhere behind those eyes, the dark memory of the terrified and agonal screams of a man dead fifteen years became again audible and real. The still-living body of Carl writhed and rolled and beat at the flames, and was consumed by them. Somewhere behind those eyes, a nine year old boy stood in the hallway in baggy underwear and spindly white legs and watched the flames consume the source of his pain. The demon Rage roared, released in the living heat and light of the inferno, and escaped, for a time, up the ladder of smoke and sparks that roiled into the wet night sky. The fearful rage retired behind those eyes, unsatisfied but mollified, leaving to Jason Grover's perception only the faint, pungent smells of lighter fluid and his mother's perfume.

CHAPTER 36

Barent brought the basket in high from above, and at an angle. The whining hydraulics, relieving at the pump forty feet below, reached his ears over the roar of the fire torching out the window. Ardi screamed and sobbed and kicked her legs ineffectually as bits of flaming, molten tar dripped onto her wrists from the burning roof above her. Still, she held her grip firm at the window ledge as they continued to flame in small spots on the backs of her exposed hands. She willed herself to take the pain, rather than release her tenuous hold on the windowsill. Release meant death. She was not ready to die.

Barent had never actually done a rescue like this, but ancient training from his line suppression days early in his career returned to him like a legend. People panicked in such situations. He knew that if he came in from below, there was a strong chance that Ardi would attempt to jump to him. There was an even stronger chance that her panic in such a situation would warp her judgment, cause her to jump too soon, miss the basket, and fall to her death. Coming in from above prevented that. Ardi's terrorized mind would not recognize the basket *above* her as a salvation, and he could get close enough to help her without risking that she would take a dive toward the platform.

He angled in until the corner of the basket nudged the side of the building, then loaded the contact point with the hydraulic control to stabilized the device against the building. He was careful to leave a working space clear of the flames that torched from the open window above, but the heat, even from the normal combustibles that now burned, was intense. He threw the toggle that disarmed the joystick control against the chance that he would accidentally strike it during rescue efforts and move the basket. He leaned out over the railing and reached for Ardi.

He gripped her firmly about the waist with one arm, clinging to the railing with the other.

"C'mon!" he grunted. "I've got you!"

Ardi was mutely hysterical. She doggedly tightened her grip even more on the windowsill, clinging with a blind will to the only safety she could perceive.

"Ardi! *ARDI*! Let go! I've got you. I won't let you fall!" Barent pulled again at her waist. "Push toward me!" Her only response was a guttural, animal whimper. He pulled again, hard, gripping her narrow waist hard enough to bruise the skin.

Her fatigued muscles were no match for his strength. She screamed, and her grip came suddenly free, like an abalone pried off a rock. The abrupt shift of the entire weight of her body to Barent's arm nearly tore his shoulder from its socket. He lost his balance; he clutched, desperate to hold his own weight against his grip with one hand and that of Ardi with his other. He had no purchase, and was unable to bring her into the basket. He just hung on for dear life.

"Ardi! ARDI!" His chest heaved with his effort. He panted with his exertion. Radiant heat from the nearby flames burned his face, added to his agony and fanned his efforts to desperation. The words came through teeth clenched in effort. "ARDI! Help me! You've got to help! I can't bring you in alone! Grab hold of the basket! For God's sake, *GRAB HOLD OF THE BASKET!*"

Somehow, the fear-driven insistence gave a magical intensity to the command. It perforated the wall of mute and dogged terror that had immobilized Ardi, and she began to make efforts to help herself. She grabbed for a basket rail, missed, grabbed again, and caught it. As she used what little strength remained in her to help, Barent added his to the effort, and together they clambered clumsily into the platform basket. Barent let her fall safely inside the railing, and threw the toggle to reactivate the joystick control. The heat was tremendous, and he had no thought but escape. He slammed the joystick back and down to drop the platform down and away, but nothing happened.

In a surge of panic, he flipped the toggle again several times, but before he could move the joystick again, the basket began to move without his control. The heat lessened as the device moved down and away from the building. He looked with relief down the basket's arm to the control pedestal at the base. The basket was being operated from the pedestal; whoever was doing it had used the override switch there and taken remote control of the hydraulics. Barent collapsed inside the railing, found Ardi, and they embraced with the strength born of near loss. He buried his burned face joyfully in her stinking, singed hair and held her tightly as the basket was lowered to the ground.

CHAPTER 37

Jason Grover became aware of the cops. There were cops all around him. He noted with relief, after his initial surge of apprehension, that they were mostly watching the fire and the crowd. Quietly, he slipped away, and found his car. He drove off into the night at a sedate and unremarkable speed.

Windshield wipers slapped fitfully back and forth in front of Jason Grover, wiping the heavy mist from his windshield. Glare from his headlamps reflected in the tiny droplets, making him squint to see the road surface. The headlights of oncoming cars, infrequent at this hour, showed first as an amorphous glow in the fog, contracting and defining into haloed points of light as the vehicles approached closer, and whined by him. He guided his own car through the misty fog, keying on the white stripes that snapped by in measured pulses like bursts of white laser light.

As he drove south on the highway, he cursed Barent with a vengeance. The man who had destroyed his life, who had put his mother behind bars, who had taken away all that remained of value in his life, was paying the price as Jason had planned. The score was not yet settled, but things were working out nicely. Barent would be once again in jail as he received the final blow, powerless to interfere, powerless to help as the final pain was inflicted. Barent could not die; he must live to suffer the total loss that Jason planned for him.

Now, the bitch who had helped the investigator had paid for her complicity in a most painful fashion. Jason smiled, gloated, wallowed in the sweetness of his revenge. The plan was not complete. Barent had a brother in Blythe, and the brother had a family. Barent would know the pain of loss of family, as he had inflicted it upon Jason Grover those many years ago. A carbon dioxide fire extinguisher filled with a mixture of metallic powder rattled and thumped around in the trunk of Jason's car as he steered into a hard turn on the off ramp. No matter. It was perfectly safe without the magnesium ribbon fuse he carried in his purse.

The late hour found only a pair of truckers at the counter of the diner Jason Grover selected at the ramp. He was hungry, and coffee would help his drooping eyelids. He would rest when his revenge was complete, and not before. A skinny, distraight waitress approached in a cloud of nearly tangible ennui and plopped down an empty coffee cup, glancing with doleful eyes for permission to fill it. Jason nodded perfunctorily, and ordered a hamburger with fries. The waitress drifted aimlessly back toward the kitchen.

Jason rose and headed for the rest rooms. As he

passed by the truckers, they turned to regard him, and the nearest slithered from the counter stool to impose himself in Jason's path.

"What brings you out so late, little lady?" he asked, grinning broadly. "Looking for a little action? We're having a two-for-one special." The second trucker, a red-haired man with pale skin and green teeth, leered from his seat at the counter.

The demon in Jason Grover roared, and without a moment's hesitation, Jason kicked the man hard in the groin. The trucker crumpled to the floor grunting in pain. He threw up. His sidekick's washed-out blue eyes widened, and he backed carefully away along the counter, retreating from the baleful glare of the young woman who stood before him.

"Fucking perverts." The voice was deep, masculine. Jason walked past the man without a backward glance. As the redheaded man assisted his nauseated friend to the door of the diner, he noted with revulsion that the girl they had just accosted went into the men's room.

"Shit, Bob," he said to his hunched-over friend in amazement. "That was a guy!"

Not until he stood in front of the urinal did Jason realize he was not only in the wrong room, but in the wrong body as well. Jason's mind looked at Jessica's body in the mirror, and realized that a horrible mistake had been made. The demon raged up inside him, and gave voice to a sound that the waitress would later describe to the police as the enraged roar of a wounded beast. The primal pain of nearly two decades of denial and repression bubbled forth like lava, spewed from the desperate, tortured psyche of Jason Grover. It welled over the protective walls of his self, propelled by frustration and the force of the snapping bands that bound his denial. It melted the mortar that held all the defensive bricks tight in the walls that kept the terrible experiences of the ten-year-old in spindly, bare legs and baggy undershorts buried under a cenotaph of rigid control.

John Barent was to blame for this, Jason thought in an irrational fury, loathing the body that stood before him in the mirror. He regarded it with revulsion. Barent was to blame. The revenge that he had planned was not nearly sublime enough for the arrogant son-of-a bitch who had stolen his mother away and tricked him into trading his body for *this*! Again the demon roared, the sound trailing off into a wail of unspeakable agony.

Jason stormed past the dumbfounded and frightened waitress to the door of the diner. He vanished into the night on squealing tires, departing at a high rate of speed for his destination with destiny, for his meeting with fateful vengeance. He headed for the home of William Barent, an obscure pipeline operator whose unsuspecting family slept peacefully in a small desert town on the banks of the Colorado River.

CHAPTER 38

"He's waking up." A mousy looking nurse stuck her head into the corridor and spoke the words to Marty Caulkin, who waited in a chair outside the door. He heaved his bowling pin frame to its feet and followed the head as it disappeared back into the private room on the third floor of Monte Vista Hospital.

John Barent had been dreaming Demerol dreams since his admission the night before for first and second degree burns on his face, neck and hands. Dopey on awakening, his first sight was the surprised eyes of Marty Caulkin peering back at him. Marty was trying, in turn, to get a look at the eyes that were the only visible part of John Barent's face. The rest was swaddled in gauze dressings. His hands, likewise mummified in bandages, lay limply on the bedclothes. Plastic tubes ran into both wrists, dripping saline solution into his veins.

"How you feelin', cowboy?" Marty asked, his eyebrows arching inquisitively to give his face an even more surprised expression. "Any pain?"

"Where am I?" Barent countered. His voice came from a hole that simply appeared through the swaddling bandages below the eyes, right where his

271

mouth should be. The pain was there, but it didn't seem to matter very much. There was still plenty of Demerol at work blocking his pain receptors.

"Monte Vista. You remember last night?"

The previous night's activities suddenly flashed into place like the pieces of a jigsaw puzzle as Barent's memory returned intact, triggered by Caulkin's query. "Yeah... Yeah. Where's Ardi? Is she O.K."

"Ardi's down the hall. She's all right, but not real pretty just now. She's got some minor burns, and some very sore muscles, she says. And her hair needs work. It's nearly singed off."

"You've talked to her?"

"Minutes ago. They're discharging her this morning."

Barent heaved a sigh of relief. He'd had no time to determine how badly she'd been hurt. When the basket was lowered to the ground, hands had pulled them apart and they had been transported to the same hospital, but in different ambulances. Ardi was a victim; Barent was still a fugitive, his spectacular rescue notwithstanding, and rated a police guard. In separate rooms, they had been evaluated and treated for their injuries, and admitted for observation against the chance that they might have inhaled superheated air or sustained other damage to their respiratory tracts.

"That's good news. What about me?"

"I'm not the doctor, but they're saying you can go home, too, if everything checks out."

"Home?" Barent figured the best he could hope for was a transfer to a bed and cell at the county jail.

"Home. You're off the hook for the Wellman Fire, and the other one. You can thank Ardi for that. You're a free man. McCabe had the charges dropped."

"How...?" Barent looked for the right question to ask, and his mind swarmed with so many that he was momentarily unable to choose one above the others.

"The little minx stole some files right off my desk," explained Marty with a twinkle in his eye. False outrage pervaded his tone. "Who'd of thought such an innocent-seeming woman would pull something like that? Anyway, I hung a tail on her and was waiting for you to show up when I saw the perpetrator set the fire at the motel."

"You saw it? Wow! You can't get a more solid bust than that. You'll make the trades if you write it up." Catching an arsonist in the act was nearly impossible. Arson was a crime of stealth. It was an investigator's sweetest dream to catch a culprit in the act. Barent was referring to the article that Marty could write and have published in one of the several trade publications that arson investigators invariably subscribed to.

"He got away," Marty said, far too brightly for the

situation as Barent saw it.

"He got away?"

"He got away, but we'll get him. We know who we're looking for, now. Again, thanks to Ardi."

"What's Ardi got to do with any of this?"

"Ardi, my dear friend, steamed open the file she stole from my office. In it she found a picture of Jason Grover. She recognized him from the photograph, and gave us a current I.D. last night. We now have a name, address, photograph, auto make and model, Department of Motor Vehicles records, fingerprints, everything. I put out an APB statewide. It's just a matter of time before the boys in blue pick her up."

"Wait a minute! What do you mean, *her*? You said 'her'."

Marty grimaced. "I don't know any graceful way of telling you this, so I'll just spit it out. The Jason Grover we've been looking for is, in fact, Jessica Collins. Ardi said you introduced them the other day, and she recognized the photo of Jason when she saw it in the file. Jessica is a transsexual. The stuff we got on Jason from Camarillo told us that, but it took Ardi to hang the new name on the old face." Caulkin went on, in a bit of a hurry to get the words out before Barent could react to them.

"Based on what I have in the files, you busted Jason's mother, Elizabeth Potter, for a fire about fifteen years ago. Since then, Jason has changed a *lot*,"

—Marty raised an eyebrow— "and he came looking for payback."

Momentarily, Barent's mind went into shock. He lay motionless on the hospital bed, stunned by Caulkin's words, unable to feel anything but numbness. His body seemed distant, remote, and not subject to his commands. Then, the shock began to burn off in a furnace of anger as feeling returned.

Barent's head reeled as the implications of Marty's words stunned him. They soaked into his mind like a blood stain on a white carpet. He felt his skin crawl, and his breathing became strained. He winced and squirmed mentally as feelings cascaded through his dazed psyche. Feelings of revulsion were replaced with horror, which in turn gave way to nausea as his mind grappled with fact. He was ashamed of his relationship with Jessica, as if it had been a matter of knowing intent. Guilt perfused in every fiber of his being, alternating with rage, frustration, and a torrential flood of self-recrimination and doubt. And he was embarrassed in front of Marty, mortified by the fact that Marty knew...and Ardi knew! He had been intimate with a male. The body may have been female, but the mind was male. It was more than he could take.

"If that's true, it means...!" Barent said weakly, the words tapering off into a renewed cataract of conflicting emotions.

"Yup." Marty said it simply, without pity or pretext.

"Fuck!" swore Barent. He had decided on anger.
"At least," said Caulkin.

CHAPTER 39

The last week on graveyard shift for Officer Walt Klingman was to be his most exciting one. Two more shifts of the eleven-to-seven variety and he could return to the land of the living, with its regular hours, open stores, and sunshine. The transition was always easier coming off graveyards than it was going on. One more week and he would be sleeping through the overwhelming craving for another donut that inevitably hit with a vengeance at three in the morning. Perhaps, he would be able to drop the half a dozen pounds that particular appetite had added to his already sizable frame. Everybody gained weight on graveyards. Boredom was the biggest enemy, and it was easy to eat to keep it at arm's length.

Of course, there wouldn't be a lot to do on days, either. Blythe was a quiet town —almost as quiet on day shift as on graveyards. The biggest difference was that he would be doing fewer single car accidents, and cleaning less vomit from drunk arrestees out of the back of his patrol car. It didn't happen all that frequently on graveyards, but it virtually never happened on day shift. It had happened tonight.

It turned out to be his own insurance agent this

time, and Klingman had decided to take the man home rather than to jail. Family problems, he knew from day watch. The guy was having problems with his wife, and climbed into the bottle now and again. In a gushing of gratitude, the man had puked all over his patrol car on the way there, dumping a foul-smelling load of half digested pizza and pretzels in an alcohol broth explosively all over himself and the back seat of the cruiser.

Klingman spent almost an hour at the police station cleaning the back seat, and changed into a fresh uniform. It irritated him. Clean uniforms were six bucks each. He thought briefly of returning to get the insurance agent and throw him in jail. He wouldn't, of course, but the fantasy helped defuse his ire.

Klingman returned to the quiet streets. The sour smell lingered in the patrol car in spite of the industrial-strength deodorant he had sprayed copiously into the vehicle. He decided to drive by Bill Barent's place. A week ago, the watch commander had directed an occasional drive-by there on request from another police department up north on the coast, to check for a fugitive who might or might not actually show up. It involved a long run out Ripley Avenue, and Klingman took it with the windows down despite the cold of the desert night air.

The neighborhood street was dark and quiet, lit only by the starlight from the clear desert sky. Smog from Los Angeles, two hundred miles west and upwind, never made it to Blythe. The sky was always clear, and the stars always bright. Klingman shut off his headlights and idled the cruiser down the street. The night was a peaceful time, still and crystalline in aspect, and there was something to be savored about driving with the lights off. A new car sat at the curb, not one of the regulars, and Klingman ran the plates. The registration came back to a Jessica Collins, from up north on the coast. It was not the name he was looking for. The Barent house was dark and quiet. He put the cruiser in gear and continued down the block.

He was a mile down the road headed back toward downtown when he realized that the Collins car was registered in the same city where the fugitive, Bill Barent's brother, lived. What if John Barent had borrowed the car, or was traveling with a friend? Klingman braked, wrenched the wheel, and made a U-turn.

As he turned down Barent's street, he saw a dark figure dart from the Barent yard and sprint toward the car he had just checked. He slapped the switch that turned on his rotating beacons and pulled on his bright headlights. He drove forward, lighting the figure in his beams. A woman dressed in black froze in his headlights like a startled deer. He keyed his microphone, transmitted "Control, Adam Twenty. F.I. stop on Bridgeman Way, sixteen hundred block."

With a nagging sense that all was not as it should

be, Patrolman Klingman replaced the microphone on its hook. Hooking a portable radio to his belt, he left his black-and-white and walked up to the woman, flashlight in hand.

"Excuse me, miss," he said with professional politeness. "We've had some problems in this neighborhood. Could I see some identification, please?"

"It's in the car." The woman was dressed in black clothing, pants and a shirt. This time of night, Klingman would have expected a party dress and a porch light on. His suspicions aroused, he flashed his beam into the vehicle before allowing her to enter it.

"O.K. Get it." Unobtrusively, he freed the snap on his holster, loosened his sidearm.

Nervously, the woman fumbled in her purse and took out her wallet. She extracted her driver's license and handed it over. She glanced nervously about as he radioed in the specifics for a computer check of wants and warrants outstanding.

"It'll just be a couple of minutes, Miss Collins." he told the woman. "Mind telling me what you're doing out here at three in the morning?"

"I have a plane to catch in Los Angeles at eight. Could you hurry things up a little?" The woman was growing more nervous by the second. The dark clothing and tennis shoes did not jive with her story about catching a flight.

"I asked what you are doing here at this time of

night."

"I was..." The woman never finished her sentence. Behind him, from the direction of Bill Barent's house, Officer Klingman heard a loud "pop" which was interpreted by his edgy mind as a gunshot. He crouched and whirled to face the direction from which the sound had come. His sidearm leapt into his hand almost of its own accord. At the same instant, the woman broke violently away from him and dashed headlong down the street.

A second popping sound came from the Barent house, and this time it was clearly not a gunshot. A blinding white light appeared from the rear of the house, and the air filled with the sound of a jet engine on afterburners. Baffled, Klingman stood frozen in place while his mind tried to analyze what was happening, and to determine what he should do next. Flames flickered at the roof of the Barent house, and his suspect was getting away. He regained his purpose, and set off at a dead run after his suspect, who was rounding the corner half a block away at a sprint. He holstered his side arm and pulled his portable radio from its belt clip.

"Control, Adam twenty! I am in foot pursuit of a suspect, west on Bridgeman Way. Send back up, and call the fire department. They have a structure fire on Bridgeman." The effort of running and transmitting his call for assistance at the same time had already winded him as he rushed after his suspect.

He cursed the three a.m. donuts, and he cursed the suspect's choice of running that forced his foot pursuit. Gathering his willpower, he forced his unaccustomed legs to dog it after his quarry. He panted and puffed with the effort, but trotted on, determined that the woman would not escape. He turned the corner, and the street was empty.

He stopped short, straining to listen between his own ragged breaths for the sound of running footfalls. The only sound that came to his ears was the distant wail of sirens drawing closer. Again, he drew his gun. If she wasn't running, she was hidden nearby. He controlled his breathing, and began to search.

Three houses down, a dog began to bark furiously, and lights came on. He headed for the ruckus.

CHAPTER 40

Marty Caulkin's prophecy of a speedy capture of the fugitive Jessica Collins had failed to manifest. Nearly a month had passed since he had uttered it, casually, to assuage a the concerns of John Barent as he lay in the hospital the morning after the Homestead Motel fire. Barent's concerns were anything but assuaged. Jessica Collins was still at large, her whereabouts unknown.

News of Jessica's attempt to burn up his brother's family had momentarily shocked Barent, and then thrown him into a grim rage. The family had escaped, but so had Jessica. They lived now in fear of her possible return, despite Barent's reassurances that Jessica was unlikely to try repeating the crime. Meanwhile, the Bill Barent family was domiciled in a cheap motel while the insurance company decided whether or not to pay the claim. Nobody was sleeping very well.

How, wondered John Randolph Barent, could any person be so vengeful and perverse as to intimately insinuate herself into another's life with the intent to destroy it? How could Jessica have maintained the lie of her presence in his own life and concealed her true purpose and intentions so effec-

283

tively? As adroit as Barent was at getting into a criminal's head, this was beyond his experience. It baffled him.

Before him, on his desk, lay the report of Officer Walter Klingman of the Blythe Police Department. It had been FAXed at his request from the desert town. There was enough of a physical description to identify Jessica. The computer cross-match of the license number of the car Klingman had seen further confirmed the identity. It listed Jessica as the registered owner. The car was gone. Jessica seemed to have evaporated.

While firefighters attacked the fire at the Barent house, and with the Barents themselves standing at the curb watching their house go to the ground, Jessica had apparently walked quietly up to the vehicle and driven it off from under their very noses. Klingman had been occupied in documenting the marks on the fence in the back yard where his fugitive had scrambled over it to escape a nasty Doberman. Blood on the fence, and on the dog's fur indicated that Terminator, the Sanderford's dobie, had been at least marginally successful in slowing down the suspect that had entered his domain without his master's approval.

Local emergency rooms had been checked, to no avail, and the California Highway Patrol and the Arizona State Police had been alerted to be on the look-out for any cars matching the description

Klingman had reported. There were only four major roads out of Blythe, and the authorities were initially optimistic about picking up the suspect. Jessica, however, had simply vanished.

John Randolph Barent had been a fugitive less than two weeks when he returned to resume his work in the office, but it felt as if he had been gone two decades. He arrived early, that first day, and cast about his office with the vague yet gnawing feeling that he was invading someone else's digs.

He opened the desk drawer, pawed through the contents in search of some talisman that would help him re-establish his ownership of the space. There was a pack of fire crackers he had confiscated from a pair of ten-year-olds who had been lighting them off in a vacant lot, reported by a neighbor. They were never booked into evidence, because he had never pressed charges. There was a magnifying glass he used to examine fire scene photos. Taped to the writing board at the left side of the lap drawer was a ratty, coffee-stained list of Penal Code sections for various fire-related offenses, and a list of ignition temperatures for common materials. He recognized these things, but did not know them.

His own office had become an alien place, a place where he did not belong any more.

Things didn't get any better when the first of the suppression crews began to arrive for the shift change. They passed by the open doorway of his office and glanced in, then quickly glanced away when they realized who the occupant was. Some muttered a hurried "Hi.", or gave a cursory nod before moving past the doorway, but none stopped to welcome him back.

He pondered regretfully the fact that Ardi had left the hospital before he could see her, before he could explain things to her, before he could thank her for risking her life, albeit unknowingly, to help him establish his innocence. It occurred to him that Ardi was apt to be mightily pissed at having been involved in something so dangerous as their recent escapades had proved to be without having been told of the danger. The idea of informed consent flashed across his mind and he considered its relevance. He had told her everything he knew, kept nothing from her. That Jessica Collins could be so unpredictably dangerous was as much a surprise to him as it must have been to her. Still, he wondered if Ardi blamed him...

The floor nurse had been cordial when Barent had wandered down the hall in a Demerol haze to Ardi's room, carrying a rehearsed explanation in his mind like citizenship papers to a third world border crossing. He opened the door to find a neatly made bed, and no sign of Ardi. He turned to head back to the registry desk, and bumped into the floor nurse, who had come up behind him.

"Where's Ardi...?" Barent stumbled, groping for

her last name. His mind had misplaced it, put it somewhere where he wouldn't forget where it was, and then forgotten where he put it.

"Campbell," the nurse finished for him. "She signed out half an hour ago. She said she had to get back home, and the doctor said she could drive." The nurse was matter-of-fact. "She seemed to be in a hurry," added the nurse as an afterthought.

"Damn!" Barent swore in frustration. "How can I get in touch with her?" Barent rolled his eyes on the realization that he had never gotten her address or phone number, then reasoned that Marty would have taken the information in the course of his interview with her. He sidestepped the nurse, and floated back down the hall on Demerol wings.

"We can't give out that information," the nurse called after him.

When he returned to his room, there was an envelope on the nightstand, propped against his water bottle. It had been delivered while he was off down the hall looking for Ardi. His name was scrawled across it in an expansive, feminine hand. He tore open the seal and extracted a simple card. Ignoring the artwork on the form, he flipped it open and went straight to the bottom of the note. The signature read "Ardi".

"*Dear John,*" he read, "*Please don't take this the wrong way, but I couldn't bear to see you in the shape I'm in. They say you saved my life, and I wanted to thank you. These last few days have been confusing to the limit, and I need some time to sort things out. I'll write you a letter once I've figured out what happened to me. Meanwhile, take care of yourself. I hope you're O.K —Ardi."*

That was it. No phone number, no address. Nothing.

Barent looked at the card, crestfallen. There was more to it than this, he had thought to himself. He couldn't have been wrong about the way he felt when he lowered her into the safety of the basket, and buried his face in her stinking, singed hair. He would find her, make her tell him to his face. He needed an address, and he knew where to find it.

It was there in the investigation files. He stared at her witness statement, taken by Caulkin and carboned to the city's files. Now that he had access to it, he balked at the idea of using it. If she had gone without stopping in to see him after all they had been through, it could only mean that she wasn't interested in a visit. Or in him, for that matter...

Andy McCabe stuck his head into Barent's office, interrupting Barent's reflections. "My office, five minutes, staff meeting," he said. "Welcome back." His head vanished as quickly as it had appeared.

Barent followed him into his office without waiting.

"Listen, Andy..." said Barent as McCabe moved

around his desk. "I was wondering when I'll get the pay for the three weeks I was gone. I'm broke, and I've got child support. I'm out of groceries. Everything in the refrigerator grew hair while I was gone." Barent dropped into a chair. "Hell, I was lucky to get my place back. The landlady was fixing to pack up my stuff and store it against the rent money."

"You won't. Sorry, but you won't be paid." McCabe thought briefly about offering a small personal loan to tide him over, decided against it. Barent was a bad risk. The idea of putting half a C-note at risk with a guy who couldn't even make spousal support payments was anathema. His frugal Scottish ancestors, several generations removed, would turn in their graves.

"But, I was absent through no fault of my own!" Barent protested. "It's not like I had a choice."

"You were absent through no fault of the city's, either. It wasn't a false arrest. We had probable cause. I'm sure you can see the city's position. It's unfortunate, but that's how it is."

"What about my Skelley rights?" Barent countered in desperation. He referred to the protection granted by a federal court decision that safeguarded peace officers from spending weeks at home under suspension without pay while complaints against them were investigated. They could be suspended, but they had to be paid until the complaint was resolved. "I'm not supposed to be suspended without pay while an investigation is occurring. You can't do that."

"We didn't. You weren't suspended; you were arrested. There's a big difference. We had probable cause. The investigation was over."

"So I'm supposed to sit back and take it, without so much as an apology?" Barent was incredulous.

"That's about it. I'm sorry, but there's nothing I can do. I can't think of anything *you* can do, either. It's best to just put it behind us."

"Shit."

McCabe's emotionless eyes looked blandly back at Barent, across the expanse of neurotically uncluttered desk. The tie was precisely knotted, and matched the suit impeccably. Every hair was in place. "You ought to be glad that we decided not to press charges for unlawful flight to avoid prosecution. You committed a different crime when you escaped, and you *were* guilty of that one," McCabe said primly.

A tidal surge of homicidal intent welled up inside Barent like a wave rushing toward the rocks. He controlled the overwhelming urge to throttle McCabe at the throat. His knuckles whitened in their grip on the arms of his chair as he considered how attractive McCabe's blazing white shirt would look spattered with bright red blood. Through clenched teeth, controlled words emerged. Barent's voice ran with venom.

"I suppose I should thank you."

Either impervious or unaware, McCabe said, "You're welcome." Bending forward he opened a drawer in his desk. From it he removed Barent's shield and weapon. He pushed them wordlessly, unceremoniously across the desk toward Barent. Barent was tempted sorely not to accept them, to tell McCabe to put the items where the sun didn't shine, sideways. He was likewise sorely tempted to take them and put a cap into McCabe's high and self-righteous forehead. The other staffers, who began wandering in at that moment, saved him from himself. He took the weapon, checked it, holstered it, and picked up his badge.

Barent stewed quietly for the duration of the meeting, speaking tersely only when spoken to. McCabe officially, publicly welcomed him back as the first item of business. The others, particularly Aaronsen avoided eye contact with him as if he were a leper, or a Medusa who would turn them to stone if they looked at him directly. If Barent's hatred were a contagious disease, McCabe should have died from it long before the meeting was over. Barent still wasn't sure how he felt about Aaronsen.

At four o'clock that afternoon, a fireman stuck his head into Barent's office.

"Mackey wants to see you," he said jerking his thumb over his shoulder. "Upstairs, right away." The fireman vanished before he could be pressed for details.

Barent put aside what he was doing, which was precisely nothing, and plodded up the stairs. As he turned the corner into the dining room, Barent saw the entire shift assembled at the long table, and was ushered to its head by the station officer, Captain Josh Mackey.

Arrayed before him on the table was a cake, decorated with a crude frosting that depicted his erstwhile rescue at the Homestead Motel. Embedded in the frosting was an open pair of handcuffs, arranged to bracket the words 'Welcome Back', which were dribbled across the cake in red. The faces of the firefighters beamed up at him from where they sat around the table, all friends, all brothers bound by two hundred years of tradition. Barent blanched, then went day-glow red.

"We wanted to make your first day back a memorable one," pronounced the officer. "A little cake, some ice cream, and a gift." With this he nodded at a fireman, who produced one of those executive toys, five ball bearings suspended in a line in a polished wooden frame. The captain swung the first ball, releasing it into the others, and the toy began clicking rhythmically as the balls knocked each other into a pendulum motion.

"We didn't know what to get you, until we found this. I'm sure you see its relevance," he said, barely controlling a smirk as the steel balls clicked and clacked back and forth. Barent looked at him with raised eyebrows, puzzled.

"Not exactly," he said.

"Balls of steel that swing both ways!" The captain broke into a wide grin, and the room filled, as if on cue, with catcalls, laughter, and off-color remarks about Barent's gender confusion, and stage-voice comments about sleeping with suspects.

Barent's discomfort and embarrassment eased. There was no mistaking the good intentions of the men before him. They all knew what he had been through. They had learned the details through the grapevine. They were bringing him back to the fold in a way that every firefighter understands—with scathing humor and the friendly flaying of a bleeding soul that actually helped it heal. It was something akin to spiritual debridement, a ritual unique to the men who run into burning buildings when everybody else is running out, men who daily face blood, death and demon fire, men who must share their feelings about death and still remain men. The good humor and camaraderie were contagious, and for the first time that day, Barent smiled. In moments, he was laughing at the wisecracks, and fielding the good-natured bow shots that were landing on him from all quarters.

CHAPTER 41

Still, it was not an easily forgettable thing that had happened to Barent. It worked on him, and he worked through it, slowly and painfully at first, then with increasing confidence.

Once he had leveled out a little, he called Kathleen from the office, asked to see the children. Holding true to form, Kathleen jumped on him with both feet. Where in the hell was the child support money? she wanted to know. He was two months behind, and how was she supposed to care for Anthony and John Junior without his help? Where the *hell* had he been? Why hadn't he *called*? Anthony and John were getting into fights with the other kids in school, it had something to do with his arrest, and she only knew what she read in the papers. What kind of an *example* was he setting? What kind of father *was* he, anyway?

He held the phone away from his ear while she discharged her outrage and rattled off the lace-curtain litany of his most recent offenses. There was little point in explaining. Hanging up the phone would only enrage her further, and make it even more difficult to negotiate a visit. He bowed his back mentally and allowed the blows to fall until she was out of

295

steam, then moved in quietly, carefully to arrange the visit with his sons. It took profuse apologies, an explicit recognition of all he had put her through, and the promise of money, but he finally got the appointment he sought. He sat on his resentment as if it were a hot stove.

On hanging up the phone, he paced quietly, raging inside at a State that would empower this woman to treat him this way. He had no choice but to take her abuse if he wanted to see the boys. He wondered what had happened to the woman that he had fallen in love with those several years ago. What made a person change so?

He suspected that the only thing that had changed was the situation. This banal and vindictive side was always there, latent. It emerged in response to circumstances that threatened her. Now, she used her cooperation with regard to the boys as a bargaining chip to extort from him the satisfaction of her own needs. *His* needs could generally take a flying leap at a rolling donut for all she cared. With an effort of will and a deeply drawn breath, he began to calm the anger the transaction had engendered in him.

He was just beginning to feel normal when he received a phone call.

"Hello. John Barent. Can I help you?"

"Yes. Well, maybe I can help you. I read all about you in the papers."

"Who is this?," Barent wanted to know.

"This is Ed Henning. You may not remember me, but I'm the clerk at IGS."

"IGS?"

"Industrial Gas Systems. You asked me a bunch of questions about that guy who bought an empty gas cylinder, and a magnesium welding rod. You don't remember? You gave me your card. You said I should call you if I remembered anything else."

"Did you remember something?"

"Not exactly. The same guy just came in here and bought another empty gas bottle, and another magnesium welding rod. I thought you might want to know."

"Are you sure it was the same guy?" Barent's heart was in his throat. This was too good to be true. Jessica was back in his jurisdiction, back in a place where he had the authority to act. "Are you sure? How long ago?"

"Yeah, I'm sure. He left about ten minutes ago. Same guy, but different. I got his plates for you—a gray Honda Civic. Real dirty."

"How? How did he look?"

"Well, he looked...nuts. He looked like an animal. His eyes were crazy, and his hair looked like he just saw a ghost. He smelled, like he hasn't had a bath in a year. He looked like a snarling dog. I mean, he didn't actually look like a mad dog, but that's how he *felt*. It was weird. Really weird."

"Did he say anything?"

"No, just the order. I got his address, too."

"I'll be right there!" Barent promised. "Ten minutes. Stay put."

Barent grabbed up the key to the unmarked car he drove on department business. He stuck his head out the door, hollered to the secretary, "I'm gone, on the air." Halfway to the parking lot, he realized he should call Marty, and spun on his heel. It would only take a minute. He returned to his desk and rang Marty's office. The machine answered, and Barent waited impatiently through the familiar recitals for the beep. "Jessica Collins is back in town," he said triumphantly into the handset after the answering machine toned, "and she just bought the makings of a device. Call me when you come in."

He slammed the receiver down, and headed for the parking lot at a lope.

CHAPTER 42

One of the reasons Marty Caulkin was so successful at his profession was favors. Favors done and favors repaid were a sort of subterranean currency in the profession of arson investigation. Later generations called this 'networking', using the very nineties affectation of manufacturing a verb from an unwilling noun, but Marty had been doing it long before the term arose to describe it. He resented the cavalier attitude that did not punish the abuse of nouns, in part because of a classical education that made him loathe the imprecise. He did not think of it as networking. He thought of it as doing favors. He always did more favors than he received, and he called in his markers only judiciously.

He sat now at his desk, his chin trebled on his chest, his fullish lips pursed into a frown, his perennially surprised eyes poring over a report. He held a document of some ten pages in length, single-spaced, typed in the inevitable government Courier 10 point font, and spaced nearly margin to margin to save paper. It was a document he would never have been able to get his hands on without the exchange of favors. It was a document he would never have been able to read except for the thick lenses perched on his nose. He frowned again.

Once he had obtained a positive I.D. on Jessica Collins, it became much easier to acquire information. Marty had assembled all the information he could lay his hands on and phoned a friend of his, a criminal analyst who worked for the FBI's Los Angeles Field Station. The friend was also one who trafficked in favors, and the deal was cut to provide Marty with a criminal analysis profile of Jessica Collins outside of normal and official channels. Favors were done, and markers called in from places and from people Marty had never seen to produce the document he now read. It was a comprehensive and scientifically derived work of art that told him things about Jessica Collins that were *probably* true. It had arrived by FEDEX™ afternoon delivery scarcely an hour ago.

He read from the concluding paragraphs of the document a summary of possible behaviors that the analyst inferred from the composite picture of sociopathic behavior constructed in the preceding pages.

"...*Given the foregoing characteristics, and in view of the subject's history and psychological profile, there is a substantial probability that the subject will act as an extremely determined predator once her prey has been identified. Acts of predation will be carefully planned and executed, since much of the satisfaction in their performance is actually derived from the mental preparation and rehearsal attendant on the acts.*

"The profile suggests a personality driven by powerful compulsive forces to extract what she feels is her due from those who she feels have offended or betrayed her in some way. The offenses and the betrayals themselves are largely products of her own mental processes, and may have little relation to externally verifiable reality. Nonetheless, frustration in the attainment of her artificial vengeances is liable to create a disproportionate rage...

"The need for control is a vital aspect of the subject's mental health. Over the course of her life, she has manufactured boilerplate defense mechanisms to protect her psyche from the pain of her childhood reality, and in fact, may have manufactured alternate personae *as well. There are strong indications that the subject may suffer from Multiple Personality Disorder (Dissociative Identity Disorder). The defense system will hold together indefinitely; it is extremely strong. If it should fail, it will fail violently. The strength of the defenses is approximately proportional to the violence of the explosion when their controls fail. In such a case, the subject's personality is likely to disintegrate into a psychotic phase, and she may become suddenly quite dangerous, both to herself and to others."*

Caulkin set aside the paper, his mind fascinated. His intellect examined the synthesis of apparently unrelated bits of information into a profile that fit with what he knew of the suspect, and he was impressed. Absently, still musing about the intricate portrait that the FBI analyst had painted, he keyed his answering machine and listened with one ear to the messages, jotting a note or a phone number now and again. John Barent's voice came up after a tone. Marty Caulkin tuned both ears and his entire attention to the terse communication Barent had left there. It filled him with a sense of apprehension and a dawning dread.

If his friend from the FBI was right, the probability was that Barent was in great danger, and was blissfully unaware of that fact.

Caulkin reached for the phone.

CHAPTER 43

Maggie Carnes, "Miss Carnes" to her second graders, had caught the duty. One week out of every four it rolled around, crunching her busy schedule beneath its oppressive track. And while she was clear on the need to perform it, she always resented it a little when her turn actually arrived. Otherwise kind, and immensely popular with her charges at Ella Springfield Elementary School, she became peevish and abrupt when she was forced to end a long and demanding day by standing an unwelcome afternoon watch at the school bus loading zone. There, every other fortnight, she would remain on her aching pins until the last child had gone home. It meant at least an hour of her afternoon was lost, and often more. If a child missed a bus, or some irresponsible parent failed to arrive on time to pick up his kid, it took additional time to hook the child up with the proper administrator who would make the right arrangements to get the student properly and safely home.

Still, she remained conscientious. When the woman in the gray Honda pulled to the curb and asked for the Barent boys, John and Tony, her appearance was sufficiently out of the ordinary to

303

precipitate an investigation of the circumstances. John and Tony normally rode the bus, unless they were going to visit their father. In those cases, rare of late, he picked them up in a rattletrap Alfa Romeo. Miss Carnes was unmarried, twenty-six, and mildly attracted by John Barent's boyish good looks and eggbeater haircut. She had been unable to break into even a casual conversation with him, and the young woman in the gray Honda Civic suggested that it might be futile, anyway.

"I'm here to get John and Tony Barent," she said to Miss Carnes, flashing an apologetic smile. "Their dad couldn't make it until later, and he asked me to pick up the boys."

"Who are you?" she queried, officiously and more than idly curious. "What is your name?"

"Jessica Collins. I'm, well, just a friend, actually. A friend of Mr. Barent's."

"I don't believe you're on the list, and we can't let the children leave with an unauthorized person. I'm sorry."

"He had to work late," Jessica persisted. "You could call him and verify me, if there's a problem. He works at the Fire Department."

"I can't leave the curb here. The boys are supposed to go home on the bus..."

"Jessica! Hi, Jessica! Tony broke through a line of children queuing up to board one of the yellow buses. John Junior tagged along behind him, struggling to keep up, but unwilling to appear to be following his older brother.

Miss Carnes turned to face the two boys. "You know this lady?" she asked.

"Yeah," said Tony. 'She's my dad's girl friend." He looked at Miss Carnes with an air of authority on the subject, innocently dashing her private agenda on the rocks. He swung his lunch box in a wide arc that nearly caught John Junior in the forehead as he hauled up short. "Hi, Jessica," said John Junior, ducking.

"Hi, guys," said Jessica. "Your dad said for me to pick you guys up, but the teacher here thinks I'm going to kidnap you."

"Nah!" snorted Tony. John Junior giggled, then looked thoughtful. "Mom didn't tell us we were going with Dad today. It's not Friday, Miss Carnes," he explained to her seriously. He knew the rules, but wasn't sure how they applied to this situation.

"They didn't decide until after you went to school," Jessica explained to him. "Your dad wanted to see you, and take you to dinner at Mickey D's." Placing an arm on each boy's shoulder, she turned to the teacher. "Well?"

Maggie Carnes waffled for a minute, then the decision was made for her. The bus the boys were supposed to be on pulled out of the yard.

"I suppose it's all right," she agreed. "Is it all right with you boys?"

"Sure," said Tony. John Junior nodded sincerely, taking his cue from his older brother. "Yeah, it's O.K."

"O.K., then. See you boys tomorrow." She watched as the boys ran enthusiastically for the car, each claiming "shotgun!" for the front seat. She wished, fervently, that she could muster such wild energy at the end of the school day. She sighed and nodded her permission to Jessica Collins. She watched as the woman walked toward the car, musing to herself that the woman hadn't an ounce of grace in her movements.

There were no other stragglers this day, and she thanked the school bus gods for an uneventful tour, returned to her room to lock up, and headed for home with papers under her arm for grading. Two hours later, a frantic vice-principal called her at home to ask if she had seen Tony and Johnny Barent get on the bus.

CHAPTER 44

It proved a short cognitive leap across the stream of events to the rock of suspicion. On hearing Maggie Carnes' story, and listening to the distraught, tearful words of Kathleen Barent, rationally there was only one suspect to consider. Detective officers Talbot and Gorman didn't know the actual statistic of parental abduction as a percentage of all kidnappings, but it didn't take a rocket scientist to zero the needle of culpability on John Barent.

They knew of his recent troubles in a hazy, non-specific way only, but they had heard through the grapevine of his exoneration, and his reinstatement. Still, there was the unspoken assumption that he must have been at least partly at fault or he wouldn't have been charged, and this present offense was most probably nothing more than recidivism. They reassured Kathleen, instructed her to remain by the phone, and find a friend to stay with her. They headed for the Fire Department offices.

"What kind of a stupid stunt is he pulling now?" wondered Gorman aloud as he drove the unmarked Dodge toward their destination. "Christ, you'd think he'd have enough trouble for a lifetime without doing something stupid like this."

"Nobody really knows what goes on between two people," philosophized Talbot. "It's just too bad that the parents are using the kids to jerk each other around."

"Story of the ages. Doesn't everybody?"

They caught up with John Barent just as he was leaving his office for the day. His interview with Ed Henning was finished over an hour ago, and he had returned to the office to document it before going home. Henning had been forthcoming, but in actuality, had been able to provide little in the way of useful information that Barent couldn't infer from the original phone contact. Jessica was in town, and up to her old tricks. John wondered who the target would be this time. His only option was to wait and see, and to try to be quick enough to catch her when she struck.

He had taken a few minutes to hunt down the station officer before sitting down at the computer. He found Captain Mackey again, and warned him to be alert to the possibility that any fire he might respond to this night might be an HTA fire, with high temperature accellerants involved. He described Jessica for the officer, and gave him a sheaf of Xeroxed photos for his crew. The more eyes looking for Jessica, the greater the chances of spotting her.

It was now a little after six p.m. The rest of the office staff, McCabe and the others, was already gone, and Barent was doing the lock up when the detectives materialized in front of him.

"Gentlemen," he said with mock formality. "What can I do for you?"

"You've had a busy day, John."

"I have. What are you doing here?" Barent was a little edgy. The last time police officers had paid him an unannounced visit, his life had been turned upside down. Detectives didn't make a habit of checking in with him to see how his day had been. Something was amiss. Barent repeated the question with his eyes, bored the gaze directly into Talbot.

"Where are your children? Your two boys." Talbot went straight to the point.

Barent was instantly apprehensive. "With their mother," he answered, glancing at his watch. While Talbot occupied his attention, Gorman had moved casually around him in the corridor, unobtrusively, to cut off his retreat option in that direction. The move was so subtle that most would not have noted it, but Barent saw it for what it was.

"Cut the crap, Barent. You had your girlfriend pick them up after school. Now, where have you taken them?"

"My...Oh, shit!" Barent blanched visibly. "Jessica..." He leaned against the corridor wall, his knees suddenly dangerously weak. The feeling passed, replaced by a fulminating, tightly controlled rage and blind, stark fear.

"You'd better come in," he said tersely. "This is serious." He unlocked the door to his office and entered, followed by the two detectives. Barent flopped behind his desk, gestured to the detectives to take seats.

"You're damn right it's serious, Barent. You want to tell us what's going on?"

Barent launched into an explanatory monologue, explaining his recent troubles, and giving the detectives enough background to make them begin to believe the incredible story. "I just found out three hours ago that she was back in town," he concluded. "And then you guys showed up."

"What do you suppose she'll do? Why the children?" Talbot was watching him like a hawk, looking for the involuntary clues that would confirm or deny the veracity of the answer.

"I don't know what she'll do. My guess is that she wants something from me, and the boys are a lever to pry it away from me if I don't cooperate."

"You think she wants money? Ransom?"

"Not likely," Barent responded thoughtfully. "She knows I don't have any."

"Then, what?"

"Control. She wants control for some reason. And she's got it. I'll do anything to keep the boys from getting hurt, and she knows it."

"Then you think she'll contact you?"

"How else could it work? She's got to, in order for

the boys to have any value to her."

Talbot looked intently at Gorman, exchanging his thoughts without speaking to his partner. Gorman nodded. "We believe you," he said to Barent. "We'll set up some equipment at your house. We want to record whatever she says to you. And, Barent..." he paused.

John Barent looked at him, waiting for him to finish.

"...if it turns out you're messing with us, we will personally dedicate our lives and careers to making your existence a living nightmare."

Get in line, thought Barent wryly. Outwardly, he remained silent. His measured glare bored into Gorman with a force of hostility just short of what would be required to trigger a response. He turned on his heel without a word. He led the detectives from the room.

CHAPTER 45

It was well after dark when the detectives Talbot and Gorman departed. They left behind in Barent's apartment a tangle of wires and a tape recorder hooked into the telephone line.

"She'll call," Talbot had prophesied, "and when she does, the machine will record everything she says. Keep her talking. You know what we need to find out, and the longer she talks, the more information we're likely to get. You call us as soon as she hangs up. Don't get heroic. Let us do our job."

"And if she doesn't call?"

"She will. Maybe not tonight; she may want you to sweat a little. But she'll call. Then you call us. We'll hook up your office line in the morning if she hasn't called before then. Don't try to do this alone," he warned.

Barent had simply stared at the detectives, and escorted them to the door in silence. Now, the house echoed with the silence of a Druid tomb. He was sick with worry about the boys, but couldn't bring himself to imagine that Jessica would ever harm them. It was inconceivable. But then he thought of his brother's family and became even sicker.

He thought about calling Kathleen, and then

313

thought better of it. What could he possibly say to her? It wasn't his fault the boys were missing, but she would blame him, and that Irish tongue of hers would lay him open. Nooo..., he didn't need that. He paced fretfully, unable to move in any productive direction and unable to remain still.

What he did need was a drink. Just a light one, to take the edge off, he told himself. He splashed four fingers of Sam Sykes into a highball glass, dropped in an ice cube, and took an approbatory sip. About halfway through the drink, with a mild buzz dulling the edge of his discomfort, he set the drink down and dialed Ardi's number. He'd lifted it out of the case records. He just needed someone to talk to, he told himself, and it would be good to hear Ardi's voice. He flopped on the sofa with the receiver in his ear and the drink within reach.

"Hello?" Ardi answered on the fourth ring.

"Hi, Ardi. It's a voice from your past."

"J.R.! How are you? I'm so glad you called. I was beginning to think I'd never hear from you again." Barent was surprised at the warmth in her voice. It had none of the coldness he had read between the lines of her hospital note.

"I wasn't sure you wanted to hear from me."

"That's ridiculous. I will admit that I didn't want you to *see* me. At least, not until my hair grew back. So, is there a reason you called? It's just great to hear your voice!"

"Well, actually, I just needed to talk. I'm going nuts down here. Jessica's back and she's got the boys. She took them from school. I don't know what she wants. The cops have got the phone tapped in case she calls."

"Oh, J.R...that's awful! Why? What does she want? Listen, you've got to get off the line in case she does call."

"If the line's busy, she'll try again," Barent snarled. "God, I'll kill her! She's evil. She's just *evil*."

"She's sick, John. Be careful, because she's not playing by the rules. There's no telling what she might do."

"She wouldn't hurt the kids. She wants something from me. I don't know what it is. I haven't got any money."

"You don't know that. She might very well hurt the kids as a way of getting you. She's sick. John, she's nuts. Crazy. Maybe what she wants is to hurt you. I read the file, remember? She thinks you ruined her life when you sent her mother to prison."

"I know..." There was a knock at the door, hard and forceful. The damn detectives were back. What could they possibly have forgotten? "Listen," he told Ardi, "there's somebody at the door. Don't hang up. I'll be right back." The knock came again. He placed the open receiver on the end table and went to the door. "Just a second," he said, loudly.

He opened the door and found himself staring

directly into the barrel of a hand gun. The narrowed eyes of Jason Grover stared back at him, burning with a wild and irrational fire he had never seen in Jessica's. Jason pushed into the small apartment, and closed the door behind him, keeping the muzzle of the weapon trained on Barent the entire time.

Restraining the urge to attack her and strangle her where she stood, Barent backed away. "Where are my boys?" he demanded. "Jessica, where are they? What have you done with them?"

"They're outside in the car. Come along with me and we'll bring them inside."

Barent stopped backing up, and came toward the door again, slowly. "Jessica, put the gun down!" he ordered in a loud voice.

She replied by cocking the hammer back. "I said, let's go get them," she hissed. Her eyes flashed about the room. She spotted the phone receiver on the end table. At the moment her eyes stopped on it, it began emitting the rapid beeping tones of a receiver off the hook. Barent could only hope that Ardi had heard his words, and would act to send help quickly.

"Who were you talking to?"

"Nobody. Nobody. I was just about to make a call."

"That's bullshit. If you hadn't been connected, you would have hung it up before you came to the door. Who were you talking to? If you want to see the boys again, you'll answer." She gestured menacingly with the gun.

"Ardi."

"Bullshit again. Ardi's dead. I burned her."

"She's not! She got out. I swear it; she got out. You haven't seen her name in the papers, have you? She got out."

"I haven't been reading the papers lately," Jessica snarled. "Let's assume she got out. Where is she?"

"San Jose. She's home."

Jessica sighed abruptly. "Let's go out to the car. You want to see the boys, don't you? Bring them in, and put them to bed. Then we'll have a little chat."

"What do you want, Jessica? What do you want from me?"

"Right now, I want you to shut up, and get the boys out of my car. Right now." She gestured threateningly, suggestively with the handgun. "And, be careful. Wouldn't want a stray bullet to hit one of them, now, would we?"

Barent edged around her towards the door, watching her intently. She followed as he went outside to her gray Honda. He opened the car door, which was fogged on the inside, opaque from moisture condensing against the cold glass. The boys were crashed in the front seat, tangled up in each other, sleeping peacefully. Barent exhaled a profound breath of relief, then turned to look at Jessica.

"Pick them up. Bring them inside."

He gathered Tony carefully in his arms, gently

untangling him from his younger brother. Tony had always had the ability to sleep through earthquakes and road construction, and he stirred faintly without waking. Barent carried him into the house, down the short hall past the tiny bathroom, and into the bedroom. He was amazed that Jessica hadn't followed him. He laid the boy down on his bed and returned for John Junior. He thought about his BD380, nestled in the nightstand's drawer amidst his socks, and decided that it represented a greater liability than an asset with his kids involved. He left it there. If Jessica meant any harm to his children, she would have done it by now.

John Junior held true to form, whining fitfully, half-awakening as Barent lifted him from the car. He smelled of peanut butter and library paste. This time, Jessica followed him into the house, and into the bedroom where he laid John Junior beside his older brother. The younger son awoke, and asked to go to the bathroom. Barent looked in the dim light at Jessica, who nodded assent.

Barent led him back into the hallway and helped him with his trousers. These he left in the bathroom and put his son back into bed when his business was done. He rose from the bedside and turned to Jessica again. "O.K.," he said. "What now?"

"Where's your automatic? The one you keep in the night stand."

"It's there. Top drawer, under the socks."

Jessica opened the drawer, retrieved the pistol. She dropped the clip out of the butt, and operated the slide to eject any possible round in the chamber. Keeping her own gun trained on Barent, she herded him back down the hallway to the living room, leaning quickly into the tiny bathroom on her way by to drop Barent's little automatic into the toilet bowl. He heard the splash and clank as the blued steel struck the porcelain.

Barent was unsure of her intentions, and unwilling to take a chance against the gun when it was not in plain view. Thinking of the boys sleeping behind a half inch of plaster, he submitted to her instructions rather than risk a struggle and the possible discharge of the firearm.

She ordered Barent to sit in a dinette chair. Working from the back, she bound his hands with long, plastic ties to the back rails. Deftly, she applied more ties to his ankles, binding them to the front chair legs. This completed, she moved around in front of Barent. She regarded him with silent, triumphant malevolence for a time. Finally, she spoke. Her voice was low, dripping with venom.

"I'm going to kill you. Do you know why?"

Barent realized that it would have been a good idea to resist being tied, but it was too late. Frantically, his mind searched for a way out, for the right words to defuse the situation. He needed to buy time.

"Jessica, I've never done anything to hurt you. Why do you want to kill me?" His tenor had turned soprano. His sudden realization that Jessica was bent on real harm iced his voice with fear.

"I don't *want* to kill you. I'm *going* to kill you. I wanted you to suffer, as you made me suffer, long and hard. I wanted you to learn to hate your life, to despise your very existence. But I'm out of time, out of patience. So killing you will have to do."

"Why, Jessica? Why? What could be so bad in your life that you want to hurt everybody you touch?"

"The name's Jason. And you know damn well why. You ruined my life, you son of a bitch. You destroyed everything I ever had that meant anything. You put my mother in prison, and I...she was the only person who ever protected me, who ever cared what happened to me. You took her away, and she might as well be dead. I hate you for it. Oh, God, how I hate you for it!"

"She killed a man."

"She killed an animal —a mindless, brutal, vicious animal that didn't deserve to live. She did it to protect me. And you put her away for it. You protected the animal, and hurt my mother instead."

Barent's mind whirled. He stifled the fear that welled up in him like gray water in a backed up drain. He held his rage down with an act of will. To meet Jason's anger with anger now might well cause him to come completely unwound. Instead, he took a reasonable, sympathetic tone. He tried persuasion.

"Jason, look. You need help. You need someone who understands what you've been through, someone who can help you through the pain. Let me help you."

"Your death will help me. And the death of your boys. That is the pain you must know. It still won't be enough."

"Jason, don't you see that you've become the very thing you despise? You're talking about killing innocent children to satisfy your own need for revenge. How is that any better than your stepfather? He used your innocence for his own selfish purposes. How is what you're doing any different? Now, you give pain to little children, just like him!"

Jason growled in frustration. The conflict tore at him like a wolf pack at a fresh kill, and he flailed his arms wildly in agitation. "Shut up! Shut up!" He laid the barrel of the gun against Barent's temple. "Shut UP!" he shrieked.

Abruptly he danced away, and bolted out the front door.

Barent, suddenly alone, struggled desperately against his bonds. The chair back was loose; it had been loose for two years, and he had never bothered to fix it. It periodically worked its way free, and Barent just shoved it back together. Now, he worked his bonds up the two chromed shafts that supported it, and pushed. If he could slip the back off the chair, he could slip the bonds off the shaft; his hands would be free.

Grunting with the efforts of his contortion, he managed to slide the seat back off on one side, and slipped one hand free. He dropped it back behind the chair and stilled his movements as Jason came back through the door, carrying a fire extinguisher.

Jason knelt in front of him, looking up at his face as he set the gun on the floor beside him and commenced to unscrew the valve assembly and remove the expansion cone. He set the cone aside. He glared malevolently at Barent.

"You know what this is?" he asked. A wild look came into his eyes. "It's a thermite device. My own little invention. So simple. So effective. Homemade, out of things you find around the house. You know what it does? It purifies. It defeats evil. In this little red bottle is a magical genie. Immense power! The power serves *me*! When I release him, he will purify you!"

Jason reached into his pocket and extracted a strip of metallic ribbon. Watching Barent, he inserted the ribbon into the open neck of the fire extinguisher. He produced a lighter and fumbled with it, trying to make a flame several times unsuccessfully. "God damn child-proof lighters," he cursed under his breath. His frustration nearly defeated his attempts as he fumbled with the device ineffectually. Finally, he mastered it, and a flame flickered in his hand.

"You're too lucky, Barent," snarled Jason. "I had you set up so tight you could never get out of it. Then, you even gave me some of your blood to use. I squeezed it from the towel in your wastebasket the night you cut your hand. Even if you had been able to explain the knife and the lighter, you could never have beaten the DNA match at the fire scene. But you did, and so I'm done with the games, and the sophistication. I'll just kill you, directly and to the point. Time's up."

He bent forward and touched the wavering flame to the magnesium ribbon.

CHAPTER 46

The ribbon took the flame with a "pop", bathing the room in an eerie, bluish-white light as smoke roiled up from the burning fuse. Barent's eyes got wide, and he glanced in panic about the room, looking for a weapon within reach of his single, freed hand. There was a brass lamp within reach, but Jason still faced him with the automatic. The timing would have to be perfect, as Jason turned to leave. Even then, Barent realized that a bullet could reach him before the swing was complete. It was a necessary chance; his only chance.

"The pain will be intense," he assured Barent, "but it won't last long. I'm sorry I can't stay to see it in your face. Your sons will probably not even wake up."

Barent looked involuntarily down the hall toward his bedroom. He was shocked to see little John Junior standing in the hallway, confused, frightened and silent, watching the scene without understanding.

Jason followed Barent's eyes and froze.

There, before him in the hallway, a kid with spindly, white little boy legs and baggy undershorts stood frozen in time as the flickering glow of the burning magnesium caused his shadow to dance grotesquely on the wall behind him. Jason stood, momentarily transfixed by a vision that he had never seen, but had *been*, those many years ago. It delivered a glance into a mirror in his own mind with the force of a sledgehammer blow, a true seeing for the first time of his own tragic and helpless childhood experience. He saw himself standing in the hallway, and heard again the screams of Carl as the bedroom vomited flames and sent his mother rushing to sweep him up and outside to safety. He saw his demon in the wavering light and knew its origin. The vision triggered a brief, unendurable pain and regret.

John Barent's free hand shot from concealment in a broad sweep that collected the brass lamp in its arc without slowing, and drove the metal base with all the force he could muster into the base of Jason's skull. Jason dropped like a stone, stunned, his automatic clattering on the floor as he collapsed. He moaned once, there on the floor, but did not move. Clumsily, frantically, Barent freed his second hand, then stood and worked the chair legs up underneath the nylon ties Jason had installed. There was not enough of the fuse left to grab and pull out. The thermite would ignite in a heartbeat, and there was nothing he could do to stop it.

He dashed down the short hallway toward his son. He scooped up the immobile John Junior as he passed, and darted into the bedroom. He slammed the bedroom door behind him as the thermite ignited with the roar of a blast furnace. The room he had just left went instantly to a temperature of over five thousand degrees. Its entire contents reached their ignition temperatures in a fraction of a second, and flames rolled and roiled through the gases cooked off from the interior finishes by the tremendous heat.

He pitched a chair through the bedroom window, and cleared the glass from the frame with an alarm clock snatched from the bedside nightstand. Though the act took mere seconds, a black stain of charring wood already grew on the door, spreading like a black, wet stain. He pitched John Junior bodily out the window, feet first. Tony had been awakened by the slamming of the door, but was not yet fully conscious. His father simply grabbed him up and stuffed out the window like a sack of oats before the boy could even begin to resist.

A beam of blinding white light cut through the door like a laser beam as combustion beyond earthly flame consumed the edges of the hole it had burned in the door. It burned at a rate so fast that the wood seemed to melt away. The searing heat drove Barent into a head-first dive out the window.

He tumbled, and leaped to his feet, searching quickly for his sons. He caught them up and half dragged, half carried them to the street in front of the little converted garage as the column of white light sliced its way through the roof and illuminated the night sky. The demon roared. Lights came on in Mrs. Forrester's front house, and at several of the neighbors' houses. Barent knelt quietly at the curb, clutching his sons to him with a steel grip, and glanced up only briefly as he waited for the sounds of sirens to rise in the distance.

CHAPTER 47

Marty Caulkin saw the glow in the sky from two miles away as he drove toward Barent's house at breakneck speed. He prayed for a miracle. He prayed that the most likely meaning of the billowing, underlighted column of smoke and flames rising into the velvet sky was somehow wrong. The color of the smoke went abruptly from gray to white, the change visible even at this distance. The white smoke told his experienced eye that the suppression crews had achieved "knock-down"; there was now more steam in the rolling, rising column than actual smoke from the burning. He hoped fervently that John Barent wasn't a cinder in a fire that he would have to investigate.

Minutes earlier, Ardi Campbell had called him on his pager from San Jose. When he returned her call, she frantically related what she had heard when Barent put down the phone and went to answer the door. Now, as he turned down Barent's street, a cluster of flashing red lights came into view in the distance. With an odd quirk of mind that such stress often brings, Marty found himself wondering if all that remained of his friend and colleague John Barent was rising in the wisps of smoke and steam that trailed lazily into the dark sky above his burned out house.

A scattering of local residents stood about in bathrobes and pajamas, their arms bundled across their bodies against the chill of the air as they watched the firemen work. The roadway was blocked with a tangle of canvas spaghetti that connected the engines to the fire hydrants, and connected the attack lines to the engines. Emergency lighting set up by the firefighters illuminated the scene with a near daytime brilliance. Caulkin parked well away, and jogged unceremoniously toward the command post. The scene was cloaked in an uncanny silence, despite the muted roar of the generators and the growling of the diesel engines driving the fire pumps. A dozen or so firefighters in yellow reflectorized bunker clothing moved about the scene, working deliberately at various tasks. The fire was clearly under control, and would be out completely in minutes. There was nothing left to burn.

He spotted Aaronsen leaving as he approached the CP, and caught his eye. "Barent?" he asked. He was fearful of the answer.

Aaronsen gestured in a general direction. "Over there," he said, tersely. "We'll need your help on this one. We've got a fatality reported, but no body. Catch up with me when you're ready to go to work." He went about his business.

Marty was stunned. Aaronsen, with an unaccustomed callousness, had directed him toward the stand-by ambulance without indicating who the fatality was. But it couldn't be Barent. Aaronsen had said there was no body, yet directed him to Barent, so Barent must have gotten out. Marty heaved a sigh of relief when he finally saw his friend sitting quietly at the curb behind the Command Post. Barent's arms were wrapped protectively around his two sons, who watched with uncomprehending awe as their father's apartment walls were knocked in toward the center by firemen wielding long pikes.

He looked up mutely as Marty approached. His eyes were vacant of any emotion. Great owlish orbs betrayed the horror of what he had just witnessed.

"Hey, cowboy!" Marty hailed him. "Am I glad to see you!"

"Marty." The voice was flat, emotionless. Barent looked down at the water that ran in a narrow stream below him in the gutter from a leaking hose coupling.

"Jessica?"

Barent nodded. "She really lost it. Wigged totally out. I bonked her with a brass lamp, and she didn't make it out. She couldn't have made it out..." He looked up with pleading eyes, seeking understanding and forgiveness. "She was going to kill us all, Marty. The boys..." He held his sons tighter at either side, unable to finish the sentence.

"I know. I got a profile on her from a buddy at the FBI. He's an analyst. It said that she would be dangerous if she came unglued. Looks like she did."

"Yeah."

"Ardi called me. You know, you ought to pay a little more attention to that woman." Marty lowered his bowling pin frame to sit beside Barent on the curb, grunting. His perennially surprised eyes regarded his friend with compassion.

"I've got nothing..." Barent nodded at the smoking hulk of his apartment.

"Bullshit, Buddy," snorted Marty. "You've got everything that's important. You've got your life, your sons. You've got a clean slate, a *tabla raza*. You would be —you *will* be— amazed at what rushes in to fill a vacuum.

Aaronsen materialized in front of them. "You ready to go?" he invited Caulkin. "They've cleared us to begin the C&O."

"On my way." Marty grunted to his feet. He turned to regard Barent, reached into his pocket, and extracted his keys. He pulled two sections apart and tossed a jangling bunch of keys to Barent. "Sit this one out. You need a place to stay tonight. Beth'll be glad to see you." Marty referred to his wife of nearly two decades.

"And John..." Barent looked up. "Call Kathleen. Right away. Then, call Ardi."

CHAPTER 48

Caulkin, working with Aaronsen and Brooks, found the signatures of high temperature accelerants in the smoking ruins of Barent's apartment. There was an area of absolutely clear floor at the point of origin, with the characteristic greenish glass puddle of fused concrete on the naked slab where the device must have been. There was not a trace of human remains in the ashes.

A search warrant served on Jessica's scorched automobile, with the usual, ridiculous knock-and-notice formality, revealed a large thermite device in the trunk Apparently, Jessica had another contract somewhere that would not now be fulfilled.

Caulkin had dropped into Barent's office near closing time on the following day at the conclusion of the investigation. He reported the findings to Barent, who listened impassively. Barent had wanted no part of the investigation, and it suited him just fine that there was a conflict of interest in his being assigned to investigate a fire in his own home. He had been happy to drop the boys with a tearful, grateful, angry Kathleen and slip quietly into work the next morning. He appreciated the fact that the suppression crews left him alone, although they were dying of curiosity about the fire the preceding night. Considerately, Josh Mackey had warned them off.

Caulkin concluded his discourse. "I guess we can close the file on this one. You should be able to sleep better now."

Barent nodded, sighed. "Yeah. I'm glad it's over," he said lamely.

"You sound about as thrilled as if you were on death row and your final appeal was denied. What gives?"

"It's...nothing. Nothing at all."

"Well, then," brightened Marty, "how about I pay up on my bet? Chili dogs at Frank's, on me."

"Can't. I've got a date."

Marty's already surprised expression intensified. "Oh?" he queried, arching his eyebrow quizzically.

"Ardi came down from San Jose to see me. She says there's a couple of things she wants to get straight between us."

"There's a double entendre if I ever heard one! Treat her right, John. She's too good for you. Go comb your hair." Marty smiled, nodding to himself.

Barent remained serious. He gnawed absently on his left lower lip.

"Jesus, John," Marty said in exasperation. "All your dreams are about to come true. Couldn't you crack a smile?"

"I suppose." Barent pasted a smile across his

mouth, but failed to put it in his eyes.

"You look like a dead 'possum. What in the hell is wrong with you?"

"Just a feeling," offered Barent after a thoughtful pause. Absently, he scratched the cleft in his chin with a thumb.

"I just wish you had found a body. That's all."

ABOUT THE AUTHOR:

Born in Jackson, Michigan in 1948, Mr. Hopkins lives with his wife Rebecca in Central California where he is fire captain.

The Fourth Corner of the 9th Room, is his second novel. Navassa is his first.

In The Fourth Corner of the 9th Room he draws on nine years as an arson investigator to weave a story of a diabolical arsonist driven by a deeply disturbed past and the investigator who must track the criminal down. He transports the reader almost subliminally into the inner circle of that unique group of men and women who call the fire ground home.

Please address any correspondence to the author in care of:

Russell Dean & Company, Publishers

P.O. Box 349

Santa Margarita, California 93453

If you enjoyed this book, read the stunning new thriller...

NAVASSA

By Bradd Hopkins

- They dosed soldiers with LSD during the Vietnam era...
- They deliberately exposed an entire nation to toxic radiation during the 50's...
- They laced childrens' breakfast cereal with radioactive potassium to measure mineral uptake...
- They fed syphilitic men placebos to observe the progress of the untreated disease...

What makes you think they've stopped? What makes you think they've told us everything?

In Bradd Hopkins exciting new novel, "Navassa", a clandestine U.S. Army germ warfare project in the early 1970's develops a weapons-grade bug by genetically engineering a virus found in African monkeys. Secret tests conducted on the population of San Francisco unleash a modern epidemic...and the cover-up extends in a conspiracy reaching to the highest levels of government.

But the Army blunders when it hires Russ Wakefield, a lanky Texan who is to environmental clean-up what Red Adair is to oil well fires. On Navassa Island, where the virus was initially developed, he discovers documents hidden two decades earlier by Dr. Paulus Harwiczki, the supervisor of the genetic engineering team and the principal developer of the virus. The rotting papers fully disclose names and dates that will inevitably create chaos at the Pentagon if the facts are revealed. And General Thomas "Bulldog" Martindale who instigated the outlaw project knows that Wakefield has found them.

Thus begins a white-knuckle adventure with the frantic pace of "The Fugitive" written with the meticulous research and intellectually satisfying meat of a Tom Clancy thriller, with plot twists and surprises that would make Agatha Cristie blush with envy. And all of it is frighteningly real, cinematically vivid, and disturbingly possible! From Navassa Island—which, by the way, does not "officially" exist and can't be found on any map of the Carribean printed since the 70's—to Desert Range Research Station in Utah, to Cabo San Lucas, Wakefield flees agents of a government determined to terminate him with extreme prejudice at any cost.

Available from your favorite bookseller, or directly from the publisher.

Russell Dean & Company
Toll free 1-888-438-4115

<u>Navassa</u> by Bradd Hopkins

ISBN 1-891954-00-8
Casebound, embossed. $24.95 U.S.

Coming soon from Bradd Hopkins and Russell Dean & Company

Mandelbaum's Donut

By Bradd Hopkins

In a world one hundred years hence, when water — pure, drinkable, pristine fresh water —is the most important thing in daily life, history discovers power and wealth concentrated in the hands of a few hidden men. Through an act of consummate heroism, Reed Yee finds himself catapulted into the stratosphere of unlimited power, mentored by Atmar Wolfe, the personal secretary of Horus Mandelbaum, the man in control of the Western Hemisphere.

As Yee hunts for clues to the identities of a ruthless band of high-tech thieves, he searches simultaneously for a balance between the demands of true power and the toll it takes on his immortal soul.

When the facts behind his fortune finally emerge into the light, Yee is sent reeling by the revelation of his true role in Mandelbaum's grand scenario, and the lie of his own ascendancy. He faces a desperate struggle between his conscience and his own blood, where both may not survive.

Underneath it all, this challenging work by Bradd Hopkins examines the nature of money, power, and social control, and their effects on our very humanity.

**Available soon from your favorite bookseller, or
directly from the publisher.**
Russell Dean & Company
Toll free 1-888-438-4115

<u>Mandelbaum's Donut</u> by Bradd Hopkins

ISBN 1-891954-40-7

Price not yet set.